Green River Saga

Green River Saga

A Novel

Rick O'Shea
and
Michael W. Shurgot

Santa Fe

Cover photograph by Michael W. Shurgot

Sunstone books may be purchased for educational, business, or sales promotional use. For information please write: Special Markets Department, Sunstone Press, P.O. Box 2321, Santa Fe, New Mexico 87504-2321.

Book and cover design › R. Ahl

Library of Congress Cataloging-in-Publication Data

Names: O'Shea, Rick, 1962- author. | Shurgot, Michael W., 1943- author.
Title: Green river saga : a novel / Rick O'Shea and Michael W. Shurgot.
Description: Santa Fe : Sunstone Press, [2019] | Summary: "Green River Saga narrates a classic Western struggle in the canyon country of Wyoming in 1866-67 for land and water between a rapacious cattle baron, Brent Tompkin, and a band of Southern Cheyenne that Sheriff James Talbot, along with Irish half-breed Johnny Redfeather and Jermiah Staggart, a Civil War deserter, tries vainly to mediate before violence destroys both Green River and the Southern Cheyenne"-- Provided by publisher.
Identifiers: LCCN 2019041727 | ISBN 9781632932921 (paperback) | ISBN 9781611395860 (epub) | ISBN 9781632934123 (hardcover)
Subjects: GSAFD: Western stories.
Classification: LCC PS3615.S367 G74 2019 | DDC 813/.6--dc23
LC record available at https://lccn.loc.gov/2019041727

WWW.SUNSTONEPRESS.COM
SUNSTONE PRESS / POST OFFICE BOX 2321 / SANTA FE, NM 87504-2321 /USA
(505) 988-4418 / ORDERS ONLY (800) 243-5644 / FAX (505) 988-1025

To:
Middleton D. Tanner
RO'S

Rick O'Shea
MWS*

*As co author of this book I dedicate my portion to the charismatic Mr. O'Shea: Los Angeles raconteur; blues aficionado; talented writer; and superb former student at South Puget Sound Community College in Olympia, Washington. This dedication, one co author to another, is certainly unusual, but then Rick is an unusual individual. He is also most deserving.

Acknowledgements

For information on some of the battles and principal leaders of the Civil War, Native American History, and the history of American railroads in the period during and immediately following the Civil War, the authors are grateful to the following sources:

Alan Axelrod, *Chronicle of the Indian Wars: From Colonial Times to Wounded Knee*. New York: Prentice Hall, 1993.

Peter Cozzens, *The Earth Is Weeping: The Epic Story of the Indian Wars for the American West*. New York: Alfred A. Knopf, 2016.

James M. McPherson, *Battle Cry of Freedom: The Civil War Era*. Oxford: Oxford University Press, 1988.

John F. Stover, *The Routledge Historical Atlas of the American Railroads*. New York & London: Routledge, 1999.

We acknowledge the superb assistance of Matthew Parsons and Christina Blomquist of the map collection at the University of Washington Library, Seattle. We are also grateful to James Strong for help with Civil War battles and weaponry; and to James O'Donnell and Nancy Keith for excellent editing. All have significantly improved this novel.

"The committee are of the opinion that in a large majority of cases Indian wars are to be traced to the aggression of lawless white men, always to be found upon the frontier, or boundary line between savage and civilized life. Such is the statement of the most experienced officers of the army, and of all those who have been long conversant with Indian affairs....[Indian warfare is] very destructive, not only of the lives of the warriors engaged in it, but of the women and children also, often becoming a war of extermination."

—James R. Doolittle, U.S. Senator, Wisconsin. Report of the Doolittle Committee to United States Senate. January, 1867.

"The American Civil War, with its blockades, crop-burnings, and scorched-earth policies, caused an enormous number of civilian casualties."

—Steven Pinker, *The Better Angels of Our Nature*

"Judgment may rack your bones."

—Flannery O'Connor, *The Violent Bear It Away*

"In the iron of every day
stars can come through the sky,
and we can turn on the light
and be saved before we die."

—William Stafford, "The Gun of Billy the Kid." in *Stories That Could Be True: New and Collected Poems*, p. 38.

Preface

Green River Saga is a work of historical fiction. As contradictory as that term appears, it is nonetheless appropriate for what follows.

Our novel begins in Green River, a town in south-western Wyoming, then Dakota Territory, in late September, 1866. In the early 1860s Green River was a station on the overland mail route along the original Cherokee Stage Coach Trail and later became an important locale for the expanding Union Pacific Railroad, which actually reached Green River on October 1, 1868. The expanding railroad at the end of the Civil War facilitated the westward migration of settlers, including war-weary men seeking refuge from the war's violence and recriminations. What Henry Nash Smith terms the "Virgin Land" of the vast American West, with its endless expanses, bounteous natural beauty, and unimaginable opportunities beckoned entrepreneurs seeking to build their fortunes. Peter Cozzens, in *The Earth Is Weeping*, characterizes this crucial moment in American history:

"The frontier army in 1866...found itself in the dual role of gate-keeper and guardian of the westering population of a nation suddenly delivered from internecine war and bursting with energy. During one six-week period, more than six thousand wagons passed through Nebraska headed west. Emigrants scoured the land along the travel routes like locusts until there was not a stick of wood with which to kindle a fire; even buffalo chips were at a premium. Along the Platte River Road, telegraph poles became more plentiful than trees. Isolated ranches offered inviting targets to Indian raiders or...to white marauders masquerading as Indians."

Among these settlers were miners, loggers, and especially cattle ranchers whose demands for grazing land created the inevitable conflicts with Native Americans and the immensely violent Indian Wars that Cozzens details so thoroughly. In the minds of many such settlers, the American West, rather than an idyllic garden, was seen as what Roderick Nash terms an "absolute wilderness" where the native Indians were considered as savage as the country itself.

After the Civil War this huge influx of settlers hastened the ravaging of Native American cultures they encountered. Among the most notorious events of the 1860s was the Sand Creek massacre in November, 1864 where the combined forces of the 1st and 3rd Colorado Calvary under the command of U. S. Army Colonel John Chivington attacked an encampment of Southern Cheyenne and Araphahos led by Cheyenne chief Black Kettle, who had settled his band on Sand Creek in a village near Fort Lyon, Colorado Territory. As advised by the Fort Lyon commander, Black Kettle had flown an American flag and a white flag at his lodge. Nonetheless, on the morning of November 29th Chivington ordered his men to attack the encampment. Men, women, and children were slaughtered. Following this brutality, most Cheyenne chiefs refused ever again to trust white men's offers of peace or to negotiate any further treatises with the United States Military.

Absent from the Sand Creek encampment were most of the Southern Cheyenne "Hotamitanio," or "Dog Soldiers" who were the Cheyenne's fiercest fighters, and here we depart from historical events. In our novel, a band of mostly Hotamitanio, led by Running Bear, have fled north from Colorado Territory and settled in the mountains and high desert northeast of Green River by early 1866. While the Cheyenne's complete disillusion with Black Kettle's efforts to achieve peace with white settlers and the U. S. Army after Sand Creek is historically accurate, Running Bear's fictional exodus from Colorado takes our novel into a landscape that is both real and imaginary, historic and symbolic. Green River is the destination toward which the railroad was driving in 1866, cutting through Indian hunting grounds and sacred lands, violating daily, both actually and symbolically, the once virgin land.

While the canyons extending east and northeast of Green River, including Greasewood, Greens, and Reiser, are real, and are where we imagine Running Bear has settled, Eagle Canyon is an imaginary, sacred refuge for the Cheyenne and for Johnny Redfeather, an iconic character in our novel. While it must be imagined as existing somewhere among the canyons and valleys winding beyond Green River, its actual location within this mammoth complex does not matter. All that matters for Johnny Redfeather is that Eagle Valley remains inviolate, even if only in his mind.

—MWS

1
September 22, 1866
Hell Rising

Unleashed on the usual mix of card games, whiskey, chaotic piano music, drunken railroad workers and cowboys, waitresses and whores, hell rose up late that afternoon to swallow the lost souls of Milly's Green River Saloon. Through open windows, lace curtains, and the swinging doors of the saloon short bursts haphazardly peppered walls and splintered wooden tables and chairs in the crowded interior. Seconds later tiny round holes appeared in the bodies of the motley assortment of customers and the employees who served them. Blood spurted out. And then the screaming, terrifying howls of pain and fury.

Sheriff Jim Talbot, whom Milly paid to canvas her place on busy nights, yelled "Get down!" Men and women, including several of Milly's girls who had had been hit by the initial barrage, fell to the floor, crashing wildly into tables and chairs. But not all of them got down soon enough to avoid the bird-shot blasted blindly into the interior or flying bits of wood and glass. The worst actual wound the sheriff saw was on a pretty brunette named Marilee. Her shoulder and chest looked as if a grizzly had taken several bites out of her flesh. He didn't have to tell her to get down again. She had already passed out upon seeing the face of her girlfriend, Roxy, spurting blood in several places and the ugly blue and black pimpled flesh where the bird-shot had lodged just under the skin. Several male and female customers sitting at tables close enough to the windows got hit in the face, neck, or upper bodies, and four or five of Milly's serving girls who had been struck in their chest, by either bird-shot or debris, were running around and crying hysterically. The sheriff barked again, "God damnit, get down on the floor!" This time all but the three or four most panicked girls did what they were told as they crashed chaotically into downed furniture.

As the random shots continued Sheriff Talbot noticed that none of the firing was loud. It was a distinct sounding "pop, pop," occasional and unhurried. He realized these were small calber shotguns, bird rifles, four-tens and whatnot, and that some of them were likely sawed off to give a wider spread, a tactic designed to induce fear, and it was working. Talbot moved deftly between downed tables that he used as cover, crawling on hands and knees amid spilled whiskey, shattered bottles, and blood, occasionally squatting to fire into the descending darkness at what he thought were the invisible attackers' positions. Suddenly Milly, her husband Frank, and her bartender Sam began firing shotguns from behind the bar. Although they hoped they were contributing to their defense, the additional gun fire only increased the general terror that now engulfed the saloon as bullets and bird-shot screamed back and forth through the shattered windows and doors. Charley dove behind his piano and Old Willie moaned piteously as he crouched behind his chair, holding up his guitar as a useless shield.

Trapped behind splintered tables, and bereft of help, much less rescue, Talbot suddenly wondered about the whereabouts of a recent acquaintance, Johnny Redfeather. He had seen the Irish Apache half breed in this same saloon not twelve hours earlier with a whore on one knee and trying to light the wrong end of an opium pipe. He recalled a bizarre incident earlier in the summer when Red had surprisingly helped him subdue a drunken mountain of a man. "Ain't no use killin' a sheriff," Red had yelled as he jumped on the drunk's back and drove him into the ground. "Never know, might need him some day." Maybe, Talbot thought, just maybe, Johnny might come to help again. Talbot had not known Redfeather long, but he already knew that Red had a habit of showing up unexpectedly in the damnedest places, and that he relished a good fight.

Then, as suddenly as the firing had started, it stopped. Sheriff Talbot, his clothes soaked in blood and whiskey and the howls of the wounded pounding in his ears, yelled at Sam, Frank and Milly to hold their fire, then slowly crept from behind a small table and looked toward the swinging doors of the saloon. Unable to see anyone in the dim light, and realizing that he had to get help soon for the more seriously wounded, he stood slowly then quickly darted back toward and behind the bar. He crouched low, reloaded his pistol, and waited. After several minutes he cautiously peered around the corner of the bar and surveyed the front of the saloon, desperately trying to locate the wretches who had brazenly terrorized it. Increasingly anxious to tend the wounded, Talbot crawled around the bar and then crept slowly down its length toward a small room several feet from the end of the bar that he believed would provide some cover. Reaching the corner of the room, he stood slowly and leaned against the door frame. Unsure if a second onslaught of bird-shot, or more lethal fire, was imminent, he surveyed the wreckage before him, increasingly unnerved by the cries of the wounded yet aware that he must proceed cautiously. Outside an eerie silence gradually descended, which made whatever came crashing through the side window that much louder as something metallic hit the floor inside with a dull thud. Talbot heard a voice yell "Ayyyyye! I'll be all go to hell!" Before he could whirl and level his gun at the shattered window a man's body was on him, slamming his own back against the sheriff's and both of them hard against the floor of the room.

"Redfeather," yelled Talbot, startled by his sudden appearance and grateful for Red's help, even if he had damn near broken his back. "How the hell did you know to show up now? You some kind of damn magician?"

"Shit man," hollered Red, "I heard a bunch of low down drunks, maybe some railroad and herder boys from up valley, talkin' over at Hal's saloon. They was sayin' they was fixin' to shoot up the place, lettin' you and Milly know who's runnin' this here territory. Figured I'd better get my ass over here. You all right?"

"Yeah, I guess," said Jim, squirming out from under Red's sweaty back and adjusting his holster. "God damn these liquored up idiots. I'm betting they're still out there, and several of the girls and customers got shot. There's blood everywhere! Get ready to fire!"

Seconds later the attackers resumed firing into the saloon's interior. Talbot and Red crouched on opposite sides of the door frame and began firing. Even with the hot, sweet glow of laudanum and absinthe welling up throughout Red's bloodstream, battling the bright, stabbing pain in his hip from crashing through the window of the saloon and landing full force on the hard, yellow pine floor, one of his .45's began firing in time with each heartbeat. Red's rapid and Talbot's resumed firing directed through open windows and the central swinging doors from where they knelt startled the attackers who suddenly quit shooting.

Talbot and Red waited several seconds, then slowly, cautiously rose to their feet. Talbot walked back toward the center of the saloon near the swinging doors, surveying the mess of wounded bodies and upturned tables and chairs. Not seeing anyone outside, yet realizing another attack could be imminent, he returned to Red who was still kneeling in the small doorway.

"Johnny, we have to act fast. No tellin' whether they'll be back. The wounded need medical help, more than you and I can give. And we got to arm some of the girls. No choice. I'll have to go for Doc Johnson as soon as possible."

"Gotcha. I'll do what I can."

Talbot turned to Milly, Frank and Sam who were still cowering behind the bar, along with Charlie and Old Willie who had joined them after the shooting stopped.

"Milly, Frank, all of you, come on out, quickly! Frank and Sam, give whatever rifles you stashed behind the bar to Red. We got to defend this place in case those barbarians return, and I'm leaving that up to him. He's going to arm some of the girls. And get some more kerosene lamps down here.

Several been shot out. I've got to go for Doc, and he'll need light to operate when he gets here. Charley, you and Willie bring down some blankets also. We got to be ready when Doc gets here."

Johnny Redfeather rose to his feet and, limping slightly from the pain in his hip, ambled to the center of the saloon. He called out to one particular girl who he knew was a damn fine shot; hell, a damn fine shot compared to most men.

"Hey, Darla or whatever that your name is, bring yourself over here," he called over his shoulder. "You and I got to decide right quick how to defend this here saloon."

Red chose five or six girls he thought he could trust, including a couple he knew could at least handle a gun, and quickly positioned them around the perimeter of the interior. He put one at the large windows at each end of the saloon, one each at the door frame of the small rooms at opposite ends of the room, and installed a brawny young woman named Stella, whose company he often shared, directly facing the swinging doors.

"You see anybody out there ladies, just fire like hell! Ain't no more customers likely for a while, not with them crazies shootin' guns like hell fire, so just assume whoever you see is just here to shoot up the place, and respond in kind. We got to take care of the wounded right quick, and the sheriff's goin' for Doc. So be steady, ya hear?"

"Yes, Mr. Red," they responded, as honored to have been handed a gun as they were terrified they might actually have to use it. "You, Stella. I'm countin' on you to shoot straight if necessary. You got that?"

"You loony redskin, don't talk to me 'bout shootin' straight. Yeah, I got that!"

Sheriff Talbot and Redfeather began helping the wounded as best they could, trying to assist the most seriously injured first. Marilee was shot in several places, and was bleeding heavily. Red took off his bandana and wrapped it around her upper arm to stop the bleeding from several bird-shots. Talbot tended to several of the other girls who had shot lodged in their upper bodies. Not enough to kill them, but enough to necessitate some painful surgeries. With help from several girls not too traumatized to take orders, Talbot, Sam and Red moved the wounded girls and the customers, mostly men, to safe places behind the bar. On the floor they spread blankets and sheets that Charley and Old Willie had brought down from the upstairs rooms and ordered two other girls to fetch water and try to clean peoples' wounds as best they could.

Talbot looked around at the many wounded men and women.

"Johnny, defend these folks as best you can. Many definitely need serious medical attention. I'm off to Doc's."

"Damn straight Sheriff!"

Talbot realized that now he had no choice but to trust everyone's life at the saloon to Redfeather. Since Talbot had come out west Redfeather was the only gunslinger he had met who was worthy of the name, and he knew that Johnny was utterly fearless. He had seen Redfeather in action in town twice. He had surprised two would be bank robbers whom he shot dead after they had wounded the previous sheriff. Then, shortly before Talbot became sheriff, late on a Friday night, Red had killed a man in Milly's saloon who had threatened her with a knife and tried to rob her safe.

Johnny Redfeather wore a buckskin tunic belted off with a two gun rig he could actually use. He was pretty much ambidextrous; his pistols were set to cross draw, so that he pulled each gun with the opposite hand. It looked impressive no matter who did it, but this man was the only one Talbot had ever seen accomplish it with speed and accuracy. Talbot also knew full well that Red endured a constant battle in his mind between alcohol and opiate addiction, and he could only hope that Red could hold himself together long enough to organize whatever defense might be necessary should the crazed attackers return. It was just one of the myriad battles in Red's personal war that Talbot knew had been going on for many years. And Red the gunfighter, so thoroughly acquainted with it, was neither, at least not at the moment, the only nor the most severely injured patient in this suddenly terrifying battleground.

Behind the bar the shooting victims, including several customers, groaned as their companions tried to minister to their wounds. Milly fired up the wood stove in back to provide boiling water, and her husband Frank and Sam tore up as many sheets as she could find for bandages. The cries of the more seriously wounded increased, especially Marilee and Roxy and two men and three women who had been sitting close to the front windows. Although Milly knew that the attackers had fired bird-shot, not real bullets, she still worried that the victims were losing so much blood that Doc Johnson would arrive too late to save them. She knew Sheriff Talbot would do everything he could to bring Johnson back as quickly as possible, but amid the din and the pools of blood Charley, Willie and her girls were mopping up Milly wondered if this night might be her last at the Green River Saloon. Why this attack, she wondered. Whom were the attackers trying to kill? Her? Sheriff Talbot, who was in her saloon most nights? How, she worried, could she go on after this?

2
Dr. Mark Johnson

Sheriff Talbot, furious about the sudden assault on Milly's saloon, hurried toward Doctor Mark Johnson's cabin two miles outside town, hoping to get there and bring him back before sunset. Although he could not know who the "low down drunks" as Red called them actually were, and while he suspected they were mostly saddle-tramps and hired guns fueled by stupidity and liquor, he also feared that the attack might have been a brazen attempt to intimidate him. He knew that many of the rail workers, miners, and especially the cattle herders and their bosses resented his recent efforts to defend Indians' land and water rights against the growing number of white settlers in the territory around Green River. Hell, he thought, if they knew I'd be there on a Saturday night, maybe I was the real target, not just Milly's "respectable" establishment.

Johnson had just finished treating a man for a snake bite and was washing his hands when Talbot burst into his cabin. "Doc, come with me right away. Several of the gals and customers over at Milly's been shot. One, Marilee, seems shot pretty bad. Grab your bag and let's go!"

"Christ almighty, now they're shooting women! What the hell is happening to this place? I'll harness my team right away and stop along the way for Maggie and Maria, they'll help with nursing."

Mark Johnson had trained at the University of Pennsylvania and in 1861 had volunteered as a surgeon for the Union forces. He had served in the Civil War in several armies of Ulysses S. Grant, but after two years had seen too much carnage, too many mangled, shattered bodies and sawed-off limbs; too many rotting, swollen corpses. His sleep was haunted by men screaming nightly in filthy, vermin-ridden, makeshift military hospitals housed in churches and barns on the outskirts of battlefields: Gettysburg and Malvern Hill and Shiloh. He had come to detest the majority of his own kind and had come west in late 1863. Like Sheriff Talbot he thought that there might be a place in this enormous country where the limitless savagery of war might not prevail among men. He too had eventually settled in Green River, in search of virgin land and rivers not polluted by human blood. The Green River ran clear, and for a year Johnson thought he had found, if not exactly paradise, at least a relatively peaceful place where the tensions that ransack human communities were less evident. Perhaps, he thought, the open spaces could convince men, Indians and whites, that there was enough room for everyone to pursue their ambitions without coveting their neighbors' possessions or cursing their politics. Since coming to Green River Johnson had treated Indians and white settlers alike, whites usually at his office in town and occasionally Indians at his cabin two miles away. Doing so, he thought, might help lessen whatever tensions existed between the Indians and the settlers, and his offices, especially the one in town, had become mutually respected oases where patients checked at the door not only their opinions but also their guns.

He had learned some of the native tongue and occasionally traveled to native encampments to aid an especially difficult birth. He had managed to do so without angering native medicine men or what among the tribes passed for nurses. Once he had saved the wife and infant daughter of a Southern Cheyenne warrior, and had thus garnered the right to pass unmolested through Indian land, a privilege that Johnny Redfeather insisted had never before in his lifetime been accorded a white man.

Now this. As Johnson crammed bandages, medications, and surgical tools into his bag, he dreaded what this latest shooting might portend. Blood was flooding into the heretofore clear waters of Green River.

3
Johnny Redfeather's Army

Redfeather inspected the weapons Milly had dragged out of a room behind the bar, five pistols and a few Remington and Henry rifles. He then walked through the saloon casually, stopping occasionally and giving everyone who would listen, especially the more hysterical among the girls, what encouragement he could. To the half dozen or so who were ready and able to help defend the place and who, in his estimation, could and would shoot if necessary and stood a decent chance of actually hitting a target, he gave sufficient arms and ammunition to mount a defense, should the assailants return.

"Now listen up! All of you! I'm guessin' those cowardly bastards who shot up the place probably won't dare return. Not after the little surprise the sheriff and I give 'em. But just in case. Don't just open fire on anything that you see move. I got you all set at important places in the saloon here, and you gotta jus' stay there and wait until I give the order to shoot and what to shoot at. But if I say fire, then god damnit fire if you see them lunatics come back. And above all, if I say cease fire, then you all cease fire! You all got that?"

"Yessir Mr. Red," yelled Stella from near the swinging doors. "You sure like given orders, don't ya?"

"Damn straight on that, Miss Stella. One damn thing I'm good at is givin' orders. That and shootin' straight."

"Yeah well, that ain't always the case, but I reckon that ain't the business here."

"No it ain't. Now you jus' keep that rifle aimed out that door there and listen and watch. I'll take care of the rest around here."

As the only real soldier in the place Red was nonetheless worried that his recruits would kill some unfortunate souls who had merely found themselves at or near the saloon under the mistaken impression that they would find what they expected on a normal Saturday evening and get gunned down for their trouble. Or worse yet, blinded by fear and fury and unable to restrain the impulse to pull the trigger, would blast away at Doc and the sheriff when they returned. He also had to dissuade a couple of the injured girls who were determined to help ("I got a big damn hunting knife in my room and I know how to use it!"). Because of their rising anxiety, he knew they would be a liability in a chaotic gun fight.

As he walked cautiously around the bar, eyeing nervously his recruits and the fading early evening light and unnerved by the constant wailing of the wounded, Red gradually realized that in his attempt to encourage his troops he was fretting as much as any of them were. To relieve his anxiety he swung over a low railing at the bottom of a flight of stairs several feet from the end of the bar and began climbing to the second floor. As he gained the top of the stairway near the middle of the second story, Red could see the girl he'd hoped would be there. She was lounging on a small couch outside one of the many rooms that lined the hallway, looking seductively unimpressed by all the commotion below her. In a tone that let him know in no uncertain terms that whatever he was doing he had left her waiting there entirely too long, she bellowed, "Now that you're finished with all that goings on downstairs, is this where you wanted me?"

"Yes mam," he owned.

"Don't call me 'mam' I'm not that old," she snapped in a good imitation of a lady offended by a forward soldier.

"Look, Darla, or what ever your-name is...."

"My name's not Darla, it's Dillard, Courtney Dillard. Of course, I'm not surprised you don't remember it, you were so damn drunk that night, it's a wonder you remember who you are." She giggled at her own quip.

"I didn't know there was going to be a test, darlin.' Uh, Miss Dillard."

Surprised, and no longer nearly so pleased with herself, she caught herself staring and not knowing now what to make of this positively savage looking man, who spoke like a gentleman of culture ("Like them New England Yankees, or a European even," she thought), with a young countenance that might even have been handsome were it not so hard worn.

"Miss Dillard?"

"What? Yes?"

"All right, put your arm down. Okay, are you ticklish?"

"Am I what? No!" she replied defensively.

"Good," he said, turning to grab a rifle propped up against the wall. Before she could protest, confused and frightened but hoping he could not tell, he bent down before her and whispered, "Be still." He sat down on the couch and eased the rifle into position on his lap, perched in the curve of his hip.

"What the hell are you doing?" she demanded with nervous anger.

"I'm not going to hurt you. Just stay calm and don't move. Just checkin' the sight on my favorite rifle. Snuffy!" he called.

Snuffy was a house orphan, the daughter of a woman who died working there in autumn, 1854. She was cared for by Madame Milly and the other girls out of compassion, to be sure, but it was also expected that should a woman die in childbirth, her death was a consequence, albeit indirectly, of working for the "house." Decency suggested that a house as prosperous as Milly's would take care of its own. The child's mother, a beautiful woman named Amanda, had worked for the house for about one year, though she was neither a courtesan, a whore, nor one of the singers or "dancing girls," distinctions that usually meant "in addition to" the world's oldest profession. Amanda worked in the kitchen or behind the bar, cleaned, cooked, and did unending masses of laundry, but she would not engage in the primary occupation of the girls at the Green River Saloon. She never revealed to Milly or to anyone else who was the father of her child, and she elicited from Milly a promise never to discuss the subject with anyone. She did not die in childbirth; she lived almost six months after her daughter was born, and then Amanda, who had never been sick a day in her life, went out walking with two of the other girls one autumn night and got a chill. She took to her bed with a fever, and three days later she was dead.

The baby girl was also named Amanda, but she had been "Snuffy," for as long as anyone could remember. Like Milly and her girls, Red was fond of her but for a different reason. What he admired in Snuffy was precisely that which frustrated the women who tried so desperately to keep her in line. At the core of her being, and what Red admired most about her, was the fact that for her age she was tougher than anybody Red knew. Even when she was made to take a switch, or was spanked with various implements of corporal punishment, Snuffy remained stoic and unmoved. She took her punishment like a man, more than any man could have, especially at such a tender age. Except for the Madame, Red was the only person Snuffy would mind with any regularity, so he tried to maintain at least the semblance of discipline with her. And so it was that a twelve year old, an outcast rebellious to all conventions and bound to no one, became heroic in Johnny Redfeather's mind.

There was an audible, "shh, thhunk, shh, thhunk..." coming from the stairs and looking down he spied the diminutive figure of a girl with disheveled, dark brown hair cut unevenly just above her eyes. She was as cute as a pixie, until she spat, and a thick brown stream landed with a smack, leaving a dark wet spot on the dusty floor and a thin line hanging on her chin. She wiped it off casually on her sleeve, then smiled up at Red.

"I reckon," she allowed, and dragging a box up the last stair with some difficulty, she put everything she had into one final push to slide it right up at his feet. Strained from the effort, she put her hand up to her brow, wiped her hair back, puffed "Here!" and stood to Miss Dillard's left.

"Eew, that's just nasty!" Courtney Dillard sniffed her disapproval.

"Naw it ain't, it's damn good, apple-wood cured 'baccy! You want some?" It was a generous offer made by the pint sized connoisseur of nearly all those indulgences normally reserved for older customers, saving the one her twelve year old mind was not quite able to understand, much less appreciate, and perhaps the only adult activity she thought was "nasty." As the older girl's horrified glare at the gap toothed child who proffered a small brown pouch in a grimy little hand made it clear she was unable to appreciate one of the truly finer things in life, Snuffy, sadly shaking her head, expertly folded it away, one handed, and sighed, "Suit yerself."

"At ease there, sergeant. Let me see what we've got. Say where'd you git to when the shootin' started?"

"Down in that damn little storage space at the end of the bar where ya always tell me to git to. Crazy Old Willie crawled in too. Him and his guitar. Weren't hardly room for no more."

"Well that's right smart sergeant. Jus' what I done told ya to do."

Red had bestowed the military "rank" upon her, who knows when, undoubtedly because he thought it sounded cute, but she took it seriously, and had come to take great pride in being Redfeather's second in command. Snuffy had her name for the obvious reason that among other indulgences, usually forbidden to youngsters, she dipped snuff. Actually, she chewed tobacco, but that did not lend itself as readily to a nickname worthy of such a precocious child. Her character and exploits, already approaching legendary in Green River, demanded a suitable nickname.

Noticing how bulky the box was at his feet and how hard it must have been for her to drag it up the stairs, Red smiled and said, "Let's see what we've got in this heavy chest." Without asking permission Snuffy sat down on the arm of the couch, brushing against Miss Dillard, who was sitting impatiently with her hands on her hips.

Irritated by what she considered an impertinent invasion of her space, Courtney hissed, "You can just leave it little boy. The adults are talking."

Red, laughing and thinking he'd throw a little kerosene on the fire, quipped, "Yeah, and it wouldn't break your jaws to call me 'sir,' now would it?"

Snuffy spat back first at Red, "No, sir, I told you I got every damn thing!" Then she turned her full four foot fury on the unfortunate Miss Dillard. "Let me tell you one damn thing Miss Princess Petticoats! I ain't no damn boy, but I will break your jaws for you if you ain't careful. If you see a boy, you give 'im five dollars!"

"Easy there, sergeant. She didn't mean nothin' by it." Red put the rifle down and motioned Snuffy over to examine the contents of the box to ease the situation as much as to take an inventory. They found nestled in a gray wool blanket a holster and two pistols, one with an elaborately carved ivory grip from what had been a custom handmade pair, and a plainer service revolver, with the cartridge belt full of bullets. Red also found a bronze spyglass and a couple of bottles, one of which held a liquor of a strange emerald color, and some smaller bottles like those found in an apothecary's shop. He picked up the absinthe and asked the child, "You didn't drink none of this did ya?"

"Hell no I didn't!

"You better not. Lemme see if them teeth are green."

"My teeth ain't green!" snarled Snuffy, puffed up now and defensive. "You're the only one I know that drinks that. I drink whiskey."

"You what?" Courtney was shocked.

"Well, I don't mind if you drink a shot of whiskey, once in a while, but don't ever drink this. It's bad for you."

"And it ain't bad for you?" Snuffy wanted to know.

"Never you mind about that. You don't do like I do, you do like I tell ya, you hear me?"

Red was spared defending his position by hearing someone shouting from the far end of the hallway. "Mr. Red, there's a buggy comin'!" It was Cornelia, a Negro girl from Alabama with an eagle eye and dead aim with a rifle. Red had positioned her at a window at the north end of the upper floor, and a woman named Stacey at a window at the south end, hoping that putting reliable pairs of eyes facing the street from both directions would prove useful.

"Snuffy, you and Darla stay here," Red barked, and grabbed his rifle and immediately dashed toward Cornelia. She was kneeling down, her rifle resting on the window ledge.

"Did you see how many?" he asked urgently.

"I, I don't know, Mr. Red, five maybe, six. They was some far off when I first seen 'em."

"That's all right," he assured her, his smile a hurried token of gratitude. "You probably saved us all."

Cornelia revealed a gold toothed grin. "I done no such thing," she said, with a small spark of pride.

"Now, let me see if I can get a fix on em." As he eased by his lookout, Red pulled out the small, brass spyglass he had found in Snuffy's trunk. The wagon in the distance, with a team of two horses, was headed their way, but in no real hurry. The wind carried muffled snatches of conversation inaudible from that distance. Damn wind out here never brought anything good, he mused.

"I figure you're right, Cornelia. Five, maybe six. From here I can't no way tell who they are." As he tried to get a sharper focus, the horses veered left, taking the wagon and its passengers with them.

"Whoever they are, Cornelia, them folks in that wagon is fixin' to come up behind the saloon, take the back road!"

"What back road Mr. Red? There ain't no other road out there!"

"Yeah there is. Supply wagons and cattle drovers use it, so's folks can get to Milly's 'Main Street.' Milly don't like no interference, if ya know what I mean. Might be Doc and the sheriff, but I doubt it. Too many I reckon in that buggy. You just stay here now, ya hear?"

"Yes, Mr. Red. I hear, but I sure am getting' scared."

"No need, Cornelia! Just be still is all!"

Red ran the length of the hall, past Snuffy and Courtney, to the south end of the second story where he cautioned Stacey to remain calm, to tell him immediately if she saw anything suspicious, and to hold fire until he gave the order. Red then sprinted back to the couch where he had left Snuffy and Courtney.

"Miss Dillard, I need you to go downstairs to the pantry behind the bar. Take these here lamps with you. Sergeant, I need for you to take this lovely lavender one, tempting as she is, down below and make sure she's out of the way in that place behind the bar, you know where I mean. You can load these two pistols for me and keep 'em, just in case. I'm trusting you to help me with this Snuff, 'cause if we don't watch after these girls, Milly will sure as hell fry our asses! Now, go!"

"Yes sir!" snapped Snuffy, her voice boasting obvious pride. The child was steadfast in the face of horrors that would loosen the bowels of grown men. All the more reason, Johnny figured, not to waste her talents on this mess.

"Damn right," Red agreed, and led them hastily downstairs to the first floor. Courtney complained as she settled into the storage space at the end of the bar. Snuffy squatted just inside the entrance, her guns ready at her sides. The pantry had the advantage of being behind structural timbers and well out of the common line of sight. Redfeather only wished that all of them, including Milly, Frank, Charley and Old Willie, who huddled along behind the bar with most of Milly's girls, were as well protected. A few moments passed, then a few more. There was a general rustling and rummaging about, whispered words spoken urgently. All that effort to move and speak quietly was noisy and distracting, and it fed upon itself, making the general anxiety in the room palpable and heightening its intensity. The wagon that Cornelia had spied would soon reveal its occupants as friends or foes. Redfeather knew that Doc Johnson and Sheriff Talbot were overdue and had damn well arrive soon. The wounded girls and patrons, their moans of pain from behind the bar punctuating the deepening silence, badly needed medical attention. The tension needed breaking, and Johnny Redfeather's experience with military commanders' encouragement to their troops led him to try something similar.

"Ladies," he began calmly, standing in the middle of the saloon,"We are in the right here, our fight is just, and we will triumph as good forever prevails over evil because we stood up against it and thereby defeated it as light defeats and disperses the darkness! So, take heart, remain steady and alert. If you see anything, cry out, and, above all, fire only on my command. Your bravery has already done you honor. I'm proud to stand with you." Johnny Redfeather felt good about his speech, but still he cried loudly,"How 'bout it, Snuffy?"

"I'm damn proud to serve with you, sir!" Snuffy declared, leaning out of the pantry door.

"And I with you, now make your ass ready in there, like I told you. Keep them guns handy!"

Redfeather didn't need to look to know she obeyed. He took a slug from the laudanum bottle and made ready, moving about the saloon silently. After checking his sentinels at all the windows, and especially Stella, who sat in a firing position facing the swinging doors, Red armed himself with his cross rigged pistols and leaned momentarily against the end of the bar just in front of the flight of stairs. This part of battle he'd always been good at. He knew he wasn't the best soldier, to be sure. Once resolved to it, though, he was the quintessential warrior, a weapon unleashed, an unshakable vessel filled with strength, courage, and singleness of purpose.

Suddenly realizing it was too bright inside, Red shot out the small kerosene lamp by the remaining front window. Everybody got quiet. Considering the fact he could have started a fire, and/or sent all the women into a panic, his impulsively killing the lamp succeeded. But then he knew it would, to the extent he paid it any mind at all. The agonizing situation was moving towards a conclusion, and Redfeather was just helping it along. He quickly climbed the stairs to check on Cornelia and Stacey, encouraging them to remain diligent, then walked back to the top of the stairs. From two large leather bags stashed against the wall next to the small couch he had shared with Courtney Dillard he removed a grey, full length military coat replete with Confederate insignia and a hat, plus several weapons. He donned the apparel, armed himself appropriately, and waited. Near total darkness now enveloped the saloon, and Redfeather was deeply worried. Sheriff Talbot and Doc were taking too damn long to get back.

"Steady, girls," he shouted, "tell me if...." A shot rang through the saloon. Red took a moment to sort it out, and decided it came from the front. One of the sentries yelled, "They're out there!" Bring it on, Red thought. Glass smashed on his left. He thought about ordering them to hold fire, more to keep them from shooting him and giving away their own position. He didn't wait for a sentinel's voice to yell "Someone's inside!"

In the dark, his spur clacked and rang only once as he lifted over the banister halfway down the stairs and floated for a moment, a dark gray cloaked apparition, landing softly near the foot of the stairs, fire spitting from the barrels of both pistols, a half dozen rounds blasted through the night at the front of the saloon before he paused. Stella fired at a huge man who had pushed open the swinging doors, wounding him and sending him crashing in agony to the ground outside. Another man outside screamed in pain. Red turned slightly to make sure his shot dropped a man who was firing through the same window he crashed through earlier, and the man howled in pain as he fell backward. One of the panicked girls upstairs fired her rifle as fast as she could into the empty evening air, and the girls stationed near the two small rooms downstairs fired through the shattered window frames. They would shoot all their ammunition before anyone could stop them. Just in case Red shot again to his right, away from his sentinel, but there was no one there. Outside there were horses and men scrambling to pull up at least one wounded man and try to escape. Red almost gave the order to open fire on "any of them that ain't us," but even the impetuous soldier he was knew better than that. Doc and the sheriff might be out there too. One of the cowards took a last shot from over his shoulder on his horse as they scattered, the bullet ricocheting inconsequentially off a rocking chair on the front porch. Holly, the sentinel on the main floor at the south end of the saloon, shot a man in the leg as he rode away, screaming in pain. Whoever they were they hadn't expected a half-breed and a bunch of women to come out shooting!

"Hold your fire, and report." Outside was panic and urgent shouting. Cornelia and Stacey raced down to the first floor from their upstairs posts. Snuffy and Courtney crawled out from the pantry and stood by the end of the bar, and most of the other girls who could stand crowded in behind. They were all stopped short, awestruck by the figure of a warrior in the Confederate cavalry officer's long grey coat, two holstered pistols positioned for quick draw and another shoved into his belt, and a carbine slung through a rifle harness off his left shoulder. He wore a nondescript hat with neither decoration nor insignia, except for a small brass tack holding up the left side of the brim, cavalry fashion, with only the butternut color to distinguish it as Confederate rather than Union issue. Under the hat, his long hair framed the truly frightening aspect of an Indian brave set off by two diagonal black stripes under his right eye. It was the war face of a man all of them knew, but no one recognized. None of them dared move or speak. Once Redfeather spoke, however, genuine gratitude that he was on their side replaced their fear. "I believe the day is ours, ladies."

From the south window Holly screamed, "They're getting' away out there."

"Let em," Red waved a hand dismissively. "We're equipped to defend this place and our own wounded. We've done that. Let the law chase down the villains," he smiled and lifted off the rifle and let it fall heavily on a table. "Didn't need that after all."

Staring and shocked by what she saw, Stella, holding a lantern, gasped, "Are you injured, sir?"

"I don't think so," he allowed, and half-spun around to see what she was looking at.

"It's just, you're smoking!"

"Well, I'll be all go to hell!" Redfeather lifted the flank of his great coat to reveal a bullet hole the blackened edges of which were indeed smoking. "Well, I'm fine but I'm afraid my long rider coat is seriously wounded."

There was some general uneasy laughter, due at least in part to the effect his war paint had on women who were used to seeing Red under entirely different circumstances. A dab of whiskey on a strip of cloth cut for bandages removed the markings altogether, and immediately almost all of the uneasy feeling. Upstairs, however, a couple of girls were arguing and calling down for Red to come up.

"It's them, they're still out there," Stacey urgently claimed. Red pushed by the women crowding the stairwell and started upstairs, followed by Stella and Holly. But before he reached the second floor landing, Cornelia called loudly from her post at the north end of the hallway.

"It's just Doc and them," she declared in a relieved exhalation. "That's his new black buggy."

"It god damn well better be! I ain't so sure we can keep this fightin' up too damn much longer!"

If believing could make it so, one man and twenty or so had conjured Doctor Johnson, Sheriff Talbot and their companions to materialize in the descending darkness on the street beside the saloon. It was Doc's voice that finally thundered through the confusion as Red and his makeshift army gathered near the shattered remains of the saloon's swinging doors.

4
The Legend of the Green River Saloon

"Hello the house! Damnit Johnny Redfeather, hold your fire. Hello the house!"

"Hello the wagon," Red returned in a jovial manner, standing on the boardwalk still attired in his Confederate coat and holstered pistols. "Y'all come right on in."

"It's a carriage, boy! Not a wagon. I had this carriage hand made in England by the Fischer Brothers. Sheriff says you got some seriously wounded victims here. Where are they?

"Behind the bar, out of the line of fire. Come on, I'll show you."

"Milly, Frank, Sam," Red shouted over his shoulder, "find whatever kerosene lamps ain't been shot out and get some light in there right quick. Doc gonna need lotta light now! Sheriff, damn glad to see you."

"And I you. Christ what all happened since we left?"

"Them no good tramps tried a second attack, but we drove 'em back. Think we killed a couple, not sure. Some of Milly's ladies a pretty good shot, but most everyone inside is still plum scared stiff. I still ain't seen Charley and Old Willie. Ain't no tellin' where they went to. But come on in!"

Just as Red and Sheriff Talbot were about to enter the saloon a large black woman shouldered her way through the door.

"Goodness gracious Boy, we come here to help y'all, but if you gonna' shoot me go ahead. Otherwise, I'm gonna' come on in outta da street!"

"Yes ma'am." Red recognized Maggie, an immensely strong African Caribbean woman with forearms as powerful as any man's and her husband Jim Smith, a giant of a man they all called Jupiter, whom Johnny Redfeather's parents had known since he was small. Maggie was not merely colored but of a skin color, people said, "so black it's almost blue." They were followed by a small woman with dark hair, Maria Santa Anna, Doc Johnson's housemaid and a curandero, a healer of Mexican and Indian descent who often worked with him and who relied on her special talents and familiarity with native women and traditional Indian medicine. Their trust in her skills was absolute, while the white man's medicine, even sometimes Doc Johnson's, was usually suspect. Given the Indians' animosity toward the white settlers and the level of care they experienced on the reservations, their respect for Maria was only natural. Doc followed quickly, and Red motioned for Talbot to enter ahead of him. The sheriff nodded politely to Red as a sign of gratitude, and Red nodded back. He knew the sheriff appreciated his gesture, and Red was grateful for Talbot's mutual respect.

As soon as Milly and Sam got several kerosene lamps lighted, Doc, Maria, and Maggie immediately began tending the more seriously wounded, especially Roxy and Marilee, and the other girls and patrons who had been nicked by the spraying bird-shot and shattering glass. Roxy's friend Susie took a lantern and rushed upstairs to fetch more lanterns and yet more blankets that she and Red spread on the floor for makeshift operating tables, while Maggie and Maria assessed who needed priority attention and administered first aid and comfort to them. Doc found Marilee lying on a blood stained blanket, groaning and cursing the "lousy bastards" that had shot up her body and her saloon. He and Maria moved her to a clean blanket, then Doc began examining the many black and blue modules of bulging skin on her arm and shoulders. He then moved her blood stained blouse down over her left breast, exposing several wounds that Doc knew would be difficult to treat.

"Jim, this will hurt. Get her some whiskey. Strong. And we'll need lots of hot water."

"Right. Susie, put a big kettle of water on the stove, and you and Red get more wood and fire it up fast."

Jim returned moments later with a bottle of bourbon, a glass, and a clean cloth he had fetched from behind the pantry near the bar. Marilee groaned as Doc examined the many small but painful bits of bird-shot that had lodged just beneath her skin on her upper torso. Jim lifted Marilee's head, slowly poured a generous shot of whiskey down her throat and placed the cloth between her teeth. With a knife steeped in boiling water, Doc began probing and then carefully lifting the bird-shot out of her left arm and then worked gradually up to her shoulder and then down to her left breast, where the shot had penetrated deeper into the soft mammary tissue. With each probe Marilee squirmed, bit hard into the rag, and tried to pull away from Doc's knife, so that Jim had to hold her against his body as more blood streamed from the cuts that Doc made, especially in the soft tissue of her breast.

Doc cautiously removed the deeper pellets and then cleaned and bandaged Marilee's wounds. He then attended to Roxy, who had several bird-shot lodged in her right cheek and upper neck. Jim looked around the room, now well lighted by several kerosene lanterns, that suddenly resembled a battlefield. Wounded men and women lay scattered across the bloody floor, many writhing in pain as he, Doc, Maggie, and Maria and some of the other girls tended to them. Marilee, Roxy, and the others; shot up, he mused for no god damn good reason. Jupiter and Charley and Old Willie, who had come out from hiding behind several barrels in the back of the saloon, helped other girls sweep up the glass that littered the interior and righted the bar stools and tables that the girls had knocked over in their panicked efforts to evade the shooting.

As Doc and his team tended to more of the wounded a slender brunette suddenly began screaming. "He's there! At the window! He's there again!"

"What's she going on about? Somebody calm her down, get somebody who knows her and remove or quiet her!" Doc Johnson barked. "I'm trying to work here. Red, for Christ's sake, see if someone is out there!"

As Red drew a pistol and sprinted toward a broken front window, Sheriff Talbot helped Maggie guide the hysterical woman to one of the small parlors behind the stairs near the back wall of the saloon. "Now then," he gently asked no one in particular, "Isn't her name Mandy? or something like...."

"It's Brandy," Maggie corrected. The sheriff was dumbfounded. "How can you remember all the girls and their names?"

"They's like my own chilren'. Madame Milly may run the place but they's my girls too."

The sheriff smiled. "They're lucky to have you."

"Well, I dunno 'bout all that. I guess we all's lucky jus' to have each other."

Brandy began sobbing and coughing with such force that Maggie feared the girl would hurt herself. "Girl, if'n you don't settle yerself down y'all gonna break yer own back. It's all right, now. Mister Johnny he done run 'em all off, and Sheriff Jim and Doc Johnson is all here now. There ain't nobody at no window no mo."

They placed her on a settee near the back of the saloon, and she gasped as if she had to snatch each breath from the putrid air in the room. In between sobs she stammered, "I could see him at the window, he was gonna kill me for sure. Mr. Red shot him through the window, and then he was just screaming and hollering and rolling on the ground. But I thought I saw him again!"

"Brandy," Talbot said gently, "you needn't be afraid. There's no one out there anymore." The sheriff meant to quiet the girl, but nonetheless glanced toward the shattered window at the front of the saloon to reassure himself that none of the attackers or their malignant ghosts remained to terrorize the saloon and its inhabitants. Only Redfeather's firm declaration, "He's dead," from his perch near the shattered window somewhat calmed Talbot.

"I know Mr. Redfeather must have got him too, 'cause he just went butt over teacup,'" Brandy giggled at her own choice of language, "and landed out there where we keep the flower bed with a smack, like that," she clapped her hands sharply. "He musta' got up, though, unless they picked 'em up, so he musta been alive, I mean why would they carry him off unless he was...."

"Brandy, he's dead."

"Well, I don't know, maybe he crawled away then came back."

"I didn't see any one at the windows," Sheriff Talbot interjected. "I suppose they could've...."

"He's fucking dead!" Red shouted back. "I shot him earlier! Ain't no one out there now!"

An unearthly howl, an animal sound, strange yet familiar, unimaginable but recognizable, pierced the night. The creature howled once more, further away now, a piteous wail that evoked a primitive fear in all who heard it. Then, as if in answer to the beastly wail, from high above terrible shrieks from a bird of prey echoed through the river valley.

The wild screeching momentarily terrified all within, reigniting the fires of imagination and the primal reflexes of fear and wild conjecture; then vanished altogether, leaving the scene eerily silent.

After the shock of the strange, chilling sounds, Doc and his team resumed tending to the shooting victims, and Milly, Frank, Jupiter and Sam, with some feeble help from Charley and Old Willie and some of the girls, continued sweeping up the debris that littered the floor. Sheriff Talbot and Maggie convinced Brandy that Red had indeed killed the man she had imagined seeing again at the window, and convinced her to retire to a room upstairs. Red walked to the bar, and stood alone for several minutes. Redfeather's emphatic "He's dead," had calmed the sheriff, and he exited the crowd cackling about the night's adventures and walked slowly toward Red.

"I believe you," Talbot said, as he approached Red at the bar.

Redfeather spun around and glared at the sheriff. Red's hands rested on his guns, but seeing no fear in Talbot's eyes, he made no attempt to draw. He allowed his hands to relax and then fall to his side, and the ivory grips of his pistols disappeared behind the folds of his great coat.

"Forgive me, Sheriff. I'm still a little wound up from our little skirmish here." The corners of his mouth curled up in a wicked smile. As he turned back towards his place at the bar, Talbot noticed the gray clad warrior moved gingerly, favoring his left side, and reaching out to the back of the bar stool he leaned heavily on it before basically falling into it.

"Oh no," Talbot said. "Forgive me. Here you've put your life on the line for our town here, twice in one day, and we haven't even been properly introduced yet, nor have I thanked you!"

"On the contrary, Sheriff, we have fought side by side against a common enemy. In my culture we are brothers."

Rather than merely taking Talbot's offered hand, Redfeather grabbed him first by the hand, pulled the sheriff nearly over a stool between them, and then caught him by the forearm and clasped his hand there. Talbot, realizing instantly Red's intent, grasped him by his forearm as well. He also realized this clasp was stronger and more meaningful than a mere handshake, as fighting and risking one's life with a man was a stronger bond than a mere greeting at a social event. Before releasing his grip, Talbot suddenly recalled the statue he often admired at the town's round-about that featured an Indian and a white man in a similar clasp. Red and Talbot held their grip for several seconds before Talbot released Red's arm.

"So, thank you, Johnny Redfeather!"

"Right welcome. See ya 'round I bet."

"Sure thing. Green River's not that big a town. Seems likely. Think now I'll see how Doc's doing." Talbot walked back to the center of the saloon where Doc and his nurses continued to attend the remaining victims.

As much as the girls wanted to put this night's terrors out of their minds, the howling of the wild creatures, real and imagined, made that quite impossible. Their bent shoulders and heads held in hands cast odd shaped shadows on the walls of the saloon. They gathered 'round each other in the parlors, just far enough away to keep Doc from snapping at them for "getting all in his light" as they ripped up laundry for more bandages. They were increasingly fascinated by Maggie. She was bold and glorious; her face radiant, halo like. She had perfectly tailored her "uniform," her dress, apron, and scarf common to cleaning women now faded to muted shades of dawn, by merely wearing it: the sleeves rolled up and out of her way, the leather sandals worn to the specifications of her comfort, their form having long since paid homage to the demands of attire.

Four hours later, Doc, Maggie and Maria, with occasionally awkward help from Sheriff Talbot, Red, and Jupiter, had removed bird-shot from some eight or nine girls plus numerous patrons, some of whom had by now left for home. Doc cleaned and bandaged the girls' wounds, and after carrying most of them upstairs to rest, Doc's impromptu medical team, thoroughly exhausted and disgusted by what they had seen, lounged against the bar and sipped whiskey or sat at tables scattered around the blood stained floor. Maria remained upstairs tending to some of the more badly wounded girls, cleaning and as necessary changing their bloody bandages. Milly, Frank, and Sam stood behind the bar surveying the wreckage, including the mounds of glass on the floor.

"God damnit this place stinks now," Milly sputtered. "Spilt whiskey and blood everywhere, and I ain't got much hooch left intact either. What am I gonna serve the fellas that come in here regularly asking for a drink? Water?

Burned coffee? Shit! Gonna take days to clean up this place, get windows replaced, fix the furniture. God damnit it all anyway! Frank, Sam, get those brooms from out back. We gotta start sweeping up some of this mess tonight. Charley, Willie, get busy!"

"Milly," Red offered from the end of the bar, "some of them moon shiners up valley might be able to supply you with some of their brew. It'll produce a damn good drunk in just about no time flat. Trust me."

"How you know about that, Red?" Milly asked.

"Being a scout, you know, I got an eye for stuff kinda hidden." Red laughed softly at his self characterization, aware of talents he knew the white men envied in him, but also sometimes despised. As Frank and his crew began sweeping up the debris, Red turned toward Doc, who was attending one last wounded man.

"We sure are glad to see y'all," exclaimed Red. "We weren't sure you was gonna get here. Seemed like it took forever."

"Well," Doc responded curtly, "I wanted to bring Maria and also stop to get Jim and Maggie. From what Jim told me I knew I would need help. We got here as fast as my horses could run. Wasn't easy."

Sensing the disgust and anger in Doc's response, Red grabbed two shot glasses and a bottle from behind the bar and walked slowly toward Jupiter, who was standing alone. Red gestured toward a small room, as he found this an infinitely more comfortable space to be in. He cleared off some broken glass and pulled up two chairs at a small table.

"How you been, Jupiter?" Red asked as he sat down and motioned Jupiter to join him.

"I'm fine, Mr. Red. I don't rightly know how long it been since anybody done calt me 'Jupiter.'"

"I'm sorry, it's Jim, right? It's just an old habit. Forgive me."

"Naw, naw, it's fine. I kinda' miss it, and that's what all y'all in here used to call me."

Red smiled and nodded, "That's true." He poured two shots of whiskey and leaned towards Jupiter, "You want one?"

"Yeah," Jupiter gladly accepted, and in the time it took him to say, "I don't reckon it'll hurt nothin,'" one fluid, graceful motion of his hand set the empty glass softly on the small table between them. Just then Sheriff Talbot, drink in hand, approached and sat down. Before Talbot had sipped his own drink, Red had filled up two more for himself and Jupiter, both of whom grinned at their own mischief. "You're falling behind there, Sheriff," Red chortled. Sensing Red's game, but unwilling to surrender, Talbot made to catch up. As the three of them huddled over their bottle, a voice boomed in from a table in the center of the saloon.

"Mr. Jim, don't y'all let me catch you drinkin' dat whiskey wid dat boy!" Immediately, the largest man the sheriff had ever seen vehemently denied his participation, like a little boy caught with his hand in the candy jar.

"I ain't doin' nothin," he proclaimed loudly. And Jupiter rolled his eyes as if to say, "Y'all know how it is...."

"I'm afraid I do," Red allowed, as he and Talbot nodded agreement.

"And y'all know yerself, Mr. Red, that's one big black woman you sho' don't want all up in yer business. Sur' 'nough!" The wizened old black man leaned back in his chair, yelped, then laughed so uproariously that Redfeather and Talbot, welcoming a moment of hilarity amid the deepening gloom of the evening, joined in a good natured acknowledgement and mutual awareness of an inescapable Truth.

To save Jupiter, and themselves, further trouble the three broke their huddle after one more drink for good measure and scattered around the saloon. Sheriff Talbot, determined to make a formal assessment of the situation, made such inquiries of Milly's girls as might be useful. Most of them had long since gathered in close knit groups reliving the night's terrifying experience. They had all been awe struck by the chivalric courage and boldness that Johnny Redfeather had displayed as their impromptu leader, taking no thought for his own safety, jumping into the fray, guns drawn and spitting fire even as the cowards fired at him while cringing in the darkness.

"It's a story fit for legend," Holly exclaimed, proud of having shot a man.

"Oh yes," Doc's exasperated voice boomed from his chair where he sat with Maria and Maggie. "This will be a legend. The Legend of the Green River Saloon! Every time we have a new legend, or add to the old, people get shot, people get killed. If we make enough legends, eventually there won't be anyone left to tell or hear them." He looked around him and noticed the bemused and puzzled looks and made a real effort to contain his anger.

"It's just hubris. Wars, between nations, states or individuals are an insult to humanity, just as gunshot is an insult to the human body. I know. I served during the war for the Union army and the so called 'ideal' of brotherhood. Hell, all armies are barbarians. No other way to look at it. Barbarians! Just like here tonight."

"Maybe so, Doc," Red interjected immediately from the bar where he and Jupiter stood, "but out here Indians got no choice. White people won't leave us alone, so what the hell we supposed to do? Got to fight. Seems to me you outta know that by now, Doc. You been here long enough I reckon."

"I know that all right, Red. There's killing on both sides. And that's what disgusts me. I'm tired of pulling bullets out of people's bodies. Red or white, men or now women! Not what I wanted when I came out here."

"Ain't what the Cheyenne wanted either!" Red scowled. "Nobody asked these god damn loggers and cowboys to come here! Be right peaceful without 'em! Ain't that right Jupiter?"

"Well, guess maybe we's all could git along better if'n we tried. We done just fought this war over slavery and what to do wid black folks an' all. Sur' 'nough terrible it was. Don't need that no more I figure. 'Specially out here now."

"Nah, Jupiter, we sure as shit don't. Now if you'll all excuse me, I'll get me some little peace here."

"Sur' 'nough, Mr. Red. See y'all again some time."

Johnny Redfeather knew Doc and his viewpoint on such matters well. He had a measure of respect for the older man and so took up a place at the far end of bar, well away from the knot of people gathered around the physician's table under one of the few remaining kerosene lamps hanging from the rafters. Red believed that such absolute viewpoints as Doc had were the luxury of isolated minds whose bodies were protected behind castle walls in lofty towers. Red took no oaths, not anymore. Let Doc believe whatever gave him comfort. Johnny Redfeather lived by his wits and his guns. He reached into his coat pocket and drew out a small bottle of laudanum. He relied on the opiate to relieve various sorts of pain, some physical, some spiritual, some he could explain neither to himself nor to others. The opiate/alcohol mixture was dulling, but had not yet sufficiently quieted the mix of pain he now experienced.

He walked slowly away from the bar and settled into a chair by a small table. As he often did to endure the present, he leaned back and, succumbing to the laudanum and alcohol, conjured memories of sunsets on the eastern coast of Florida, where it took its sweet time and one was treated to the entire spectrum of shimmering color. Even after the glowing orange globe had rolled beneath the horizon there were myriad sprays of subdued light. It left the impression that some things, be they of sufficient majesty, truly did go on forever. Even after darkness had crept up and surrounded it, the light due west lay determinedly on the horizon, so that one could never be sure when it had at last given way. Here, he reflected, the sun just flat went down. And dawn was not a soft, sleepy awakening through pink and lemon hued phases as Apollo's chariot ascended to its zenith (or so he had read somewhere). Here, night's serenity ruled absolutely until it yielded suddenly to merciless, glaring light.

Red hated it; which, admittedly, seemed rather unlike an Indian, even for a half breed, but this particular half breed much preferred the east coast of Florida, the cobble stone paved streets of St. Augustine to the burgeoning

"West" of "Manifest Destiny." He also preferred Greek myths to the many tales he heard on reservations, all of which were apparently "true" and compelling, always depending of course upon the teller. Perhaps because he was a half-breed, a loner, dangling between two cultures but belonging fully in neither, in a new world not yet properly defined, he could see clearly neither who he was nor who he might become. What he desperately wanted to find in this wind-swept wilderness was a place where he believed he belonged. As absurd as he often feared that wish was amid these vast, crushing mountains, it could still occasionally seem possible. It gave one hope, and to Johnny Redfeather d'Argent O'Shaughnessy, hope was every bit as important as the old empirical truths, especially these days. All the more so tonight, as fading images of sunrises and sunsets in St. Augustine were suddenly banished from his mind by lingering moans of injured men and women.

5
Johnny Redfeather's Story

Sheriff Talbot walked to Doc's table and sought to alleviate the tension by engaging him in discussion and perhaps the better to understand the half breed Irish-Indian crumbled at the far end of the bar who sparked such emotion from every corner. A few minutes later Jupiter and Maggie ambled over and sat down next to Doc.

"Maggie," Talbot asked, "what about you and Jim? You known Red a while?"

"Yes, Lord," she replied, "we have. I done knowed his mama and daddy and him since he was a baby down south, mostly Florida. Ain't that right Jim?"

"Sur' 'nough, Maggie. I 'member him from way back, 'way fore the war I reckon."

"His daddy was the Irish part, O'Shaughnessy if'n I 'member dat name rightly," Maggie continued. "Mama was Indian all right. Not quite sure which tribe, maybe Timucua or somethin' like that. Ain't one bit sure 'bout the name, tho' she always said way back she was Cheyenne. Said her Mama, Red's Gramma, was daughter of a chief or holy man, so's I reckon Red's legit Indian all right. Don't kno' nothing 'bout Red's Grandpa, tho' he coulda' been Indian or white, seein' as how them peoples was all mixin' wid each other, y'all know what I mean. Anyway, we knowed 'em in St. Augustine. Johnny got his name 'Redfeather' cause one day his Mama found him, when he was jus' 'bout one year old mind y'all, standin' toe-to-toe and starin' down a red-tailed hawk in a field. Ever since his Mama done called him her 'red tailed Indian boy,' but Johnny decided later for 'Redfeather.' His Mama always told him 'Never forget the Indian part in you. Don't never let no white man ever try to cut that part out of you. Promise me.' Dat what she say to him, over and over. She one proud Indian woman I'd say. Never did take no shit from no white folk that woman, an' I don't figure Johnny Redfeather ever will either. You agree Jupiter?"

"That sur' 'nough sounds 'bout right I'd say. Red don't take nothin' from nobody."

"From what little I know of him," added Sheriff Talbot, "I'd have to say I'd agree with that part. How long you and Maggie been here in Green River, Jim? And how is it you found Red here again and Doc?"

"We left Florida after the war, y'all know, some 'leven months back. Figured South weren't gonna be no place for black folks. Got work on wagon trains an' such, cookin fer da railroad once they was runnin' pretty good again, workin' our way west you see? Whatever work us black folks could git ya unnerstand? Finally come out here, Sheriff. Then lawd almighty but don't we see Johnny in this here saloon one night sittin' with Milly 'bout four months back. Craziest dang thing I ever did know, seein' him way the hell out here! I never had known what happened to him, or his folks, and he don't like to say much 'bout his comin' an' goin' so me and Maggie don't ask. Seems he just shows up every once in a while, like he drop down from the sky or somethin' crazy like that."

"That's quite the coincidence all right, you finding him way out here. Yeah, I get that sense about Red. Just never know where he's at. What about you, Doc? You known Red long?"

"Well, yes, a few years. I knew his father and mother back during the war. Johnny's father was a fine, courageous man, a tracker and Indian liaison for the Federal army in the South. I met him in Georgia some place, late eighteen sixty-two. But by then Johnny was off fighting for the Southern cause, so I did not meet him during the war. I've known him here only since late sixty-five, about two years after I arrived. It was Maria here who told me about him. She had met him at the Indian camp up in Greens Canyon and told me he knew the Southern Cheyenne tongue. I was eager to learn enough so I might be able to treat some of the Indians hereabouts. Red knew Running Bear had settled into the canyons up north, and he and Maria gradually arranged for me to help the Cheyenne when possible. Not too often, just once in a while. I was finally glad to be able to help when I could."

Doc leaned back in his chair. "Sheriff, have you known the boy long?" he asked.

"No," Talbot admitted. "I hardly know him at all really. Like Jim says he pretty much comes and goes as he pleases. I mostly know of him by reputation, and we both knew Colonel Bill Swanson in the war down south. He knew Colonel Bill better than I did, and they had known each other longer. I'm afraid, however, I had the unhappy chore of informing him of Swanson's death. It hit him hard."

"Yes, I'm sure it did," Doc responded. They had survived many dangers. And then, it was just so senseless...."

"I couldn't say," Talbot remarked. "I wasn't sure how Swanson died. Certainly it was tragic. Red was convinced he was murdered, but there was little or no evidence either way. I mean there was a suggestion he was killed by a stray bullet from a fight between a few drunks, or one man who was drunk and firing blindly in the dark."

"Of course, it's all senseless," Doc added, "but men war with one another by choice, even if they have no grasp of the horror they bring upon themselves or others. Johnny is lucky to have you as such an honorable companion."

"Thank you," Talbot responded, then paused. "For my part, I consider us friends. Come to think of it, every time I've seen him in person up to now, he's fought by my side, at no small risk to his own person, while the rest of the town has been content to watch their new sheriff uphold the law or perish in the attempt. The first day I met him, sometime in early July as I recall, he helped me fend off a man who was apparently the victim of unrequited love. I felt for the poor cuss, but he was very drunk, and shooting out windows all along the street, crying and carrying on. And my God he was strong! The Federal Marshall hasn't sent out a deputy yet, and nobody here has got the sand to volunteer. I wouldn't have been able to subdue that brute by myself. We damn near lost him together."

The sheriff paused to pour himself and Doc a drink. "Jim, you up for one more?"

Jim cast a wary eye on Maggie, who nodded gently to her husband and murmured, "Jus' one more. Guess it can't hurt none. I'll have me one too, Sheriff, if'n y'all don't mind. If I do say so myself, Maggie girl, you done worked yerself to your bones tonight. I normal don't like to indulge no whiskey, but tonight maybe jus' a bit."

Talbot walked to the bar and returned with three extra glasses, then filled everyone's before resuming his story. "Well, anyway I thought I'd have to shoot that big ape. He seemed to quiet down at one point. I went to walk him off the street and over to the jail. He was blubbering like a baby. Then he spun around, grabbed my arm, damn near broke it off! Red jumped past me and knocked his big ass over. Next thing you know, he's over Red, poundin' on him with them beefy arms. I pulled my pistol, didn't have no choice. Don't know if Red had a gun, but he didn't shoot it if he did. He just reached a vicious looking hunting knife strapped on his knee and planted it in big boy's thigh. He couldn't do much but roll and moan after that. I figure you had a look at him, Doc. They said he's going to be all right. Big ol' boy, ain't he?"

"Yes," Doc allowed. "He'll have a limp, but there were no arteries or veins cut, and the boy must keep his knife clean. No infection to speak of. If the fellow keeps the wound reasonably clean, he'll live to love again."

The chance to laugh wasn't lost on either man, and if both were guilty of laughing longer and louder than Doc's observation warranted, they could be forgiven. Another round was also appropriate. Any reason to laugh in the eerie darkness was cause to celebrate.

"Oh lord," Sheriff Talbot wiped his eyes. Still chuckling, it took some effort to recall where he was and so carry on. "I saw Red in here much earlier today with a lady on his knee, then suddenly again when that bunch opened fire through those windows." He waved, indicating the remaining front windows and swinging doors of the saloon. "I was standing over there, with Milly and two other girls. I tried to get them down on the floor, couldn't tell who, what, or where, but next thing I know Red slams his back against me, and I won't lie, I was glad to see him." Talbot laughed and added, "He said he'd heard some nasty talk about shootin' up Milly's from a bunch of drunks at Hal's saloon, but that he also just came lookin' for a quiet place to get drunk! I didn't half believe what he said, but either way his bein' here was a blessing. Damn, but that man can shoot!"

"Oh, you can believe it," Doc responded solemnly, "The Indians and the Irish race have in their blood an unfortunate proclivity and inordinate fondness for libations and a pronounced tendency to indulge at the cost of their health, well-being, and sanity. Johnny Redfeather O'Shaughnessy is thus doubly cursed. I've warned him about it. But as his father's countrymen might say, 'Better to save your breath for the cooling of your porridge.' The injuries he's suffered from all this gun-fighting nonsense have made him a laudanum addict as well. The war inside is the more lastingly injurious, in my estimation. But forgive me Sheriff, I did not mean to interrupt."

"No, no, that's all right. Well, back when Jones was sheriff I had seen Red in action twice. Killed a couple guys trying to rob a bank, and later another fool in here trying to rob Milly's safe. But tonight was just the second time I guess you'd say I've actually met him and spoken to him in person. No, that's not quite right. That was several nights ago, up the street a little. I had just heard about Colonel Swanson, and he must've heard something too, 'cause I saw him running from one person to the next asking questions about Swanson until he got to me. I got the feeling it was all he could do to keep from grabbing me, and demanded to know what happened to the Colonel. He looked beside himself, but he spoke real polite, called me 'Sir,' which was unnecessarily formal, I thought. So, I told him what little I knew, that maybe it had been an accident. And then, he just blew up, started shouting that he was sure it hadn't been an accident, like he knew, but he couldn't have. He was plum torn out of his frame though. I guess he was good friends with the Colonel, and the death hit him real hard. It was just so..."

"Like I said, senseless," Doc interrupted, making no attempt to hide his disgust. "And Johnny will wind up the same damn way, for the same reason, which is no damn reason." The anguish in his look had diminished, and Talbot could see that despite the gruff voice and grim condemnation, "the boy," as Doc insisted on calling Red, meant something to him. "Did Colonel Bill Swanson tell you about himself and Johnny?" Doc asked.

"Only that Redfeather had once been his captive in Georgia during the war, escaped, and then later, after Johnny and his calvary had captured Swanson and his men, Red actually turned around and helped them escape from the Rebel prison," Jim admitted. "But not too many details. Damnedest thing I ever heard."

"Oh, it is that," Doc agreed. In hopes that Doc was warming to it, Talbot proffered him another drink as incentive for him to tell the story.

"Yes, Sheriff, I believe I will join you. Maggie, you and Maria had better check on the two girls we had to sedate. Set rounds for every three hours. Tell me if anything unexpected happens. We're lucky we got here when we did. So are they. And please remind Milly that we'd all like to stay here tonight, all of us, just so's we can be sure the girls will be all right in the morning. We can check on them during the night if necessary."

"Yes sir," Maggie replied, and then she leaned over towards Sheriff Talbot, smiled, and added softly, "Y'all wanna kno' anythin' 'bout the boy, you jus' ast me, ya hear?"

"Yes, Mam," Talbot said, "I sure will."

"We'll leave y'alls now and go check on them girls. Jim, come along wid us now." As Maggie, Jim, and Maria stood up to leave, Doc had finished his whiskey and lit a cigar. Talbot poured another for both of them, and sat back, giving Doc the floor.

"Well, Johnny had no business joining the Confederacy, especially considering his father was a Union tracker. But some friends of his, from Kentucky I think, convinced him that theirs was the nobler cause. These folks preached a kind of 'state sovereignty' that persuaded Red to join their cause. Anything anti government appealed to him. The boy always feels things strongly as you have seen here tonight. Anyway, he joined one of those irregular, all Irish light calvary units that fought light skirmishes, fire and retreat. Johnny made a reputation as a crack shot. He'd climb trees and shoot officers in the Union lines. Not proper conduct for a soldier, if you ask me. And that's how Swanson caught him. Red had this little spy glass he wore on a lanyard off his hip, to spy on the unsuspecting soldiers across the line. Swanson discovered him in the North Georgia mountains when the glimmer of his spyglass betrayed his position and led to his capture."

"Red was furious at being caught. Guess it just tomahawked his ego you might say. Well, from what I know, Red decided that anyone clever enough to capture an Indian scout, even a half-breed, might be worthy of some respect. Red escaped, but not before expressing his admiration for

Swanson as a soldier and a man, thereby establishing mutual respect between soldiers who are supposed to be sworn enemies."

"This turning into quite a story, Doc."

"It gets better. Later in the war, Redfeather and a small band of renegade Confederate calvary caught Colonel Swanson and his Company unawares. Red, now an officer, treated Swanson and his men with respect. However, once Red turned his captives over to a higher command, the prison guards, embittered, Swanson believed, mostly by their sense of inevitable defeat, brutishly abused Swanson's men. When one of the guards threatened to sodomize one of Swanson's young soldiers with a cattle prod, Johnny suddenly turned on them, grabbed his guns and killed or wounded all ten guards in seconds. Swanson said he had never seen anything like it!"

"God help us, sounds like so much I remember and want to forget."

"Exactly, you and I both, Sheriff. 'Where we going now, you crazy Indian?' Swanson said he remembers screaming at Red."

"'Don't make no fucking difference! Anywhere that ain't here!' Red fired back.'"

"Well, Swanson said they traveled all night through thick forests and swamps, dodging tree limbs and wary of the snakes that crawled all over the country. Swanson said he was terrified, but Red insisted he'd tackle a cotton-mouth any day or night over Confederate soldiers. 'Hell, worse a snake bite can do is kill you right quick. God damn rebels would torture you for days, and then piss on your dead body just for insult. No tellin' what I've seen them barbarians do. Snake ain't nothin.' They didn't stop till two days later when they approached the Yankee garrison Swanson had been working for. Swanson and his men returned to their unit. He told me he never said a word to anyone about what Red had done for them. Johnny just disappeared. He had to. Swanson knew that the Confederate soldiers would torture Red viciously if they ever caught him, and for the rest of the war Red became a hunted man on both sides of the conflict: a 'traitor' to the South and a 'cold blooded murderer' to the Union."

"My God what a story. How the hell did Johnny survive?"

"Swanson figures he roamed around the mountains in Georgia and gradually worked his way up north, through Tennessee, keep going till he got into Indian Territory further west and what he figured was far enough away from everyone who wanted his scalp. He lands here, holds up a while with the Cheyenne, and now he just seems lost whenever I see him, which isn't too often anymore. Though I guess he spends some time here at Milly's."

"Seems Red is good at saving the lives of white men," Talbot said, after Doc's emphatic retelling of Swanson's tale and recognizing in it the man who had earlier crashed through the front of the saloon and saved his life.

"Seems like a fellow you would want on your side in a tight spot, especially out here. Well, thanks for that story."

"My pleasure I assure you. Think I'll see how Maggie and Maria are doing with their charges. Thanks for the whiskey, and for listening."

"Sure thing, Doc. I'll check back tomorrow. See you then."

Doc Johnson walked to the bar where Milly, Frank, and Sam were sweeping shards of glass and splintered wood into tin buckets.

"Looks like a war zone, Milly. Are all the girls upstairs now? Did Red and Jim carry them up all right?"

"Yeah, mostly Jim. Red's up there now with his favorite, the one he calls Darla. She wasn't hurt, so she's takin' care of him. Seems he's drifted off somewhere, don't quite know where."

"Yeah, I know what you mean. His self-medication again. Guess that's how he copes. We can all stay here tonight, right, so we can check on the girls in the morning?"

"Yes, I got Frank and Willie and Charley up there making bed rolls on cots for you all. He'll show you where to bunk. We'll sure have a full house tonight, but I figure we'll manage all right."

"Right grateful, Milly. I'll just head up then. See you in the morning. Good night."

"Good night, Doc. Thanks for comin' and for all you and Maggie and Maria and Jim did here tonight. Me and Frank sure do 'preciate it."

6
Passion and Warfare: Gentleman Jim Talbot and Miss Abigail Delacourte

Sheriff Talbot slowly walked outside through the bullet-scarred swinging doors into the quiet night. He leaned against the front of the saloon, removed his hat, somewhat disheveled from the evening's violence, and held it in his hands: a black, wool felt Jasper. He twirled it slowly between his fingers, dusting first the bowl and then the wide brim. He tightened the two black leather thongs at the base of the bowl, fitting them tightly against the wool and stretching the ends until they were of equal length. He ran his right thumb down the length of the valley at the top of the hat, then gingerly pinched the creases on either side. Convinced that they were symmetrical, and the valley of proper depth, he slowly put the hat on and pulled down the front brim. He stepped off the boardwalk into the dusty street and began walking slowly toward his office a half-mile away. Since he had left his horse at Doc's cabin, he decided he would wash and change his filthy clothes at his office, then sleep on one of the cots he kept there for emergencies. He would ride back with Doc in the morning to retrieve his horse.

A refugee from the Civil War, Sheriff James Talbot, although originally from Virginia, had nonetheless been with the Union Army since just before Bull Run and had fought bravely with Lieutenant Winfield Scott Hancock's First Minnesota Regiment at Gettysburg, where he was one of only forty-seven men to survive the regiment's valiant defeat of an Alabama brigade on Cemetery Ridge on July 3, 1863. For the next two years, moving gradually south with marauding Union forces, he had seen more barbarity in combat, more landscapes drenched in human blood, heard more hideously wounded men howling for death, than he could have imagined possible. After the war ended he had settled briefly in Philadelphia while he tried to fathom the violence of the Union Army and its generals in the name of eliminating the barbarity of the "Southern way of life"; i.e., the abject enslaving of thousands of terrified black souls on the huge plantations owned by the "educated" Southern aristocracy. The unmitigated violence of the war, especially during the final months of Sherman's rapacious campaign, had permanently scarred his soul. Rather than an aberration, war now seemed to him endemic to humankind.

In late January, 1866 in hopes of finding spiritual solace, Talbot had again been visiting the small Presbyterian church in Philadelphia he had attended before the war. At a social event sponsored by the church he was unexpectedly reunited with Miss Abigail Delacourte, a young woman originally from Richmond, Virginia. He had met her at this church in April, 1862 and, before joining the army, had become quite infatuated with her beauty and her charming personality. Her father, a Presbyterian minister, and her mother, a school teacher, were fierce abolitionists who, like Talbot, had left Virginia at the start of the Civil War and had come to Philadelphia to preach against slavery and to work for the Union cause. During the war Abigail had also been a school teacher and had taught Sunday school in her father's church. Having mistakenly believed that Talbot had been killed at Gettysburg, she was stunned when she saw him standing alone drinking a cup of coffee at the small gathering in the church hall.

"Why my Lord in heaven," she exclaimed, "have you come back from the dead James Talbot? I never did expect to lay eyes on you again! Wherever have you been all these days?"

From that moment on Talbot had resumed the courtship he had tentatively begun nearly four years earlier. Aware of Miss Delacourte's formal education, the emotional hardening in himself caused by two years of constant battle, and her parents' positions as church and educational leaders, he had courted Abigail so politely and so hesitantly that she labeled him "Gentleman Jim Talbot." When he finally proposed nearly two months later she accepted readily. "Why gracious heaven above James Talbot, how awfully long you can make a Christian woman wait. I was about to give up on you. Told my daddy I'd be a right old lady before I ever heard the word 'marry' come from your lips. When exactly are you planning on this wedding day?"

"Why Miss Abigail," he had responded shyly. "Begging your pardon, I had not wanted to seem too forward. You are a fine and pretty and educated woman, and I'm not too much more than an ex soldier fixin' on improving my book learning some and trying to get myself more balanced with the Lord at this little church after that awful war. Wasn't at all sure your daddy would see much in me to like as a son in law."

"Well, Gentleman Jim Talbot, there comes a time when a man just has to state his case and let his prospective bride make her decision herself. My daddy and I, and mother too, been fixed on you since before the war. I'm quite surprised you had not figured that out yet. Besides, since I am their only child, they would be right glad to have me marry a gentleman who knows how to talk politely to a lady. They and I believe that bodes well for a marriage."

"Well I sure am glad to hear that, Miss Abigail."

Abigail's father married them the first Sunday in April. Three restless weeks later, haunted as he still was by lingering memories of violence and disturbed by the recriminations and social unrest lingering from the war years even in a northern city, Talbot hesitantly began explaining to Abigail that he felt they needed to get away from such memories and that he could no longer remain in Philadelphia. He thought they should seek the innocence he dreamed of finding in the western territories. "Peace and prosperity," he had promised her, "a new life out west. Way out west, away from all this." She was furious at his sudden decision, and doubtful of his idyllic vision of what she imagined as unfathomable wilderness. She was also fearful of her parents' anger at her husband's reckless plans. Nonetheless, a week later she finally agreed.

"If I did not love you, I would never agree to leave here for God knows what. Do not disappoint me, Jim. Please."

"I'll head west first, and when I find the perfect spot, I will send for you," he promised.

He left Philadelphia in late April and headed west, mostly by train, occasionally by stage coach and borrowed horse, seeking that elusive paradise for him and his betrothed where everything would be new and fresh and free of the battle scenes that still wracked his dreams. He heard talk from travelers and Army scouts about the virgin lands of the Dakota Territories, and heading west from Denver he became increasingly sure that somewhere in this vast wilderness he and Abigail could build a new, safe existence. The sheer majesty of the landscape, the mountain spires spearing scattered clouds; streams tumbling from glistening glaciers onto arid mesas seemingly dropped from the sky; a relentless sun scouring the stones and shrubs of the endless high desert, both awed and terrified him. "This sure isn't Philadelphia," he muttered when the creaky and hideously uncomfortable stagecoach finally stopped outside the hotel in the shabby metropolis of Green River, Wyoming, population 376.

"Won't be going on for a while, I figure," Jim told the coach driver, who, puzzled by Jim's statement, stared at him in disbelief before climbing to the top of the coach to fetch his bags.

"You sure about that?" the driver asked.

"Yep," Jim answered. "This looks fine for now. Thanks."

Within a week Talbot had found work as a deputy sheriff, mainly because of his war experience and his knowledge of and aptitude with guns, especially his Colt Navy 44 and Spencer rifle. Shortly after securing the post he had sent for Abigail, and when she alighted from the smelly coach on the twenty-sixth of May, Jim, ever the gentleman, had greeted her with a western version of a bouquet: wild yellow daisies.

"My word!" Abigail exclaimed when she alighted, obviously annoyed. "Wherever have you brought me Jim? I must have asked the stage coach drivers ten times if we weren't in Green River already. Every town we come to the buildings look so untidy, and the streets are so dusty! Whatever will we do here, Jim? Really! Even the railroad doesn't come quite this far yet."

Having imagined a warmer welcome and perplexed by her sudden dismay, Talbot struggled to pacify his wife. "You'll see my dear. I've fixed up a small place out near a stream that runs into the river, got decent soil and the water we'll need to plant a garden, grow corn, beans, maybe some potatoes, squash. It's got some trees and some shade, and the cabin, well, it's not just too bad, though I'm sure a woman's touch will round it out a bit. Month or two I think you'll grow to like the place, once we get the garden planted."

"Hmm, we'll have to see about all that, Gentleman Jim! For right now see to it that this tired lady gets a bath and a room with a real bed to sleep in. And if you do not mind for tonight, alone! I do not recall the last time I slept more than three or four hours a night, what with traveling on noisy trains and these terrible horse-drawn contraptions. My goodness mercy! Now you'll be pleased to get down my traveling suitcases and allow me to refresh. We will talk tomorrow." And after kissing him she strode deliberately into the hotel.

"Yes Mrs. Abigail Delacourte Talbot. Right away," said Jim, stumbling up the hotel steps after her, his arms wrapped precariously around three suitcases and a hat box.

They had settled in a small cabin on Brown's Wash about two miles outside of town. Abigail immediately set about lending the place that "woman's touch" that Jim said she would surely provide. Barely a week after she arrived she gave Jim a written order for muslin that she needed for making curtains and told him to order new cotton sheets and pillow cases from the general store.

"Curtains? Whatever for? Wolves and coyotes and rattle snakes don't much care what happens in our cabin. And we don't have any neighbors. That's part of why I bought this place for us, far outside of town."

"Well, coyotes and wolves notwithstanding or, God help us rattle snakes, which by the way James Talbot you never told me about, if this lady is going to share a bed with her husband she is going to do it in absolute privacy. I will take no chances whatsoever!"

Abigail's "touches" quickly transformed the rough, barren cabin into a place of pleasure and tranquility. Abigail made curtains and also cushions for two wooden chairs in the cabin and also for the love seat that Jim had built on the small porch where they spent many cool evenings huddled together watching the sun sink behind a far peak. As night fell they would then rise and walk into their cabin where Jim would warm water on the wood stove for quick baths in an old tub Jim had convinced Milly to give him. "For Abagail's sake, Milly, you know," Jim had told her. "She's a real fine lady. Fine ladies don't bathe in a stream." Ensconced in their small bedroom behind Abigail's carefully sewn curtains, Jim would undress and then slowly disrobe Abigail who fell willingly into his arms as they embarked on passionate journeys that neither could have imagined without the other. "Now do you understand the curtains, Gentleman Jim?" Abigail would whisper. "We enclose each other, and they enclose us. They keep us safe."

He had purchased a horse and buggy for Abigail, and once she mastered it Abigail rode often to town to buy seeds. She planted that garden that Jim had envisioned when she arrived. He dug a well and a channel to divert water from the stream into a pond to irrigate their garden. Abigail brought with her cooking skills from many years in her mother's kitchen, and she would fill the cabin with aromas from meals that, especially riding home from town, Jim swore he could detect a half mile away. She also established a morning ritual that Jim came to cherish. She would arise before him and prepare on the wood-burning stove two steaming cups of coffee they would share together in the morning light on the love-seat. "Darn fine cup of coffee," he would say to her every morning, as if for the first time, and then kiss her softly.

As sheriff Jim had quickly learned that the western territories were hardly as peaceful as he had imagined them to be. Although he would not admit this, his vaguely "eastern" attire, the vest, clean shirts, jacket and clean boots, his prized Stetson, and the dignity with which he carried himself around town, were a desperate attempt to ward off with the formality of appearance his sense of the chaos and terror of everyday life that war had ingrained in him and that he desperately tried to hide from his beloved Abigail. He nonetheless believed that their little Eden was sufficiently isolated from the drunken revels at the saloons and the occasional disputes over land use and related "Indian matters." These last he saw as mostly rightful rage at cattlemen driving their herds over established Cheyenne hunting grounds and what Indians had long considered sacred land, and miners digging up grave sites. When Sheriff Richard Jones dropped dead of a heart attack in late June, Jim was offered the post by the federal marshal. He accepted immediately and assumed the post on July first. He cautiously hoped that this might be an opportunity to bring order to what he feared was becoming a more chaotic landscape. If he could calm their little corner of this vast territory, maybe he could put behind him the grim violence of the war years and secure the lasting peace he had promised Abigail in exchange for her agreeing to come west. On the love seat and within their curtained room they would love and share for all their lives the morning light and the setting sun.

Four weeks after being appointed sheriff he and Abigail were riding through town under a calm summer sky headed back to their cabin after a Sunday evening dinner at a small restaurant in town. A drunk stumbled out of Hal's Saloon, firing wildly at everything that moved, including their buggy. A bullet tore through Abigail's skull. Jim tried frantically to staunch the bleeding, and when he realized he could not, he cradled Abigail's body in his lap while furiously whipping his horses toward Doc Johnson's cabin just outside town, racing against the inevitable. It was just like the war, Jim had told himself: the random violence of the battlefield, the endless, senseless shooting, the indescribable maiming that would not only cripple men's bodies but also poison their souls that pursued him everywhere. Driving the horses furiously with his wife's body in his lap, he knew deep in his soul that he would never forgive himself for bringing Abigail out here to die so horribly.

Nor would Doc Johnson ever forget the evening Jim stumbled into his cabin carrying Abigail's body in his blood soaked arms. Never before, despite two years of brutal combat, had he seen as much anguish in one man's face as he had seen in Talbot's. He drew a sheet over Abigail's mutilated skull. He could only confirm what Jim already knew. But what Doc had not told Jim, because he could not, was that the bullet that killed Abigail had taken two lives.

***

Talbot walked slowly down what passed for Main Street in the business district of Green River, which in 1866 qualified as a boom town in the vast Dakota Territories, especially in southern Wyoming. He contemplated several stalwart and sensible businesses along the main and side streets that he knew were owned by decent folks simply trying to earn a living for themselves and their families: a bank, grocery store, butcher shop, bakery, barber shop, laundry service, haberdasher advertising "The Finest in Men's Wear" and a companion store featuring "Fine Ladies Wear," feed store, printer's shop, a small theater advertising "Live Music & Dancing Girls," the post office offering telegraph services at $.05 per minute, Doc Johnson's office, welder's shop, farrier, a few small restaurants, a small café offering "Saturday and Sunday Specials," Hal's "filthy no good saloon" as Milly called it, a tiny school next to a Presbyterian church with a neatly printed sign proclaiming "Sunday Services at Ten O' Clock," a general store that sold household goods, and a supply store selling the products and services that residents might purchase, such as loggers' saws, picks and pikes, gardening tools, harnesses and saddles, and of course hunters' rifles. He passed the largest outfitter's warehouse in the territory that catered to the more lucrative trades, mainly the drovers, railroad laborers, and miners who cherished the riches they were able to pry from the creek beds, outcroppings of ore rock, and sluice drains of the larger mines. Since becoming sheriff in July he had locked up several miners for their own good after drunken boasts of having "struck it rich" in Hal's or Milly's saloon. Miners followed their passion for gold, at no small risk to their already perilous lives, because, as Sheriff Talbot knew, in Green River ownership meant everything.

"And didn't Milly Waters understand that!" he shouted, laughing. As Doc had told him their story, Milly and her husband Frank had arrived in 1852, from somewhere in New York, and had invested in property and business as the town grew. He passed the colorfully painted Confectioner's and Ice Cream Parlor on his left and the equally attractive storefront of Milly's Beauty Parlor directly across the street. Milly and Frank owned both of these going concerns in addition, of course, to the Green River Saloon just down the street. Talbot admired them for investing in such sophisticated commerce. Using the new "pot freezer method" she had learned about from its inventor in Philadelphia, Milly sold ice cream at the last store on the left as one approached the round about, and did the ladies' hair and make up on the other side. As Frank was fond of saying, "She gets 'em comin' and goin'!"

Talbot knew she was a church going Christian woman. She and Frank appeared promptly every Sunday morning at the Presbyterian Church for the ten o'clock service. Despite vocal protests and disparaging frowns from some of the righteous ladies of the congregation, they were always welcomed by Pastor Bartholomew Aloysius Simpson. Every Sunday morning he relished the thought that this might be the day when he would convince the Waters to abandon their sinful ways and surrender their souls to the Lord. Sheriff Talbot figured it was the righteousness of the Lord God Almighty, as much as the fear of the Almighty should anyone harm His servant, that Mrs. Milly Waters tendered on both sides of the street. Maybe it was just that; the fact her little shops didn't interfere in the daily concerns of the town and its decent inhabitants and those pleasures that can be indulged in by those who can afford them. So they wisely left Milly to her "parlors" (as she insisted on calling them, including and especially her Saloon), which was the only trace of vanity or pretense of any sort in her. Feeling self-justified and confidant in their necessary place in the community, Milly and Frank attended Sunday services regardless of others' opinion of them.

Sheriff Talbot marveled too at Milly's sheer upright manner of living. She held her head high, though she now toddled around her saloon with a black enameled cane, inlaid with vines of green gold filigree with leaves of Jade and little Mother of Pearl. It was, as far as anyone knew, the only expensive possession she owned. Though she boasted all the latest styles in her beauty parlor, Milly always wore her hair in the neat bun that respectable women, especially Christian matrons such as herself, all wore. Neither did she wear make up, save for lipstick that might have been the same color as her lips for all the difference it made. In fact, for a woman who runs a beauty parlor and a saloon in a town with two whorehouses, and myriad other establishments in which pleasures of the flesh were also on sale, Milly looked downright plain. She did cater to some of the girls in her beauty shop. Or, that is, some of the girls went to Milly to have this or that done, but they didn't carry on or behave in any way that might be offensive. Same thing was true for the ice cream parlor; anyone could go in there, as long as they behaved.

Talbot approached the round-about near the center of town, just up from his office, and sat on its circular bench. The night air, cool and moist, only partially soothed his rattled nerves. He realized, as he had the night Abigail was killed, that this sudden, senseless attack had demonstrated again that no fear of legal punishment or justice held sway over the town's criminals and cutthroats. He knew there was as much potential violence seething beneath the sweetness of the evening air in Green River as in any other self respecting boomtown. The gold and silver and cattle and railroad had remade this small town into an explosive collection of wealth and poverty rife with potential violence and revenge on both sides of the badge. Worst of all, the general decency exhibited by most residents of Green River, as in other places in the territory, could all too easily be overwhelmed by the fever that consumed all those ranchers, loggers, panners, and sifters looking for one thing at the expense of everything else. And thus there was in Sheriff Talbot's mind, and he knew in Doctor Mark Johnson's as well, a sense of just how easily the town could become so dangerous to live in that some federal law enforcement agency would have to invade just to keep the peace. Since the end of the war Union soldiers, many of whom were now part of the federal occupation force in Fort Laramie, were deployed keeping the peace between Indian tribes and settlers in several problem areas, and Green River might soon become one of those. In the midst of this growing turmoil, the one man Sheriff Talbot most feared was Brent Tompkin, a reckless, angry cattle rancher whom he suspected might be somehow behind the assault at Milly's Saloon.

"Lord I stink," he said out loud, as if hoping maybe the coyotes he now heard in the distance or an owl that darted overhead might take pity on him. He rose and, before turning down the side street toward his office, looked at the statue in the center of the round-about that he had admired many times before. Doc once told him that Milly and Frank had paid for it, and for the oak archway that partially protected it from the elements. The bronze statue boasted an anonymous white man with an equally anonymous

Indian chief, replete with the full length head dress that had become popular in painters' renditions of the "noble savage" and in front of cigar stores. The unknown worthies clasped each other's forearms in apparent solidarity. Talbot relished the ideal of brotherhood embodied in the figures, and longed for the peace that it signified even as he feared its impossibility.

Suddenly the Green River Saloon girls, Marilee and Roxy, loomed in his mind. Their wounded bodies were their own; but each had the face of Abigail. He sighed deeply, then began walking slowly toward his office, accompanied only by his moonlit shadow moving silently before him.

7
Jeremiah Staggart's Journey

Jeremiah Staggart was a burly, twenty-five year old infantryman from rural eastern Tennessee who had enlisted in the Confederate Army in January, 1862. He was the only child of deeply religious parents who firmly believed that the Southern cause was righteous and divinely sanctioned, and that white Southerners were justified in fighting for its survival. On September 19th, 1863 Jeremiah was with Major General Thomas C. Hindman's contingent, a furious fighting force within General Braxton Bragg's Army of Tennessee, when they routed Major General William Rosecrans's Army of the Cumberland on the second day of the fierce battle at Chickamauga Creek. Despite General Hindman's failure to act on General Bragg's specific orders to attack at McLemore's Cove, Staggart still considered Hindman to be a military leader worthy of his loyalty. Before the Confederate army's eventual victory, during the two day carnage crazed soldiers fought in ferocious deadly combat. By the night of September 20th Staggart had seen so much bloodshed that he wondered if anyone could survive this war, and whether any cause could be worth all the killing. Thousands of mutilated men and horses littered the battlefield, and the hideous howling of wounded soldiers along LaFayette Road and between the final battle lines and Missionary Ridge punctuated the night air. Here, Staggart thought, is hell.

The remaining Union troops, exhausted and starving after their retreat, were trapped in Chattanooga and cut off from their supplies by Confederate artillery on the heights above the Tennessee River. The siege ended with the arrival in late October and November of additional Union troops led by General Joseph Hooker and General William T. Sherman. For three days in late November fighting raged at terrifyingly close quarters and hand to hand combat. As the combined Union contingents finally pushed the remaining forces of General Bragg's Army of Tennessee out of their defenses atop Missionary Ridge, the Union troops, screaming "Chickamauga! Chickamauga!" enacted vicious revenge for their comrades' earlier losses. On the second evening of fighting, during a furious assault by General Hooker's Union troops up Lookout Mountain, Staggart, mad with terror and sensing disaster, took advantage of the encroaching darkness and fog that frequently enveloped the battle grounds to flee. Carrying his rifle and a small pistol, he ran north through the pine forest toward Lookout Creek and the Tennessee line, trying desperately to remain hidden from the advancing Union forces. After walking and often running in sheer panic for nearly six hours Staggart lay down amid thick undergrowth in a small clearing just south of Lookout Creek. Sickened by the terrifying sounds of screaming men from the day's butchery that he could not silence in his mind, but too exhausted to continue, he pulled his Confederate overcoat over his shoulders and fell asleep immediately on a hastily assembled bed of leaves and pine needles.

He awoke just before dawn. Cold, wet, and hungry he carved his way through the thick underbrush until he came to a dirt road. As a native of eastern Tennessee, he was certain that he remembered a railroad depot in the small town of Wauhatchie west of Chattanooga and determined to try to reach it. He began walking west, hoping that a branch line of the Nashville & Chattanooga Railroad still ran from Wauhatchie onto Bridgeport and then Stevenson in Alabama. From there he believed trains ran north to Nashville. He knew that if he were going to survive he would have to depend on his gall and wits, and that he would have to carve for himself an alternative identity and leave behind him the horrifying battles he had barely escaped. He also knew that no one he was likely to meet would tolerate a deserter, especially now when Union soldiers were penetrating deeply into the South. The Union army threatened not only to overwhelm the Confederate army but also to obliterate all that Southerners cherished.

He walked for several hours, drinking occasionally from the small streams that flowed through the fecund farm land of southern Tennessee. He passed several farms, most small but a few larger, where he knew the work was done by slaves. Hunger gnawed his bones. He knew he would have to eat soon, and resolved that if he had to kill in order to get food and to escape, he would.

Around what he guessed was near twelve noon Staggart spotted a small farm house off to his right. Convinced now that he could go no further without eating, he left the road and approached the house through a dense grove of trees. He heard the voices of a man and a woman coming from behind the house, and noticed a Negro and two young children, a boy and a girl, working a field along the side of the dwelling. He crept closer to the field, then saw the woman come around the corner of the house and approach the field. As she began walking toward the Negro and the children, he burst from the trees and ran towards them with his rifle pointed at them.

"Don't move, any of you, or I'll shoot! Just stand there and don't do nothin! Do what I say and ain't no one gonna get hurt."

He moved closer to them. "You there, little girl, come on over here.

Don't be scared. Just come on over here and keep quiet and ain't no one gonna hurt you. You, lady, jus' stay there and keep quiet. Send that little girl over here, now!"

The woman, trembling violently, looked behind her toward the back of the house, but could not see her husband. She turned toward Staggart, and, wrapping her arms around her daughter, said quietly, "Please don't hurt my little girl. She ain't done nothin' wrong, mister. You're a soldier, aren't you? Why you want to hurt us? We're good people here."

"Lady, I ain't gonna hurt your lil darlin' none. I just wanna be sure you folks here and that big darkie over there do like I say, that's all. Yeah, I'm a soldier, and I know where I am, but my situation's kinda peculiar now, and I just gotta be sure y'all understand that so nobody here gonna git hurt none, that's all. Now we're all gonna march over yonder by your husband, and your little girl's gonna walk with me and y'all gonna walk ahead of me and you gonna be sure that your husband understands the situation here so, like I said, no one's gonna get hurt. Now send that pretty darlin' over here so's I can have her walk real nice with me."

"All right now Emma, you go stand by the nice man and walk with him whil'st we go fetch Daddy over behind the house. Go on now."

The woman slowly, reluctantly unwound her arms from the little girl. She released her mother's hand and, crying, stepped slowly toward Staggart. When she stopped just in front of him he grabbed her wrist with his left hand and pulled her to him. She yelped in pain. "Hush!" he shouted, and pointed his rifle toward the back of the house. He motioned for the others to begin walking, but the large Negro stood firm.

"What y'all wan' wid these folks mistah? They ain't hurtin' nobody. Just farmin', tha's all. Why y'all wanna harm these here peoples?"

Staggart pointed the rifle directly at the Negro's chest. "Just shut up and walk, nigger. You be a good nigger and nobody's gonna get hurt. Go on now!"

They started walking slowly toward the back of the house, the woman and her son in front ahead of the Negro, and Staggart and the girl behind them. Just as they came around the corner of the house, the woman's husband, barely ten yards away, turned toward them.

"Priscilla, is anything wrong? Where's Emma?"

Suddenly he saw Staggart holding Emma hard by the wrist and the gun in his right hand.

"Priscilla," he yelled, "who's that man? You there, what you doin' with my daughter? Let her go!" He ran toward them.

"Stop!" Staggart yelled, pointing his rifle at the man. "You just stop there, mister, and your little girl gonna be jus' fine. You just stop now, ya hear?"

"Joshua, please! Do like he says!"

The man froze twenty paces from Staggart. "Just don't you hurt my Emma, ya understand? She's as innocent as the day is long. She ain't never hurt nobody."

"I gather that, mister, and if y'all jus' cooperate here with me your little girl's gonna be jus' fine. I need clothes and food. You give me what I want and y'all gonna be jus' fine and y'all can go back to tendin' your little farm here and ain't nobody ever gonna know I was even here, ya understand?"

"Okay, whatever you say, mister. But I see by that uniform you're a Confederate soldier, so I don't git why you comin' here threatenin' us folks. We supposed to be allies in this here war. Why you come in here with that gun pointed at us like we was some kinda Yankees?"

"That ain't none of y'all's business. Let's just say I had my fill of this god damn war, and I'm fixin' to git as far away from it as I can, and now ain't nobody stoppin' me. Now you and your missus here and these youngens and your darkie we all gonna go into your little house and you're gonna git me some plain clothes and fix me a meal and gimme some food for the road. Ain't nobody else gonna mind my business or yours. Now y'all git over there with him!"

Staggart released Emma's hand and she and her brother and mother ran to Joshua and huddled behind him. The large Negro stepped back, and Staggart motioned him to join the group. With his rifle he waved them toward the house, and they walked through the back door into the small kitchen. Priscilla took down some eggs and bacon from a pantry and then lit the kindling in the stove. Staggart sat at the small table with his rifle in his lap. The children, their father and the Negro stood several feet away.

"You, mister Joshua, go fetch me some clothes now, and a sack, and don't try nothin' stupid. Remember your wife and young ones is all here with me."

Joshua went into a small room at the back of the house and emerged several minutes later with a bundle of clothes and a cloth sack that he dumped on the table.

"This here's all I can spare. Winter's comin' on and I gotta have clothes to git through it. There ain't nothin' else extra."

Staggart poked through the small pile of clothes: two cotton shirts, a pair of heavy overalls, two heavy wool undershirts, a well worn denim jacket, and a pair of old leather boots. He stuffed the clothes into the sack.

"This an't much, but I guess it'll have to do."

"Like I told you, winter's comin' and I got to keep workin' this farm. Gotta be able to keep warm or I can't work this place. I'm responsible for my family. You got a family you might understand that."

Staggart's lips quivered as he leaned back in his chair, then looked at the family huddled before him.

"Had, oncet. Up by Collins River. Whilst I was gone some men, Union soldiers I reckon, come through, killed animals, took food, tied up my wife and son and set the place on fire. Burned 'em alive."

Staggart stopped, choking back tears and gulps of air as he tried to continue.

"All's I found was bones and ashes. Rats, dogs, vultures picked clean what the fire left, which weren't much. That turns a man's mind inside out. Ain't no revenge big enough for that."

"Oh my Lord Jesus Christ," Joshua muttered, "we're right sorry for your terrible loss, mister. God have mercy! But runnin' won't beat them terrible Yanks. You got to stand and fight 'em or they'll burn everythin' we got!"

"I done my share of fightin'. Two years' worth. I can't do no more. I got to get away, out west maybe. Forget, or try to. Try to make a new life, anythin' away from this god damn war. Anythin'!"

Priscilla laid a plate of scrambled eggs and bacon in front of Staggart. After hearing his tale, she was less frightened for herself, though still wary for her children. He's mad with grief, she thought. No tellin' what he's liable to do to other people's children. As he ate she gathered some bread and apples and put them on the table for him.

Staggart finished eating, rose form the table and, taking his rifle and the food and pile of clothes with him, walked into the small living room. He took off his Confederate uniform and stuffed it into the sack on top of the bread and fruit, then dressed in Joshua's clothes and strapped on the boots. He then pointed his rifle at the family.

"Y'all been real good, real cooperative. Now y'all got to forget I was ever here, ya understand? Some colonel come ridin' by on his horse and askin' lotta questions, you ain't never seen nor heard of any damn deserter. I'm just running from hell's fire and a pile of bones, and what I can't understand no more. That ain't no crime in my book. Y'all understand that, right?"

"Yes sir, guess we do," Priscilla mumbled softly.

"Good, 'cause right now you ain't got no choice but to understand that. One more thing. How far to Wauhatchie? Seems I recall a railroad goin' west from there. That right?"

"That's right. 'Bout four, maybe five miles I figure," Joshua told him. "Stay on this here road a spell, then north on Crawford Road then clear to Wauhatchie. But I hear Yanks been there, 'bout end of last month. I reckon they's still there."

"Yeah, think I knowed that. Them Yank bastards everywhere now!

Come down from Chattanooga, routed us southern boys from Missionary Ridge, Lookout Mountain, every which way, real bad. But the trains still runnin', tracks ain't been tore up?"

"Far as I know, trains still runnin'. Don't know nothin' different, least ways not yet."

"Well, that's where I'm headed, but y'all never heard me say nothin' 'bout that. Just remember that! I'll be off. Y'all been real kind, and I thank ya."

Staggart grabbed the sack and his rifle and walked to the front door. "You nice southern folk and your blackie there relax now and get back to what you was doin'. Just pretend like this little visit never happened. You do that and you'll never see me again. Promise." He opened the front door, looked back at the group once more, and walked quickly toward the road.

Forty minutes later he turned north along Crawford Road. If, indeed, the trains were still running on the Nashville & Chattanooga Railroad, he was sure he could get to Nashville and hopefully from there further north and west. Perhaps, he thought, all the way to Denver at least, if not further. He hoped if he could get to a completely different place he could banish from his memory the scorched shell of his farmhouse and his wife's and son's hideous screams that he heard nightly.

One mile after turning onto Crawford Road he heard noises behind him. He turned and saw two men on horseback and a third man driving a heavily-laden wagon coming toward him. They were Yankee advance scouts. He dashed into the woods and watched them approach, his pistol aimed directly at the two men on horseback. As they came within range he fired twice, killing each with a single shot. He leaped onto the road and ordered the wagon driver to stop. The man reached for his pistol and fired once before Staggart shot him in the shoulder. He fell off the wagon seat, and Staggart rushed toward him. The man rolled over, fired again, missed, and Staggart shot him in the head. He grabbed the reins before the horses could bolt and steadied them.

In the wagon Staggart found provisions, a cash box, rifles, pistols, and several crates of ammunition. He took several cans of beans, some salted pork, three loaves of bread, a pistol and ammunition, and stuffed everything into his sack. He dragged the bodies of the soldiers far enough into the brush so that the vultures and coyotes would find them before any Union soldiers did, and then scattered the rifles in the woods on the other side of the road. He took the bridles and saddles off the horses, carried them several yards up ahead, lugged them into the heavy underbrush and left them there. When he returned to the wagon the horses were waiting, and he swatted them on their rumps and sent them back down the road. Let the murdering Yankees find them, he mused with a sense of vengeance, and wonder what happened to their riders. He opened the cash box, took the money and stuffed it into his pockets, then threw the box deep into the woods. He whacked the behind of the draft horse and resumed walking toward the small settlement of Wauhatchie and the rail line that ran west from Chattanooga. He could only hope that the marauding Union soldiers had not yet destroyed it.

Hours later he was riding in an empty box car headed for Bridgeport, just over the Alabama border. In a corner of the car he stuffed his Confederate uniform under a pile of discarded tarps and ragged blankets, the detritus of criminals, vagabonds, and deserters. Carrying the pistol he walked to the center of the open freight car. He lay back on bales of hay, placed the pistol by his right leg, opened a can of beans with his knife, and poured them onto several slices of bread he cut from one of the loaves. Looking through the open door at the landscape passing by, he tried to imagine a peaceful autumn harvest. Instead, the smoldering remains of his house and barn, the slaughtered live stock, and the charred bones of his wife and son lacerated his vision.

Hungry, dirty and cold he jumped from the box car the following afternoon as the train crawled into the Bridgeport rail yard. Picking his way carefully among the freight cars and belching steam engines, he arrived at the back of a small shed. From there he watched as men and women alighted from the single coach at the front of the train. If he was going to ride in coaches to the western territories and the freedom he imagined he would find there, the farmer's worn pants and shirt would not suffice; he would need more clothes. As Bridgeport was now occupied by Union forces, he knew he would have to be as inconspicuous as possible, especially since that supply wagon he had ambushed was probably headed for Wauhatchie and perhaps eventually for Bridgeport. He also knew that he could not linger.

About a mile from the station he walked into a general store and bought two shirts, a pair of wool pants, underwear, a jacket, and, to give himself a sense of respectability, a Stetson Hat. When he took the roll of Yankee bills from his pocket the clerk looked surprised, but if he thought to question where Staggart, beat up and smelly, got the money he did not ask. Staggart's fierce gaze at the clerk's expression of incredulity was enough to convince him to conclude the substantial sale, for which the clerk was grateful, and not to inquire further. Staggart placed the clothes in a sack the clerk gave him and, as if recognizing the merchant's passive acquiescence, rapped the counter twice with his knuckles before ambling out the door into the late afternoon sun. He stopped at a dry goods store and bought a leather suitcase, assuming that would ease his way among the respectable passengers on tomorrow's train. He walked to a small hotel, booked a room for the night, and again drew suspicious looks from the clerk when he pulled the roll of bills from the pocket of his ragged pants. He washed, changed into his gentleman's attire, including the Stetson, and walked down the street to a nearby saloon. Recalling how hungry he had been on the train, he ordered two steaks, potatoes, green beans, and two large glasses of beer. After dinner, before going to bed, he went back outside and tossed the sack of dirty clothes into a garbage bin several yards behind the hotel. From now on Jeremiah Staggart would travel as a proper Southern gentleman.

A train left Bridgeport for Stevenson, Alabama at ten the next morning. Jeremiah was at the depot at nine, and when he learned that trains were still running north on the Nashville & Chattanooga Railroad he purchased tickets for the short ride to Stevenson and also for the much longer journey to Nashville. From there he would make plans to travel further north and eventually as far west as he could get on the existing rail network. After buying his tickets, also surprising the attendant with his roll of bills, he ordered a cup of coffee and rolls at the little station cafe, and sat in a corner waiting for the passenger car to open. Among the travelers were several fashionable young business men Jeremiah imagined were looking to establish trades in the booming western territories; a few Union soldiers he thought were probably sent from Chattanooga for reconnaissance purposes in Alabama; and families carrying their belongings in bulging cotton sacks, presumably expecting to homestead. He knew that a search party would be sent out soon to find the three Yankee soldiers he had killed. Later today or early tomorrow soldiers would get here to Bridgeport and begin asking questions, either at the dry goods store, the hotel, the cafe, or the train station, and somebody would be sure to recall the Southerner in dirty farm clothes with the large roll of Yankee money. He found a seat in one corner of the depot and huddled under his Stetson until he boarded the departing train. Within his growing confidence in his ability to escape west emerged, just at the frayed edge of consciousness, the bloodied faces of a woman and a child locked in contorted silence.

Next day in Stevenson he was second in line at the station window waiting to board the train for Nashville. He thought he might stop there a day or two, rest, and decide where to go from there. Staggart could not know how extensively search parties might already be prowling the vicinity, but he knew that he should avoid conversation with his fellow passengers at all costs. Best to appear solitary and pre-occupied as best he could.

Two days later Staggart's train rolled into Nashville at 3:30 PM. He alighted from the coach, and gazed around him at the unfamiliar city. Wanting to continue further north and west if possible, he inquired at the station and learned that he could buy tickets for several days of travel on mostly reliable trains that would get him to St. Louis, Kansas City, and eventually Omaha.

"Be kinda rough riding that far mister," the short, balding ticket agent said. "'Course no train travel is entirely reliable, but I figure with some luck and a lot of patience you might make it to Omaha in four to five days. I can sell you tickets right here if you want. First train would be out of here at nine tomorrow mornin'. Hotel's just up the street, cafe for good food."

"Sounds good enough," Staggart said. "I'll take tickets clear to Omaha, hopin' like you said the trains actually can get me there. Suppose that's the best I can hope for now. Imagine lots of folks tryin' to get away now, seein' as how this here war's still ragin' and the Yankee soldiers movin' down from up north. Can't no one see clear what's comin' now."

"Nope, don't reckon no one rightly can. That'll be twelve dollars even please."

The clerk looked up sharply through his gold framed glasses when Staggart handed him Yankee dollars but, given Staggart's gentlemanly attire, did not question him about how he came to possess them. He handed Staggart his tickets, looked up at him suspiciously again, then thanked him for the sale and wished him a safe journey. As he walked out of the station Staggart decided that he could not linger in Nashville any more than one night. Already too many people had scrutinized both his person and his money, and he imagined that soon people would begin talking about the Southerner spending Yankee dollars freely on clothes, food, and train tickets. Now only flight could save him. Omaha was far enough west that he figured Yankee soldiers would not bother looking for him there. Still, he was a deserter and a murderer with a price on his head and if he were ever caught the law, Confederate or Union, would be merciless. Better to lay low for a good while, maybe even, he thought, until the war ended and his crimes, like numberless others committed during the terrifying slaughter, might be forgotten. In the chaos of Lookout Mountain he doubted that anyone realized he had deserted, and he prayed that as long as no one could connect him to either that battle or the killing of the scouts he might remain relatively safe. If necessary he would just start walking north toward the endless plains and disappear into the wilderness that cared for neither his name nor his crimes.

Four days later his train pulled into the Omaha station. "A man could get good and lost up here," he thought, and hoped the screams he still heard most nights would finally disappear forever in the extensive landscape before him. On his way past the ticket office he noticed a poster advertising jobs for laborers on the newly expanding railroad. "Inquire within," read the last line, and Staggart decided he would do just that tomorrow. A railroad job in this growing city full of strangers would enable him to earn money for his further travels west while helping him establish a new identity as distant as possible from his past. Right now he needed food and a room, and he hailed a horse-drawn buggy with a sign "For Hire" painted on the side.

"Where to?" the driver asked

"Nearest hotel, wherever the hell that is."

8
Green River

On Saturday, August 4th, 1866 Jeremiah Staggart, eager now after three years of hard labor to leave the city, stepped briskly to the ticket window in Omaha. He had heard from travelers a year back that at Appomattox on April 9, 1865 Colonel Robert E. Lee had surrendered his Army of Northern Virginia to the forces of Ulysses S. Grant, and that all during April and into May various armies of the Confederacy had collapsed and surrendered. Travelers related that the capture of Confederate President Jefferson Davis certainly signaled the end of the war, and hearing this news Staggart decided that he would stay in Omaha one more year to allow armies to disperse and the country to settle after four violent years. On July 20th he had given notice at the depot, then wasted little time packing his belongings and collecting his earnings. He thought of himself as a man now free of his crimes against the Union Army, though not of his memories of what he believed rogue members of that army had done to his wife and child.

"Green River, Wyoming, Dakota Territory" he said when the clerk at the depot asked him where he was headed. "I've heard from folks it's real pretty, peaceful like. This here city's gettin' too crowded."

"Green River, uh? Well, ain't no rail quite there yet, though it's gettin' close. There's rail work there too if you want it. Graders gettin' the route ready, that sort of thing. Hard work, but decent pay I hear. But ain't too much else. How about Denver? Got a line that runs damn near all the way there now. Big bustlin' town I hear tell."

"Nah, I've had enough of big bustlin' towns. I'm lookin' for a quiet place, where I might take my earnings and start over, maybe homestead somewhere quiet and peaceful. Somewhere I ain't never been to before."

"Well, I'm sure Green River fits that bill all right. Like I said, out in them territories there's not too much to do nor too many folks livin' there. Cattle ranching I'm sure, mining, logging, probably prospecting for gold, plus the railroad's headin' out that way pretty fast now. Still lots of Indians too I believe, especially up in them big mountains. Place is pretty dry so there's bound to be conflicts over water. Usual stuff. With some stage coach rides it'll take you four to five days, figurin' in a few layovers of course. Sure you want to do this? I can sell you a round trip for just twenty dollars 'case you decide to come back here."

"I'll have me a one way," Staggart replied firmly.

At seven o'clock on August 11th he stepped off a rickety coach onto a bare platform in front of a small building with "Stage Coach Tickets" painted on the front window. Spread for miles before him was an endless expanse of high desert and towering glaciated mountains, their sheer walls glazed gold and crimson by the early evening sun. Cumulus clouds danced above the highest peaks, crowning such stunning beauty that Jeremiah stood transfixed, wondering if he had traveled through a time warp back to some forgotten mountain paradise. War, he thought, could not linger in such a landscape. Maybe a man could even be redeemed here, enough so that he could take to preaching among some folks. He recalled his daddy telling him a long time ago that there would come a time and place when he knew why he had been given a prophet's name. Maybe here was that time and place.

The Green River station wasn't much to look at; hardly a station at all, he thought, more of a shack. Can't be too many people get here, he reckoned, so why waste wood and nails on anything fancy? The ticket window was shuttered, and there weren't any horse drawn buggies available. Staggart noticed a wooden sign with "Green River" painted, he thought ironically, in red, hanging from a nail underneath an arrow pointing west. He checked that his pistol was secure in his jacket pocket, then picked up his luggage and began walking down a dusty road toward a cluster of buildings silhouetted against the blazing sunset. He hoped to find something remotely resembling a town.

Twenty minutes later, ambling down what he assumed was the main street of Green River, he passed a scattering of shops and businesses that he decided might qualify, if one were judging generously, as a respectable frontier town. He noticed especially the barber shop, which he decided to visit soon; the bank, where he thought he would deposit his remaining money as soon as possible; the welder's shop where a man labored over a broken buggy frame; the supply store, post office, several small restaurants and Hal's Saloon; a battered, abandoned building to which barely clung a wooden sign reading "Wyoming Hotel"; and a large outfitter's warehouse. Down a side street he noticed a small church with a sign proclaiming "Sunday Services at Ten O'Clock." "Might be a place I could spend some time," he thought. At the far end of the dusty street a tall windmill turned gently in the summer breeze.

Hearing laughter and music coming from further up the street he quickened his pace and came upon the swinging doors of a large, sturdy building over which hung a carefully painted sign in big black letters: "Milly's

Green River Saloon." On a rickety chair besides the doors sat a tall, thin man wearing a greasy, lop-sided top hat, a dirty, white cotton shirt, a red bandana and a string of beads around his neck, leather pants and old boots so worn that Staggart wondered what kept them on the man's feet. Beside his chair was a tin can in which lay several coins. He lazily strummed an old guitar, and nodded at Staggart as he stepped up to the boardwalk in front of the saloon. Staggart nodded back and tossed a few coins into the tin can. Numerous horses stood tied to hitching posts the full length of the long building.

His curiosity now fully aroused, as well as his hunger and thirst, Jeremiah stepped inside the saloon, placed his suitcase on a small table near the bar, and sat down. The saloon was busy, with small groups of men standing at the bar or sitting at tables, drinking and talking loudly. He picked up bits of conversation about cattle drives and wolves, hunting rights and burial grounds, railroads and miners. Several young women, most wearing wide-hooped skirts and sleeveless, low-cut blouses and fancy ribbons tied in their hair, moved quickly to and from the tables serving whiskey and the occasional meal, while men hooted at them and asked for room numbers for, he guessed, later in the evening. A woman Staggart took to be the Milly of "Milly's Green River Saloon," dressed in a shabby, neck-to-ankle dress that once might have passed for an evening gown, prowled among the tables reminding men that "Not all my girls work the night shift," and insisting that her's was a "respectable establishment."

"Jesus, Sam," Staggart heard her complain to the man behind the bar, "ain't two men in here can think past their fire hoses, and ain't I grateful one of them is Sheriff Talbot!"

"Right so, Milly. You know sweet little Abigail wouldn't have tolerated Sheriff Jim foolin' around with none of your girls. Besides, he's too much of a gentleman for that."

"Ain't that nothin' but the truth. You can fry bacon on that one, Sam. Lord have mercy!"

Staggart ordered a whiskey and the "house special," a hefty hunk of well-cooked beef and some potatoes, from a pretty waitress who introduced herself as Marilee. As he waited for his order, the noise level in the saloon increased, fueled by the whiskey consumption around him. He finished eating, ordered a second glass of whiskey, and sat back as the spectacle of a Saturday night in the bustling saloon unfolded before him.

Amid the general clamor of men shouting orders for more whiskey, women yelling "Yeah, yeah, be right there. Hold onto your ass!" and a man wearing a straw hat and spectacles banging out dance hall tunes on a dilapidated piano, Jeremiah picked out the voices of three men at a table in the middle of the room shouting vigorously over a poker game. One of them shouted "Straight flush!" Another player, a huge man, obviously very drunk, suddenly slammed his hand on the table and spilled two glasses of whiskey, then wiped the table with his hand and scattered the pile of cards.

"You god damn idiot, now look what you done!" the first player shouted. "What'd you do that for?"

"Grant, you cheatin' son of a bitch," the huge man shouted. "You can't get no two straight flush! You didn't shuffle them cards for shit! I seen you. You kept them five cards right together so's when you dealt 'em you'd know where they was. Fuck you twice over! Ain't possible no two straight flush with them same damn cards! I got full house here, I win."

"Weren't the same five cards. You're too god damn drunk to see straight. It's a straight flush with different cards." Grant turned to the man at his left. "Ain't that right, Joe?"

"I couldn't rightly tell," Joe stammered. "Seems though that Grant won with two different sets of cards. I didn't see nothin' different."

"I win I tell ya! Full house!" the drunk roared.

"Hell you do," Grant cried. "That money's mine, you lousy drunken Kraut. Get your filthy hands off it."

As he reached for the coins to his left, the drunk suddenly stood and whipped a knife from the back of his belt and pointed it at Grant. Men at nearby tables scattered and several women screamed. Joe pushed his chair back and yelled, "Rensfeld, you crazy bastard, put that knife away!"

As Rensfeld lurched forward Sheriff Talbot grabbed him from behind, knocked the knife out of his hand, and slammed him to the floor, all in one swift motion. He stood with his left foot on the man's neck.

"Look here mister," Talbot said, "I've told you too many times if you're gonna pull knives on people just because you lost another crummy poker game you're not welcome here. Now when I take my foot off your neck you're gonna stand up and walk out of here and you're not coming back here, you understand? Milly doesn't want you here and neither do I. So scram! Go on back to your bunk in that railroad camp and sleep it off. And leave the knife here!"

"He was cheating with them cards," the man mumbled as he staggered to his feet and, hanging on to the edge of the table, rubbed the sore spot on his neck.

"I don't know that and you're too damn drunk to know that either, so just clear out. Now!" the sheriff barked. With that Rensfeld stumbled toward the swinging doors.

"You fuckin' son of a bitch sheriff," he yelled, "you ain't so damn smart neither!" He lurched awkwardly down the steps and, still hurling curses, grabbed the reins of his horse and tottered into the darkness.

Sheriff Talbot turned to Grant "You, Grant, take that money and your cards, and you get out too. Seems like you are being just a bit too lucky in here tonight."

"I won the money square, Sheriff. Honest."

"Yeah, well, maybe you did and maybe you didn't. No way tellin' now, and I'm sure your partner here isn't about to volunteer any information on that score. So let's just close up this little card game for the night, and if you two want some more whiskey at the bar that's fine, but no more card playin'. You hear?"

"Whatever you say, Sheriff. Come on Joe, one more." The sheriff picked up the knife and, when Milly and a couple of the girls came over and began wiping up the spilled whiskey, he gave it to her and told her to keep it in a safe place. "Just in case," he said, grinning.

"Thank you, Sheriff. Me and Sam and the girls so glad you were here tonight."

"So am I."

Staggart greeted the sheriff as he walked back toward the bar. "That was quite the exhibition," he said as he gestured toward an empty chair at his table. "Like a drink? Name's Jeremiah Staggart. Just got into town tonight."

"Don't mind if I do. I'm Jim Talbot, sheriff here in Green River and some of the Dakota Territory. What brings you here?"

Staggart hesitated and looked away. Searing images of fire choked his voice as he stared at Talbot. "Well, I, I been workin' on the railroad some, back in Omaha, then after the war I wanted to start again somewhere far away. Figured I'd try out west."

"Well," Talbot said, "you can't get much further away from anywhere than Green River. This part of the Dakota Territory is mostly open space, big mountains, high desert and rocks, rivers running here and there out of the canyons. Folks try to get along. Course they don't always succeed. Men like that goon Rensfeld come in here, get drunk, start fights, rail against me, some maybe curse Indian treaties. But I'm trying to keep the peace as best I can."

"Peace. Well, that's just what I'm lookin' for. Say, where can a man get a room around here?"

"Dakota Hotel is around the corner and up a short way. Can't miss it. Decent place. Usually has a room available, seeing as how we don't get too many visitors out this way."

"Glad to meet you, Sheriff. Thanks."

"Don't mention it. Welcome to Green River. Now let's see about that whiskey you offered."

9
Settling In

On a windy morning two days later Jeremiah Staggart sat in the lobby of the Dakota Hotel nursing his second cup of coffee. He noticed a very tall, muscular man sitting at a table across the lobby whom he had seen the day before. He had heard the man talking to others about needing someone to mind a small cabin he said was part of his cattle operation. The man wore intricately carved, dark leather boots and spurs, black leather pants, a grey shirt, a black leather vest, and a distinctive black Stetson with red and blue ties similar to the one Staggart had purchased in Omaha before he headed west. In a black holster on his right hip he carried a nine round Lemat Revolver, a weapon Staggart had not seen west of the Mississippi since the end of the war. Strapped to his waist on the left side was a long, curved hunting knife with an ivory handle. Staggart finished his coffee, then decided to inquire about the position and walked across the small lobby to the man's table.

"Excuse me mister, my name's Jeremiah Staggart. I heard you talkin' a day ago 'bout needin' help with a cabin somewhere out here. I just got into town a few days back and I'm lookin' for some kinda work. I done farming for a while, been around horses and such. Be right grateful if you'd consider me."

The man turned to Staggart, and he immediately noticed beneath the rim of the man's hat an ugly scar just above his right eye. Half of the index finger of his left hand was missing. He looked Staggart up and down, then invited him to sit down.

"Yeah, I'm lookin for a man to stay out at this cabin I got out a ways from here toward the mountains. 'Bout two miles. I keep horses and some guns there, plus ridin' gear, bedrolls and blankets, that sort of thing. I can't be there all the time so I'm lookin' for someone to tend it for me. Not much pay but it'll keep a man, just so's he don't demand too much. Ain't a whole lot to do most times. Men come and go pickin' up horses they can ride when tendin' cattle. That sort of thing. Maybe do a bit of cooking for them. You interested then?"

"Suppose I could be. Ain't got much else to do out here right now."

"Can you handle a gun? Some bit of trouble with Indians out there. Never sure what the hell they're liable to be up to. Might have to defend yourself a bit."

"Yeah, I can handle a gun if needs be. Was in the war for a while."

"War, huh? Well, who wasn't? All right, meet me here tomorrow nine o'clock. I'll take you out there and you can look over the place. See what you think. Won't take but a short while. I'll have an extra horse for you. Name's Tompkin, Brent Tompkin."

The men shook hands, and a flicker of hope sparked in Staggart's eyes. "Sounds good. See you then."

A week later Jeremiah lay on a bunk inside a small cabin near the edge of a clearing above the Green River valley. Amassed to the north and northeast several miles away was a vast, seemingly limitless complex of mountains and canyons that to Jeremiah seemed equally appealing and forbidding. As he was anxious to make some acquaintances in this unfamiliar, ominous landscape he had readily accepted Tompkin's offer and asked nothing more of him. Having seen untold, unimaginably mangled bodies in the war, he thought little of Tompkin's scarred face or damaged finger. He assumed the injuries resulted from some nightmarish battle much like the ones he had fled, indeed was still fleeing, Chickamauga and Chattanooga. He suspected that in the vastness of this wilderness there might be dozens of other men like himself trying vainly to bury memories they knew they never could. In his solitude at Tompkin's cabin for the past several days, as he tried to sleep, Jeremiah had begun seeing again, all too vividly, images of his burned house and the hideous remains of his wife and son amid the ashes. Not even the terror and madness of endless battles haunted his memory as vividly as his first sight of the incinerated land that had been his family's home. He had told himself that he had come west, very far west, to escape the infernos of war and to find peace within himself. Yet here in this astonishing expanse of land and sky these terrifying images still pursued him.

Neighing horses roused Staggart from an afternoon slumber. He rose quickly, grabbed his rifle, and edged toward the cabin door. He saw two men standing near the corral, tying their horses to a railing. He opened the cabin door slowly.

"You fellas here about some horses?" he shouted.

"Yeah, that's right. You Staggart?"

"Yeah, that's me. Jeremiah Staggart. Right glad to meet you. Tompkin send you?" Staggart set the rifle against the side of the cabin and walked to the corral.

"That's right. We need two fresh horses and grub for some riding out to the range for a few days. Boss says we need to check on part of the herd far out in the grasslands near Reiser Canyon. He says you got provisions for us."

"Sure, just take what horses you want. I'll get your grub and bedrolls in a minute. I'll be here when you return so's you can just bring the gear back." Staggart thought for a moment. "Say what's this I hear from Tompkin and this sheriff I met at a saloon last week 'bout trouble with Indians? Tompkin warned me to be on the lookout for 'em. I ain't hardly heard about them before. Hear they try to steal horses."

"Them redskins claim we got no right to use this territory for our herds," shouted the older man, a gruff, heavy-set cowboy with fat jowls and a shaggy beard. "Claim treaty rights or some such shit. Ain't nothin to do but kill the bastards if they don't leave us alone. We need these lands and water for our herds. That god damn sheriff in town, Talbot or turd box or whatever his lousy name is, fuck him! Says they got rights too and we need to respect 'em, but this territory is gettin' settled and ain't nobody gonna stop that."

The man started to tighten the saddle straps on one of the horses just inside the corral. "Him and them Indians don't look out one of these days all of em's gonna be in for a big surprise. I'm Benedict, by the way, call me Benny. This here's Williams." Benedict pointed to a tall, lean man with huge hands, several years younger, putting his saddle on a horse further inside the corral. "He ain't like me. I'm mean and nasty, but he's a nice fella."

Williams walked his horse to the corral entrance and stood by Benedict. Jeremiah shook their hands. "Like I said, right glad. So what y'all know about this Tompkin fellow I hired on to? He don't seem to wanna talk much 'bout himself when he comes by. Just says he needed a man out here at his cabin."

"Well mister," responded Williams gently, "out here sometimes the less you know about a man the better. Don't seem to matter none what you done before you got here, long as you do what you're asked and don't cause no trouble. If there's any kind of golden rule out here, that's it. Most of the country real peaceful like, 'cept for rattle snakes and some of them Indians Benny's always goin' on about."

"So who are these Indians?"

"Up in Greens Canyon there's a tribe of Southern Cheyenne. Their chief's Running Bear. Guess they been there a while, don't quite know for sure, but some few years I hear tell. Warriors call themselves 'dog soldiers.' I heard some Indian name for them once but I can't say it. Benny here thinks we got us another war comin' with the Indians in these parts, maybe like in Fort Lyon a few years back that I heard was real bad. They claim lots of this territory around the canyons is theirs by some treaty and that it's sacred ground, especially up around Eagle Canyon. Anyway that's 'bout all I know. Tompkin wants 'em out, says he needs the canyon lands and creeks for his herds. They're gettin' pretty damn big now, and the Indians say it's their land and we're killin' too many buffalo and the miners are diggin' up burial grounds and railroad's runnin' everywhere. I sort of understand that, but I keep hopin' we can settle this without another shootin' war. I keep tellin' Benny here and Tompkin that, but they don't listen much. Most of the herders tryin' to avoid trouble, but at the same time we got work to do, and we got to defend ourselves. But like I said, 'cept for a few wild Indians and the rattle snakes, rest of this country real peaceful like. Ain't that right, Benny?"

"Yeah, suppose so. Leave them Indians to me and Curly we'd get this trouble over with right quick."

"Oh yeah, I almost forgot about Curly," Williams said to Staggart. "He's poison like a snake. Got to watch out for him too. Now can ya get us this gear we need? We need to get ridin' out."

"Sure thing. Be right back."

Twenty minutes later Jeremiah handed the men bedrolls, blankets, and several cans of food. He shook their hands again, then watched as they rode off, wondering about the different opinions of the country and its inhabitants he had just heard from them.

10
Festering Wounds

The freedom of unimaginable space among huge mountains and canyons looming to the north and east of the river appealed to Jeremiah Staggart in more ways than he could fathom. His farm had nestled between gently rolling hills and two creeks, a little valley, he used to tell his wife, like that between the Tigris and Euphrates he had read about in the Bible. But three years before, when he stumbled among the smoldering ruins, putrid water flowed from decaying carcasses in the upper pastures, and bones picked clean by ravenous animals littered the landscape. The Union soldiers, or whoever the killers were, had turned his little paradise into Golgotha.

Here, the sheer expanse of this high desert amid endless, rugged vistas signaled utter indifference to whatever or whomever lived here. The morning sun painted the foothills dragon fire red; scorched the noon-day dust; then so gently purpled the distant ridges before suddenly plummeting that one almost believed, the evening air so refreshing, that tomorrow would bring rain and coolness. But not now, not in late summer. The land just burned, day after relentless day.

During the last few weeks Tompkin had come by frequently, and each time he was more agitated and more caustic than the last. At each visit he brought more guns and ammunition and constantly warned Staggart about Indian trouble. He was especially adamant during a visit near the end of the month.

"Keep them guns handy! Night and day! No tellin' what to expect now."

"Tompkin, you ain't told me much about Indian troubles when I signed up for this cabin work. I wasn't plannin' on fightin' another war."

"Ain't gonna be no war if I can help it. God damn Indians just gotta back off, leave my men and cattle alone. If my men are armed and you guard these horses, Indians won't try nothin' stupid. You just do what I tell you and we'll be all right. Don't ask too many damn questions and don't relax your guard, that's all you gotta know right now. I'll be back in a few days and my men will be comin' by more often now. Just be ready, ya hear?"

"Yeah, guess I do all right. I'll stash these rifles where they'll be handy."

"You do that! See you later."

At the butcher shop in Green River several days after Tompkin's last visit Staggart had heard about a confrontation between Cheyenne hunters and several of Tompkin's herders. It had occurred at Casper's Bluff several miles west of town near Eagle Canyon, a steep canyon he had been told was especially beautiful. Williams had told Staggart that herders liked to lead their cattle to a stream above the canyon. Later he had heard that Indians believed cattle were fouling the stream that runs into the bottom of the valley, which they claimed was a sacred burial site. Two days after Jeremiah's visit to town, Tompkin arrived at his cabin and provided Staggart with more horses and several more Spencer rifles and boxes of ammunition.

"Give these rifles to whoever comes by!" Tompkin raged at Staggart. "Ain't no god damn way I'm gonna allow a bunch of redskins to stop this cattle operation just when my animals most need water in this heat. You keep all of them rifles handy and be real careful now. Make sure you give my men plenty of ammunition too when they head out. Don't want to take no chances now. Just be extra alert all the time!"

"I will be all right, but if'n what you and the men say is true, I'd sure appreciate havin' some help out here. I'm pretty much alone most of the time, and a man has to sleep some of the time or he goes plum loco. Y'all can understand that, right?"

"Yeah, I can understand that all right, and I'm workin' on getting another man to stay with you a spell, but right now I got to have most of my men with the herds. I'll see to sendin' someone soon as I can."

"I sure hope so. Meanwhile I guess I'll just do what I can."

"Yeah," Tompkin scowled, heading out the door. "You do that and remember just who you're working for out here."

Since fleeing Chattanooga Jeremiah had not thought much about land holdings or who had rights to them. In Omaha he had seldom ventured beyond the rail yard and his boarding house, biding time and hoarding cash until he felt secure enough to venture safely further west. What had been his was now a wasteland, burned beyond recognition, fit only for scavengers. Tennessee territory had once been Indian land too, but in Jeremiah's mind that was so long ago, and so little had been done with it, that he had no qualms claiming his plot and working it to support his family. He told himself that accommodations had been made, that Indians had been mostly pacified, and that the land had been put to profitable use. Yet looking out over the vast distances and towering peaks from his small cabin as he tried to justify his past, he felt the shattering insignificance that this landscape could impose upon anyone.

A man can be driven equally by what he has gained as by what he has lost. And during the lonely, brooding weeks of late summer and early autumn of 1866 Jeremiah Staggart became what he had lost. Jeremiah's father Amos, himself the son of a preacher, was a stout, stern tobacco farmer from eastern Kentucky. He and his wife Judith had married late in life and felt blessed that the Lord had nonetheless sent them a child. They had raised Jeremiah to believe fervently in hard work and the word of the Lord. On Saturday nights Amos would sit at the rickety kitchen table with Jeremiah and read to him from the Bible, mostly the Old Testament, because he wanted his son to know about loss and vengeance and a harsh Deity who had no particular reason to be kind or to keep promises. The best story his daddy used to say was not Abraham's or Isaac's, or even Cain and Abel in Genesis. It was Job's.

"Job loses everythin' he had, and weren't no good reason for it," his father would begin. "All them counselors give him useless reasons for what God did to him, and ain't one but makes any damn sense at all. Which is the point. You got to git that and figure it's gonna happen to you unless you're damn lucky and there won't be no good reason for that neither. You just got to be ready and don't bother askin' no damn questions, 'cause God ain't gonna give no answers. Counselors never know nothin' about all this, so don't waste your time goin' to them. Just accept and git on with whatever you're plannin' on. That way you might git somethin' back someday."

Jeremiah imagined Job wandering aimlessly over this scorched land teeming with snakes and stones, searching vainly for herds and wives and children and reasons, and finding only madness. Long nights he gazed from the tiny porch at the west end of his cabin at the dancing colors in the high clouds just before the merciless sun sank like a shot behind the highest peak. Where, he thought, would God find him, or Job, for that matter, out here, even if he did have something to give back? "The Lord giveth, and the Lord taketh away." He remembered his daddy reading that too. And "Vengeance is mine, saith the Lord." Was there ever vengeance back in Tennessee? He knew the South had lost, so he assumed not. Who then would exact it? Who would find the Yankee killers anyway? Not he; not anymore.

Loss festers, then grows. Deep wounds do not heal. Where in this unforgiving wilderness could a man find what he had lost? If the Lord hath not yet given back, how could He here? If the Lord promises vengeance, but does not exact it, whose duty does it become? Must vengeance remain an empty word, a grain of sallow dust? Whence justice? Whence judgment? Must the sword remain bated?

Night after night, week after week, Jeremiah stared across the forbidding emptiness to mountains and canyons seemingly a million miles away. One night he saw his wife and child herding their animals into a small corral. "Samantha, Seth," he cried out, "it's me, Jeremiah! I'm here! I'm coming for you. I will save you!"

11
Thieves

Jeremiah now occasionally shared the cabin with a herder named Zachary Brown whom Tompkin had sent to help guard the horses and ammunition. In addition to tending the cabin, Jeremiah often rode with some of the herders to the numerous valleys where Tompkin grazed his sprawling herds. He often rode with Williams and Benedict, the men he had met initially at the cabin. During a ride four weeks later, as they sat near a brook eating beans and watering their horses, their conversation turned immediately to the Southern Cheyenne up in Greens Canyon. Benedict had spotted a hunting party riding near Eagle Canyon two days before.

"Ruthless savages, nearly sub-human," Benedict raged, "war's the only way. Whites gonna rule all of the Dakota Territories sooner or later, so why wait? Me and Curly we'll kill every last one of 'em ourselves if we have to. Just like the fuckin' wolves. Kill em all! Won't need no damn sheriff."

"Come on, Benny," replied Williams. "No use talkin' that way. I done my share of fightin' and killin' in the war, like most men my age, and I know it don't solve nothin'. That's not why I come out here. If we can find another way to solve this, we should. I just want to herd these cattle. You think we got to have all-out war, but I'm hopin' for a more peaceful way. Seems all these huge canyons ought to be big enough for everyone."

"Yeah, well, I ain't never been in no war, but I still done my share of fightin'. All's I know is, sometimes it's the only way that works. Ya waste too damn much time talkin' and pretty soon the situation gets outta hand when you coulda fixed it earlier if you'd just acted when ya could. Ain't gonna do no more good talkin' 'bout this Indian shit. Jus' come out shootin' and get it over with!"

"Benny, you startin' to sound more and more like Curly," Williams snorted angrily. "That man's temper is red hot. Hell hot, if you know what I mean. Like he almost come from hell. All he knows is hate. You know what I mean, Staggart?"

"Suppose I do, yeah," Jeremiah murmured, looking straight at Williams. "Suppose I do all right."

"Curly's all right. If you're smart just don't get in no fight with him. Don't cross him is all," Benedict snapped, dumping his uneaten beans into the brook. As they gathered their gear together and mounted their horses to ride out, Williams wasn't sure what Jeremiah had meant about hate and being from hell, but he kept his curiosity to himself.

By mid-October Tompkin had secured more horses for his herders to use, and had given Staggart and Brown more guns for the cabin, including three more Spencer six-shot carbines and several additional boxes of ammunition. Tompkin told him that in the last week of September two of his men had encountered several Indian hunters a mile or two south of one of the creeks where they often watered their cattle. The Indians had shot two of the cattle, including a pregnant cow, before they rode off. His men had fired at them, but missed, although one of his men, Stuart, said that he thought he had wounded one of the Indians' horses. A day later, about half a mile from the spot where the cattle had been killed, three cowboys found the dead horse. Its throat had been cut, apparently to put the animal out of its misery. Tompkin thought the Indians might seek revenge for the killing of one of their prized stallions. He assumed that if the Indians raided Staggart's compound they would come at night, so he told Jeremiah that another of his men, a sharp shooter named Bridges, would be coming by to stay with him and to help protect the place. He would bring several more guns, including four lever action Henry repeating rifles. However, after two days when Bridges failed to show, Jeremiah wondered if Tompkin was lying to him about providing extra manpower, and began to wonder if he were being played for a fool in a larger struggle. Then again, maybe the man he promised was either a coward or dead somewhere on the wind swept wastes.

On a cold night under a brilliant full moon a week after Tompkin had promised Jeremiah that Bridges would arrive at the cabin, Jeremiah lay on his bunk fighting fierce fatigue yet eerily sensing the need to remain awake. Assuming Bridges had by then arrived, Tompkin had sent Brown to herd with Williams and Benedict in a distant high canyon. Under Jeremiah's bunk lay the pistol he had taken from the Yankee soldiers he had killed, and his new Spencer carbine rested on a shelf against the wall just above his bunk. He drifted in and out of sleep, in and out of memories of the wailing of war and wounded men, a woman and child. A deadening slumber finally enveloped him until nearly too late. Gun shots and shrieks of panicked horses roused him, and he grabbed his pistol and rifle and bolted for the door. As he opened it a bullet screamed past his head, lodging in the door frame just past his left ear. He fired the pistol in the direction he thought the shot had come from, then grabbed the rifle and leveled it and began firing into the front of the corral. He could dimly see three Indians on horseback. Two of them fired rifles at the cabin, forcing Jeremiah to crouch in the doorway. From there he fired again at the Indians, and a yell told him he had hit one of them. The other two, who had been untying horses in the corral, immediately resumed firing toward him and Jeremiah ducked back inside the door frame to avoid the hail of bullets. "Christ," he wondered, "where the hell did they get those guns?"

From where he crouched Jeremiah could see the wounded Indian, who had fallen off his horse, struggle to his feet and a warrior turn swiftly, reach down, and scoop him up on his horse and gallop away. The third Indian lingered to shoot again at the door frame, just missing Jeremiah, before he too fled into the darkness with two of Tompkin's horses in tow. Jeremiah raced into the open, firing three times at the fleeting men on horseback. Before he could reload the rifle, they were but swirls of dust in the moonlight.

The corral had been broken open, and several horses had been driven out. Inside the corral Jeremiah found a severely wounded horse. He had been in enough battles to know what he had to do. He aimed his pistol at the head of the panting animal, and fired.

"Fuckin' redskins," Tompkin raged the next afternoon. He was accompanied by Curly, a small, taut man with deep-set eyes, a thick moustache, broad shoulders, and a twisted upper lip that exposed a broken tooth. They sat at the small table inside Jeremiah's cabin.

"Williams came by and told me, said you had been surprised at midnight. Didn't Bridges show up?"

"Nobody showed up! I was here alone, god damnit!"

"Son of a bitch, I told him where to find you. What a fuckin' mess! Looks like you was right, Curly. Them red bastards are determined to have a fight!"

"Maybe now you'll start listen' to me, god damnit!" Curly fumed as he stood up and paced back and forth across the cabin floor. "How much more it gonna take, Tompkin? We jus' gonna sit here and get shot at like rats in a cage? That your idea of runnin' a cattle business out here?"

His anger rising, Curly picked up a chair next to Jeremiah's bunk and slammed it against the wall. "Me and Stuart and Benny and the others signed on 'cause we figured you was gonna fight for this land, not sit and wait to be shot or scalped in our bunks! Fuck this! You think we're stupid?"

"Nobody's stupid around here, Curly!" Tompkin yelled as he stood and confronted Curly. "This ain't the last of it. I promise you that! And quit bustin' my chairs! That ain't gonna solve nothin'."

"I'm warning you, Tompkin. You don't do something real quick either me and Benny and the others gonna do it ourselves, or you ain't gonna have nobody to run your lousy cows. You can damn well herd them yourself. Seems like you 'bout runnin' out of options now."

"I got plenty of options, Curly. Don't you worry none about that. You just settle down and help me and Staggart drag that carcass as far away from the corral as we can. Ain't no damn use trying to bury an animal that big. Wolves and coyotes and vultures will pick it clean in a day or two. Just leave it. I'll try to find out what the hell happened to Bridges. Then I'm gonna see what I can do about gettin' this damn sheriff to do somethin'. Maybe now he'll see what we been talkin' about for months. Maybe get the calvary out here before it's too god damn late. Next thing you know gonna be bodies of men shot up all over the place! Then maybe he'll listen to us. God damnit!"

"Sheriff? What the hell you wanna ask the sheriff for again?" Curly raged. "The hell with him! He ain't gonna fix this! I done told you that ten times already. We gotta fix this ourselves, now! It's getting' too god damn late for that stinkin' sheriff!"

"I'll decide that, Curly. Just get some rope and get on your horse so's we can drag that dead animal away from the corral. After we're done, you stay here tonight with Staggart. I don't wanna take no chances on losing more horses. There's four horses let loose or stolen last night, including two of my best stallions. You two can take turns keepin' watch tonight. I'll figure somethin' else out for later. Now let's get goin'!"

***

"So what's your story, Staggart?" Curly asked two hours later as they sat around the small table in the cabin. "You ain't said much, an' you been out here alone away from the rest of us further up the valley in the bunkhouse. What brung you out here, if you don't mind me askin'?"

"Nah, I don't mind too much. Had me a little farm in Tennessee before the war. Did my share of fightin', lost most everythin', like most folks, so I come out here lookin' for somethin' new, thinkin' to just start over. Figure this place as good as any. Ain't too much more to say I'd guess. What about you?"

Curly twisted his mustache and leaned back in his chair. "I ain't got too much to tell neither. Worked some before the war, Ohio and them parts, some ranchin', lumber mills, some railroad. Seen lotta killin', come west, like you say, after the war. Been in Denver, Colorado Territory, Dakota. Met Tompkin, hired on. Ain't too bad work, 'cept now for these savages rovin' all over the place again. Don't seem to be no end to it."

"You know much about Tompkin? He didn't seem willin' to tell me much about himself when he hired me. He ever tell you much about himself?"

"Jeremiah, let me tell you something you better remember for your own good. Out here best not ask too damn many questions. I'm surprised you ain't figured that out yet. Yeah, I know a thing or two 'bout Tompkin. He ain't no saint, seen the inside of a few jails, like a lotta men I know, myself included. So what? That don't make no damn difference to me or him, and you best never mind that neither. He made honest money prospectin', struck gold, made more money, bought out a rancher named Dickerson, and now he's fixin to grow his cattle business. That's all you need to know, 'bout him or me. So now just do what he asks, especially if this here Indian crap gets worse. I'm guessin' it will right quick. We don't need no one askin' more questions and not doin' what he's told. You got that?"

"Yeah, Curly, I got that alright. I won't ask no more. Let's fire up the stove and cook some bacon. I'm gettin' right hungry."

That night the smell of rotting flesh still permeated the autumn air, adding to the decay that Jeremiah began to sense all around him.

12
Canyon Rendezvous

Three days later, while riding south toward one of the herds, Jeremiah found what the coyotes and vultures had left of Bridges's body. He had been scalped, and his half-eaten horse, its neck sliced wide open, lay ten yards away.

"Bloody damn redskins must have known where Bridges was headed," fumed Tompkin next day back at Jeremiah's cabin.

"So that's where they got them rifles!"

"Yeah, god damnit," Tompkin raged, "I gave Bridges six rifles, four new Henry and two Spenser repeating rifles, like the ones I gave you earlier, and them red bastards took every damn one of them, plus all that ammunition. Now they're really armed, and it'll take several days to replace them."

"Tompkin, now they'll be back here, aimin' to steal the rest of the horses, or maybe try to kill who's ever here," Jeremiah insisted. "Curly and I can't defend this place by ourselves."

"Curly needs to get back with me to the bunkhouse, so Williams and Benedict will stay here with you. There's room enough for three in this cabin. I just gotta have someone to guard this corral so my herders have a place to keep horses and grub. I gotta have an outpost somewhere close to that herd in the south and near enough to the canyons east of here. They'll be here before sundown."

"You sure about that?"

"Yeah Jeremiah, I'm sure about that! You just keep alert and those rifles you got handy at all times. They won't be long now."

Two days later Jeremiah, Williams and Benedict, along with Curly and two more of Tompkin's men, Stuart and Bradford, rode the remaining horses in the corral out to the herds north and east of Jeremiah's cabin. As always now, they went well-armed with rifles Tompkin had stashed at his larger bunkhouse. When, for several days they didn't encounter any Indians, the men, especially Jeremiah, began to relax their vigilance. Around three-thirty on the Wednesday of their week patrolling the eastern herds, Jeremiah decided he would venture out alone toward Eagle Canyon, the "beautiful place" he had heard so much about in town and from Tompkin's men.

"I'm gonna go check out this canyon y'all always talkin' 'bout," he told Williams. "I won't be long. Curly told me where it's at."

"Keep your guns ready, especially that rifle, and don't linger. And don't do nothin' stupid out there. We don't need no more dead people around here," Williams scowled.

"I ain't worried. I know how to use this rifle."

After riding leisurely northeast into Greens Canyon for nearly two hours Jeremiah came to the top of a wide, rocky, gradually descending slope. The vast, eerily silent canyon opened before him. To his left Casper's Bluff, a massive wall of scorched rock, hovered over the landscape. He urged his horse forward slowly down a worn path. As he descended a bubbling stream running down the cliff on the opposite side became audible. As he listened his mind wandered to rivers he was convinced the Lord had given him and his family to tend. The few trees he began to see growing alongside the stream's edges seemed transplanted from a different time and place. As the stream quickened its cascade into the canyon, a child's laughing voice emerged above the sound of the water circling around rocks and thirsty tree roots.

On the other side of the stream an Indian woman and her young child sat on a ledge. She was dipping clothes into the water, then rubbing them against rocks before hanging them on tree limbs to her right. The child saw him first. He screamed, and when his terrified mother saw Jeremiah she abandoned the clothes, grabbed the boy, and ran upward, carrying him in her right arm and balancing her body against the canyon wall with her left. Without thinking Jeremiah immediately yelled, "Wait, wait, I won't hurt you! I won't hurt you!" She continued running up and stopped only when she could look back and saw that Jeremiah had not moved. He guided his horse slowly across the stream to where the woman had been crouched, dismounted, and began gathering in his arms the clothes she had left behind. He bundled them together inside a large shirt, and as he tied the sleeves together he noticed blood stains. He looked up at the woman, who was now kneeling twenty yards above him and clutching her child to her bosom.

"I won't hurt you," Jeremiah called again. "I won't." He was not sure if she understood him. From where he stood she seemed to be trembling. She looked at him, then up and behind her, as if expecting someone. Realizing that she did not want to abandon the clothes, Jeremiah began walking slowly up toward her, holding the bundle out in front of him, as if offering her a gift. She did not move, but as he came closer she looked back desperately, and seeing no one began scrambling further up the canyon, looking back frequently. Jeremiah continued walking cautiously toward her.

"Stop!" a voice thundered above him. He looked up and saw a large

Indian brave standing at the top of the slope pointing a rifle at him. Jeremiah froze. The woman ran hurriedly to the Indian and stopped beside him. Both stared at him, and when the Indian motioned downward with the rifle, Jeremiah understood. He lay the bundle of clothes at his feet, then slowly, carefully backed down along the rocky trail, glancing over his shoulders only to avoid rocks he had passed on his way up.

"I wasn't tryin' to hurt her," he implored. "I was just returnin' her clothes. I'm sorry I scared her and the boy. Didn't hardly mean nothin'."

The man leveled the rifle at Jeremiah's head. For several seconds they both stood motionless; one frozen in hate, the other in fear. The man motioned for the woman to descend and retrieve the clothes, then fired a shot over Jeremiah's head that ricocheted off the canyon wall behind him. As Jeremiah crouched, the woman scrambled down to the bundle and carried it back up the ledge. She and the child then hurried to a waiting horse tethered to a protruding tree root, followed by the man who walked very slowly backward with the rifle still aimed squarely at Jeremiah.

He did not move until he glimpsed them riding swiftly away at the top of the canyon rim. As he looked up, darkness descended. From a roaring inferno two skeletons appeared before him. Naked, bleeding soldiers danced in a circle around a burning structure, firing randomly. He sprawled on the ground, pressing his temples between his hands as if to erase the visions.

He awoke thirty minutes later, covered in dust and shivering in the chilly air, sweetened now by a hint of rain. He rose swiftly, realizing that the others would be angry that he had lingered way too long. His horse had not ventured far, content to nibble on grass by the stream. Jeremiah mounted quickly, checked that his rifle was loaded, then hurried back toward the herders' campsite. They would wonder where he had been.

13
Jeremiah Staggart and Jim Talbot

"I did everything I could to save him, Jim, but by the time they got him to me, he'd lost way too much blood. It was three in the morning out at my cabin. Damn hard to work there. Would have been easier here in my office."

"Sure, I understand, Doc. When did this happen?"

"Five, six days ago."

"Know who shot him?"

"One of the Indians said his brother was shot at that cabin that Tompkin maintains for his herders' horses. One of the Indians claimed they were just looking for some of their horses that he claimed Tompkin's men had stolen, but I'm guessing it's a whole lot more complicated than that. I don't trust Tompkin at all. He's been trying to run his cattle all over this territory and deliberately ignoring Indians' claims about sacred sites and water. And the railroad builders don't help either, cutting trees and chasing Indians off their supposed 'right-of-way,' then raising drunken hell in the saloons. If this keeps up, the whole Cheyenne nation out here is going to rise up, then the next thing you know we'll have federal marshals and the U.S. Calvary and a full blown war. We don't need that."

"I know, I know. I've tried before to talk to Tompkin about where his men drive their cattle I've told him there's lots of room out here for both his damn cattle and the Indians. But he can't, or won't, see it that way. He just says he's got a business and he and his men need room for their herds. Keeps talkin' about the railroad coming and being able to ship cattle back east. Cares about nothing else."

"Do you know where this cabin is?"

"Yeah, it's two miles west from town. I don't know who's livin' there now, but has to be one of Tompkin's men. Maybe more by now. Tompkin's own place, plus a bunkhouse he keeps for most of his men, is another two miles from there. I'll ride out tomorrow and see what I can find out. I figure I'd better get on this before it's too damn late and we get more violence than either of us bargained for when we came out here. Thanks for your help."

"Sure thing. Any time. Any way I can help, just let me now."

"I will. Keep that fire goin.' Winter's comin' on pretty quick now."

***

Sheriff Talbot arrived at Jeremiah's cabin at 10:30 the next morning. As he rode up, Jeremiah burst through the door, rifle up, cocked, and aimed at his head.

"Stop there! Who are you?"

"Sheriff Jim Talbot, that's who. Not much point in aiming that rifle at me, mister. I didn't ride out here to get shot. And I don't reckon you want to start your day by shooting a sheriff. Real bad idea."

Jeremiah glared at Talbot, then slowly lowered the gun.

"Sheriff? Ain't I seen you before? We had us a whiskey at that saloon in town night I arrived, ain't that right? Seems we talked a bit."

"That sounds about right. I don't reckon I've seen you since then. Or if I have I don't rightly recall. Jeremiah, right? Didn't know you were staying here in Tompkin's place."

"Yeah, that's right, Jeremiah Staggart. Well, Tompkin offered me this cabin and a job of sorts. His men run cattle, as I guess you know, and I tend to his horses, maybe put up one of his men, store rifles and grub, cook up meals once in a while. It's okay, I guess. Least ways I figure for now. Most nights one or two other fellas bunk here, on account of a raid a while back, but you got me alone here today."

"Well, that's right nice of him, and I guess good for you. I come lookin' for Tompkin, but I guess you'll do for a spell. Got some questions I need to ask him, or maybe you too, 'bout this raid you just mentioned. Mind if I get off this horse now?"

"Sure thing. Sorry about the gun, Sheriff. Just wasn't expecting any of Tompkin's men back so early, and I ain't studyin' no more surprises, 'specially since Williams and Benedict ain't back yet. I got some coffee. Come on in and sit a spell."

Talbot dismounted, tied up his horse, walked into the tidy cabin, and sat down at the small wooden table. He removed his hat, brushed it lightly, and placed it on an adjacent chair. As he sat down he noticed Jeremiah's own Stetson hanging on a nail over a bed.

"That's a right fine hat you got there," Talbot said. "I noticed it back at Milly's that night. Where'd you get 'er?"

"Omaha, I was...." Jeremiah paused, suddenly aware that he may have already said too much. "I was there after the war, worked on the railroad for a few years. Made pretty good money for a while. Real hard work, so I quit after a spell and come west."

"Yeah, that's right. I recall now you tellin' me about workin' on the railroad some. We didn't talk for too long that night. I recall you bein' plum tired out and lookin' for a room. Don't recall you sayin' where you come from. You sure do sound Southern to me. What'd you do during the war?"

Jeremiah tensed. "Coffee?"

"Sure thing. Don't mind if I do."

At the stove Jeremiah, his hands trembling, carefully poured out two cups of steaming, pungent coffee. He then carried the two cups to the table, placed one carefully in front of Sheriff Talbot, then sat down.

Talbot sipped his coffee, settling comfortably into his chair, waiting for Jeremiah to respond.

"So, what about the war? You are southern, right?"

"Yeah, southern," Jeremiah mumbled over the lip of his mug, "that's right. To be exact, we had a farm oncet, in eastern Tennessee, some good land, water, nice little place."

"We?"

Jeremiah peered into his mug. "Wife, little boy. Come back on leave after a wound, found them and everything else burned and dead. Just bones." After a pause, he added, "Yanks, I figured."

Sheriff Talbot sat back and groaned. "Oh God help us, Jeremiah, I sure am sorry. No man should have to face that. Why would anyone want to do that to womenfolk and children? Wasn't them that started that god forsaken war, and they sure as hell weren't fighting it. This near the end of the war?"

"More like the middle, April of sixty-three. Nothin' left, so...after, I come out here. Got me to Nashville, then up to Omaha where I worked."

"Lot of the southern railroads got torn up during the war, especially near the end. Must have been hard gettin' to Nashville, much less up to Omaha."

Jeremiah squirmed in his chair, fidgeting with his coffee mug. "I managed. Weren't easy anyway you cut it, but I managed."

"Yeah, seems you did. I noticed back at Milly's that night you were wearing a mighty fine Stetson, the one you got hanging on that nail over the bed. You must've done real well in Omaha."

"Might say I did. Worked a lot, three years and then some. Didn't have nothin' to spend my money on, just room and grub. Easy life for one."

"So I gather. Three years you say."

"Yeah, got wounded again at...at Chickamauga, then discharged. Couldn't fight no more. Figured I'd had enough, worked like I told you, then just started headin' west. Figured I'd find somethin' sooner or later I could do, maybe try to start over. Guess that's what I'm trying to do here. Trouble is I hadn't knowed 'bout Tompkin's run-ins with them Indians. I ain't exactly bargained for that."

"So I gather, seein' as how you're tendin' his cabin now. Don't suppose he told you too much about himself or his cattle business when he hired you."

"Nah, not too much. But then I wasn't about to ask too many questions neither. Been told twice now not to do that out here."

"Guess I can understand that all right, seein' as how you just arrived."

"You know more about Tompkin then? I'm getting damn curious 'bout him. And about some of his men I've met. Williams seems all right, but this guy Benny, and this little guy Curly especially, they both seem full of hatred and violent as all git out. Seems all them two want is war, and they talk about goin' against the Indians all by themselves, without askin' for no help, yours or anybody else's. Benny keeps sayin' he and Curly, just them two, could kill 'em all. Don't make no damn sense to me, though I was scared to death by that raid. Had no idea that was comin'. Tompkin warned me, but I was all alone out here and just didn't expect Indians to come out here stealin' horses and tryin' to shoot my head off."

Sheriff Talbot leaned forward, embracing his warm coffee cup. "What I know from the last sheriff is that Tompkin arrived here sometime in 1861, I gather just as the war started, but from where I don't exactly know. He did time somewhere back east, Kansas maybe, I think for robbery, got out, been arrested a few times since, spent some few months locked up in Denver. Guess when he arrived out here he had money, not quite sure how he got it, but he made more, some say he struck a gold or silver vein in Colorado Territory, then bought into this cattle business a few years later. I also know that he has a violent temper, a craving for alcohol, and a hatred for what he calls 'authority,' by which he means anyone who he believes stands in his way. Most folks in town know him as a disgusting troublemaker who boasts that someday he'll own this town and the whole Dakota and Colorado Territories. He buys liquor for his herders and gangs of railroad men and miners and they rampage through town and sometimes fight in saloons. Milly Waters, who owns the Green River Saloon where you and I met that night, hates him because of the fist fights he starts over which girl he believes should be 'his' for the night. Truth is no woman in the place wants anything to do with him, despite the money he flashes before them."

Jeremiah's face darkened. "So, seems like he can be a mean son of a bitch when he wants to be. How'd he get that scar, you know? It's right awful lookin'. You want more coffee, by the way?"

"No, thanks, this is just fine. Don't know about the scar. My guess is one hell of a fight somewhere. Maybe with a grizzly or a mountain lion, who knows? Man with that kind of temper as likely to fight with wild animals as with men any day. I've had to lock him up several times for his troubles since I became sheriff in July. Each time in his drunken rage he vows bloody revenge as I slam the cage shut in his face. Best be wary of him I'd say."

"I see. Thanks for the warning. That's right good of you. What about Tompkin's other men I mentioned?"

"Well, I don't know too much about the rest of his herders, though I've had, shall we say, 'encounters' with many of them around town, often at a saloon called Hal's and a few times at Milly's. This Williams fella you mentioned, and Benedict, maybe one or two others. Seems I recall a Stuart also. But I sure do know this Curly guy you mentioned. Look out for him. Real nasty bastard. I've had to lock him up a few times too. Like Tompkin he's got a nasty temper, and quick, like a rattlesnake."

"Hmmm. That's what Williams said about him. Poison like a rattlesnake. Guess I better avoid him if I can."

"Yes, I would. Well, seems like you're tied into Tompkin's cattle operation now more than you figured, and you best be careful. I'll do what I can to stop this trouble before it gets any worse, and I've made inquiries about getting a few deputies and a posse quickly if I need one. I just hope I'm not too late. Best idea for you is to lay low and, like we said in the war, 'keep your head down.'"

"Don't I know that one! Say, who are these Indians Tompkin is always cursing?"

Talbot leaned back in his chair and paused a long moment before he resumed speaking. "They're a band of about thirty five Indians, maybe a few more. Southern Cheyenne. So'taeo'o, Doc tells me, originally from the Black Hills in the Dakotas. They like to camp separate from other Cheyenne tribes. Their chief is a fierce warrior named Running Bear. They settled in the Greens Canyon complex northeast of Green River about two years ago on what they consider traditional Cheyenne sacred land. From what I gather, like several other Cheyenne tribes in the Colorado and Dakota Territories, they were outraged by the Sand Creek Massacre near Fort Lyon, in the Colorado Territory, back in November '64. Since then they refuse all treaty or peace offers and are determined to fight to the death all incursions into their lands. Among Running Bear's braves are numerous "Dog Soldiers," or Hotamitanio. They're utterly fearless warriors, and they despised the efforts of the older Cheyenne chiefs, such as Black Kettle, to make peace with whites."

"Williams used the term 'Dog Soldiers,' but he said he did not know the Indian word."

"I learned it from Doc Johnson, who knows a good bit of the Cheyenne dialect. I know that Tompkin's men have had tense encounters with Running Bear's hunting parties in recent months, and I gather this raid on your cabin is retaliation. Guess there haven't been any casualties yet, but Tompkin knows the warriors' penchant for violence. I gather he's become increasingly worried about raids to steal his horses, or worse. I'm guessing that's why he hired you. He decided he needed someone here most of the time to watch the horses."

"I figure so, yeah. He told me his men would be around, to keep a look out and guns at the ready, and said that I'd be fine. Trouble is I almost wasn't. That bullet in the door frame came awful close."

"Yeah, I hear you. What's Tompkin telling you now?"

"Says two other men, Williams and Benedict, will also be here for now. They should be back soon now. Least ways I hope so." Jeremiah looked away, exhaled deeply, then, anxious to change the subject, looked straight at Talbot.

"Say, what about you? How'd you get here? You don't sound like one of them Yankees. I think I hear a bit of a drawl from you too."

"Virginia born, but I fought for the Union. After the war spent some little time in Philadelphia, then came out west several months ago. Seen too much bloodshed, too much hate. You know, new place, new folks."

"Sure 'nough. I hear you. You out here alone I take it, like me?"

"Am now. Wife was killed just the end of July. My Abigail, a fine, lovely lady I met in Philadelphia. We fixed up a little cabin out by Brown's Wash. Real nice place. One night some drunk come flyin' out of Hal's saloon firin' away. Bullet tore right through her head." Talbot paused. Choking, he looked down, slowly unfurled his hands from the coffee mug, clenched them, then drew his fists to his temples where he held them for several seconds before looking up at Jeremiah.

"You know, I'm sure," he said softly, "a man never forgets that sort of thing. Especially since I brought her out here, promised her a new life after all the hatred and killing in the war."

Jeremiah lowered his head, and exhaled deeply. "Yeah, I know that right well. I sure am sorry, Jim. Know who done it?"

"No. Some god awful no good drunk," Talbot sputtered. "Maybe a railroad worker, miner, one of Tompkin's cowboys, firin' every which way, one just found out Abigail's pretty face. Tore it.., tore it clean away!" Talbot looked away, sighing heavily, before turning again toward Jeremiah.

Jeremiah sat back in his chair, gazing at Talbot's anguished face.

"Sheriff, there's somethin' I should probably tell you, seein' as how you've told me 'bout your wife. Not pleasant, but I figure you should know. I've heard tell from Benedict and one or two others 'bout men goin' into town and gettin' drunk in the saloons, fightin' over girls. That sort of thing. On a ride few weeks back Benedict bragged about a rowdy night in town last July, said some railroad guy said he was out shootin' in the street and feared he hit some lady in a buggy, then ran like hell. Maybe him what killed your Abigail, though Benny ain't mentioned any names. That's right terrible, and I'm sorry to have to say this. I hadn't thought this Benny would talk about somethin' like that if'n it really happened. I'm right sorry to have to say this, Sheriff."

Talbot stared at Jeremiah "Benedict! You say Benedict told you about this shooting."

"Yeah, that's right. 'Bout two weeks or so ago."

"Well, guess I'll just have to look into this, find this Benedict fellow again. I did not know anyone who knew about the shooting, seeing as how I had to race our buggy out to Doc's as fast as possible. I appreciate you telling me this. No need to tell Tompkin, or Benedict especially, that you told me this. This is my business from here on out. Understand?"

"Yeah, I understand," Jeremiah murmured. Talbot looked down, overcome by memories of the kind he knew both men would spend the rest of their lives trying vainly to suppress. He also knew that neither could ever sufficiently comfort the other.

Talbot turned to Jeremiah. "Doc Johnson tells me he treated an Indian last week that was shot here. He died, and the others say you shot him. Mind telling' me what this was all about? It's my job to stop any festering violence out here before it explodes way beyond my or anyone else's control."

"Well, that night I was dozing when I heard gun shots. Got up, grabbed my rifle, went to the door and damn near got killed by a bullet that struck the doorframe just above my head. They broke into the stable and stole a couple of Tompkin's horses, so I just started firin' at whatever I could see in the moonlight. I hit one I guess, 'cause I saw one of the other Indians reach down from his horse and pull him up before riding away. I was afraid they were gonna kill me. I had to fire back."

"So it appears. But you have to understand that the Indians have been complaining for years about herds on sacred land, chewing up grasslands, tromping stream beds, driving off buffalo. Seems they been putting up with a lot from these miners and cattle drivers. And now this railroad comin' from east of here. Just seems to me there ought to be room enough out here for everybody. Don't need any more killing. Been more than enough of that in the war. Don't you think?"

"I seen more than one man could imagine possible. I hear screams damn near every night, see fire everywhere.... "

"I'm not saying you don't, and for what you suffered I am right sorry. But what's happening out here is approaching what neither of us wants. If Tompkin knows what's good for him and the rest of his cowboys, you all will have to stop trying to settle these disputes with the Cheyenne with guns and running people off their land. Indians been here for centuries, way before you or I or Tompkin or any other white man ever got here. We don't need blood running in the Green River. If there's a way to save folks from more bloodshed, and maybe save a few souls from self-destruction along the way, then that's what has to happen."

"You gonna arrest me then?" asked Jeremiah, suddenly aware of the possibility.

"Not this time, seeing as how some Indian's bullet just missed splitting your skull wide open. But be forewarned, it might be different next time. I'm not tryin' to take sides in these skirmishes. Not yet anyway. I'm heading over to Tompkin's own place to tell him that, but in case I miss him and you see him before I do, give him that message. And tell him we don't need any more damn shoot ups at Hal's Saloon or Milly's or anywhere else in town. That clear?"

"Yeah, Sheriff, that's clear." Jeremiah stood, then walked Talbot to the door of the cabin. "Here's the notch the bullet made. It just missed me."

"I see," Talbot answered, running his finger down the split in the doorframe. "Thanks for the coffee, and remember what I said."

"I'll do that, Sheriff."

Suddenly recalling his lost family, Jeremiah touched Talbot's shoulder as the sheriff approached his horse . "And one more thing. Remember there's women and children up there with them Indians. They're innocent. Like my missus and little boy, like your Abigail. Ain't hurt no one. They's not all 'dog warriors,' or whatever they call themselves. Not by no long shot. You got to remember that if trouble starts. Tompkin got to remember that too."

The sheriff stood, brushing the left flank of his horse, then turned to face Jeremiah. "I hear you, Jeremiah. That's one real good reason why I'm trying to head off any serious trouble here before it flames up, like elsewhere in the territory. The Cheyenne won't harken to any more talk from whites if people like Tompkin ignore what few treaties we got. I figure Running Bear sending his warriors to steal horses and damn near shoot your head off means he's about out of patience. Can't say I blame him. Anyway, I'm headin' for Tompkin's compound to try to talk sense into him. Now that you know more about Tompkin and the Cheyenne, be careful, and like I said, keep your head down."

"I'll do that for sure. Thanks for comin' by. Good luck talkin' with Tompkin. Sounds like he ain't the kinda man be liable to listen too much."

Talbot turned to face Jeremiah, and shook his hand. "Reckon I'll be seeing you around some now, maybe more in town. Thanks for the talk, and the coffee."

"Right welcome I'm sure. Seems likely I'll see you again. Anyway hope so."

Sheriff Talbot nodded, walked to his horse, mounted, and, tipping his hat, began riding slowly south.

Jeremiah watched James Talbot leave, his words about "saving folks' souls" and his daddy's words about his having a preacher's name blending strangely in his mind. He now realized that he had again found himself between warring parties, and he sensed that Brent Tompkin, who both Curly and now Talbot had told him had served time in jail, was a man he could not trust. He also sensed that should hostilities erupt between Running Bear's warriors and Tompkin's herders, innocent lives could easily be sacrificed. Beset by his growing fear, though grateful for shelter in this alien land, he was determined to seek peace amid the simmering turmoil around him.

14
Tompkin Meeting

Approaching Tompkin's cabin and large bunkhouse around noon Sheriff Talbot tried to imagine Staggart's Tennessee farm before and after the raid that Jeremiah had described. It was, he knew, but one of hundreds of atrocities that had been committed against civilians during the war by Union and Confederate soldiers alike hell-bent on revenge and senseless destruction. Virgin land torched, woman raped, children shot, bodies tossed on a pyre, sacrifices offered to the scourge and madness of war. The faces of two women appeared before him, one he recognized, the other he did not. Both opened their mouths as if to plead, but neither could.

At his cabin door, his right hand on his holster, Tompkin scowled as he watched Sheriff Talbot dismount, tie his horse to a tree limb ten yards away, and slowly approach him. "Hey Benny," Tompkin called behind him, "look who's come to visit! The lousy no good sheriff!"

Benedict appeared, leaning against the door frame, and adjusted his holster on his right hip. They watched Talbot walk toward them, his right hand also on his holster.

Talbot stopped a few feet before them, glanced at Tompkin, then at Benedict.

"Well, Benny," Talbot spat through clinched teeth, "how nice to see you again. Here tell you and a bunch of the boys been out target shootin' a while back at Hal's Saloon."

"Fuck you, Talbot. I don't know nothin' 'bout no Hal's saloon."

"Really? Well, I figure we'll have to have us a little chat about that some day real soon."

"Talbot," Tompkin yelled, "never mind Hal's now! God damnit, where the hell you been? Seems like you're always late when we have trouble with these murderous Cheyenne. You got any idea who scalped Bridges yet? Whoever killed him took the rifles and used them over at Staggart's cabin. I told you this was about to get a whole lot worse. Why the hell you always too late? Why? They're stealin' my horses and now killed one of my men. Ain't it about damn time you did somethin'? You gonna take a posse out to Greens Canyon, or am I?"

Furious at Tompkin's threat, Talbot bolted forward and stopped directly in front of him. "Listen damnit," he barked into Tompkin's face, "Staggart shot one of the Indians that night, and he died out at Doc Johnson's cabin. This tension between your cattle business and the Indians is getting way too dangerous, and I don't have to tell you what could happen to a lot of innocent folks if this situation gets any worse. How many times do I have to tell you to keep your cattle off Indian land? You know where that is, don't you? Why the hell is this so hard for you to understand?"

His right hand still on his holster, Tompkin stepped back and spat near Talbot's boots. Sheriff Talbot smirked, but did not move.

"So," Tompkin stammered, almost too furious to talk, "an Indian dies and you come runnin' to me complaining about Staggart defending his cabin and our horses. Seems you did basically nothin' when I told you 'bout Bridges being scalped and all those rifles stolen. Mind me askin' whose side you're on here?"

"Listen to me Tompkin! I asked Johnny Redfeather to see Running Bear just two days after the raid at the cabin. He told me Running Bear is willing to meet with me and Johnny, and as soon as I can get a posse together we're headin' up there. We will try to find out who killed Bridges, and maybe retrieve those rifles and your horses. I don't hold out much hope there, but I can sure as hell predict what they will say about your cattle. And as I've said before, if you all just try to act reasonably and respect what they want, there's plenty of room out here for everyone, cattle included."

"Oh, is that right?" Tompkin screamed as he suddenly lurched forward. "Room for everybody? That's what you think?" Benedict, slouching against the door jamb, moved his right hand to his pistol.

"Benedict, one more move and you're dead!" Talbot yelled, his pistol pointed at Benedict's chest. "Drop that hand. Now!"

"Benny, not now, god damnit!" Tompkin roared. "Use your fucking head, will ya?"

Benedict dropped his hand from his pistol and slouched back against the door jamb. "It was just in case," he muttered.

Talbot returned his pistol to his holster and turned to Tompkin. "Yeah, Tompkin, that's what I think. Room for everybody. Shouldn't be all that hard I'd say. You don't need to water your damn cattle in Hoover Creek, or anywhere else near that canyon. There's plenty of grassland and water closer in. You're just provoking the Indians because you think you can ride rough shod over all this land out here, and you don't like me tellin' you that's not the case. Do you?"

"No I fucking don't! Not when I'm tryin to run a cattle business and you're tellin' me that a bunch of savages deserve rights to empty land that's perfectly good for cattle grazing. Don't make no sense. You see them Indians, you tell 'em leave my men alone, and give me back those rifles. Then we'll see about whatever they claim is theirs. All I know is my cattle need feed and water, and for now I ain't got no more to say beyond that."

Eyeing Benedict, Talbot backed a short distance away from Tompkin. "That so? Well, guess we got a ways to go before we get something settled out here. Like I said, I'm gettin' deputies and a posse together, and if you think I won't use them as I see fit you're sadly mistaken. I know more about you and men like you and Curly and this crazy Benedict here than you think I do. I'm headin' back to town now. Meantime, you and your men steer clear of Indian lands. And Benedict, lest you want to die young, keep your hands off those guns."

Sheriff Talbot turned to leave, stopped, then slowly walked back toward them, stopping a few feet away. "Just so you know. I talked to Staggart earlier today at his cabin. Be careful of him. He lost his wife and son in the war when Union soldiers raided his farm in Tennessee, and I got some sense of what that might do to a man."

Talbot darted his eyes toward Benedict, then back to Tompkin. "Maybe you know I lost my Abigail to a drunk's stray bullet back in town in July, and no man is absolutely sane after losing his wife that way. We weren't married nearly long enough to have children, so I can't speak specifically to that kind of loss, but I figure in Staggart's case, given how his family died, he's hurt real bad somewhere down deep. Never know what a man in that state might do."

Benedict stood bolt upright. His right hand quivered near his holster. He glared at Talbot, who glared back and slowly shook his head at him. Benedict relaxed his hands, and Talbot turned again to Tompkin.

"He tell you that?" Tompkin asked. "I did not know that 'bout Staggart. I think I heard a while back you lost your wife, somethin' about a shooting in town, but nothin' else. Sure sorry for you both."

"Well, I must say that's right considerate of you Tompkin. Yeah, Staggart told me about his family just a bit ago. Can't quite imagine that. Just be careful is all. No need to tell him I told you."

Talbot shifted his weight, glanced again at Benedict, then stood upright.

"You just remember, both of you, what I said here. No need to create more trouble than we already got. No need at all. And about Staggart too."

Tompkin looked directly at Talbot. "Yeah, and you remember what I said 'bout my cattle and my men and them rifles. I'll attend to Staggart all right."

"Just be sure you do."

Sheriff Talbot turned slowly to his right, paused to glare again at

Benedict, then walked to his horse, mounted, and rode briskly back toward town.

"Benny, what's this about Hal's? What's Talbot talkin' about? Did someone shoot his wife when you and them railroad guys was cuttin' up that night in July? You never told me nothin' 'bout this."

Benedict leaned against the door and looked down, shuffling his boots in the dust. "I ain't knowed for sure," he stammered, "but I think someone comin' out of Hal's shootin' off his pistol shot some dame in a buggy and the driver turned 'round and took off real fast. Didn't stop to find out who did it. Lucky for the shooter, I guess. Shit, had no fuckin' idea it was Talbot's wife! How'd he know I wonder? I ain't told too many 'cept the herders and some railroad guys. All I said was some of the men like to go into town and get real pissed and raise a lotta hell. Nothin' more than that, I swear! Figured best keep it quiet."

"Yeah well, ait't exactly quiet now! Damnit to hell anyway! Now Talbot's gonna be on you 'bout this too!"

"Staggart! I mentioned it on one of the rides when Staggart was there," Benedict blurted. "Maybe he blabbed to Talbot."

"Well maybe, but why would he? I can't figure it no way. We just gotta watch Staggart real careful like. Make sure he's doin' what we tell him. You and Williams watch him, you hear? And don't mention to nobody else how he lost his wife. No need to do that."

"Yeah, I hear. I'll talk to Williams and Curly when they get back here."

15
Sandy Bluff

Nine days after the raid at Staggart's cabin, under overcast, early November skies, Sheriff Jim Talbot and five other men rode north-east out of Green River. He had requested three men from Rock Springs who had arrived the day before. Among them was a younger man named Butch Grogan who would remain with Talbot as his permanent deputy in Green River. The two others were sharpshooters whom the sheriff knew, had been a temporary posse after the attack on Milly's saloon, and whom he had specifically requested: an Englishman named Samuel Cunningham, and a Kansas man with a temper almost as fast as his draw named Lenny Devonshire. Anticipating Running Bear's anger at the death of one of his warriors the night of the raid, and recalling the bullet that narrowly missed Staggart's skull, Talbot figured he'd need a few crack shots in case he spotted a potential assassin lurking among the rocks above them.

Besides the deputies Talbot brought along Doctor Johnson and Johnny Redfeather. Talbot knew that Johnson often treated Indians, and that he knew enough of the Cheyenne dialogue to engage them at some basic level of understanding. But the man he was really depending on for communication with the Cheyenne, to say nothing of his bravery and his gun, was Johnny Redfeather. Talbot considered him the best damn shot west of the Mississippi, drunk or sober. Talbot still remembered Redfeather's suddenly bursting onto the scene at Milly's in September, seemingly out of nowhere, both guns blazing like some fiendish killer sprung from the depths of hell. Saved his ass, Talbot reckoned, and several of the women's and patrons' as well. He didn't want to chance this expedition to Running Bear without Red's sure fire fury. Besides, Redfeather knew the Cheyenne language well. Talbot knew that many of the Indians distrusted Red because they thought he spent too much time with white men, but Talbot also knew that only this half-breed could manage enough talk with the Indians to avoid more bloodshed on such a dangerous gamble. Redfeather had told Talbot that Running Bear and several warriors would meet them at Sandy Bluff, although Talbot was not sure that he believed Redfeather's word that the Indians would appear unarmed.

Around noon, nearly five miles out of town, as they rode slowly around a rock formation near the top of Sandy Bluff, Talbot and Redfeather spotted Running Bear and three of his men on horses twenty yards away. They were armed.

Talbot and Redfeather halted. "God damnit Red," Talbot yelled. "You told me the chief said he would come unarmed! What the hell is this?"

"That's what he said. Unarmed. I'm sure of that!"

"You sure you understood him right?"

"Yeah, I'm sure. I was cold sober and I heard what he said. I swear I did!"

Instinctively the three deputies reached for their rifles slung on their saddles and pointed them at the Indians.

Talbot swirled in his saddle to face his men. "Hold your fire! Put those guns down!"

"Sheriff," Devonshire yelled, "you fuckin' crazy? Wanna get us killed? They're pointing their guns right at us!"

"I can see that! But there's no need to provoke gunfire if we can avoid it. Let Red and me see what we can do. Red, you and I will dismount, keep our hands at our sides, and slowly walk toward Running Bear and his warriors."

"You god damn crazy white man! I ain't exactly their favorite Indian ya know! You fixin' to get us scalped? You got any idea what you're doin' here? This ain't no game! Just 'cause I'm with you don't mean they won't shoot us!"

"I know that, Red. I also know without some resolution in these mountains about land and water we'll never have peace. We don't need no more killing! We've got to talk! Now dismount and walk with me!"

Redfeather looked at Talbot for several seconds; then back at the Indians, rifles cocked. He then slowly dismounted. Talbot dismounted, then looked back at Doc and his deputies.

"Devonshire and Cunningham, stay mounted, and wait here. Have your rifles ready, just in case, but pointed down. Grogan, wait right here also. Red and I are going to the top of the bluff for a little chat, aren't we Red? Doc, dismount and come up here with me and Red."

"You're mad, Talbot! Mad!" Devonshire screamed. "They'll cut you to ribbons!"

"I don't think so. Just do as I say. Red, Doc, come on."

Doc Johnson dismounted and walked up to Talbot.

"Jim, are you sure about this? I trust you but I'm not sure at this moment I trust Running Bear. Or any Indian here for that matter."

Redfeather whirled and glared at Johnson. "Careful, white man!"

"Easy, Red, easy. Doc didn't mean you," Talbot cautioned. "Yeah, Doc, I'm sure about this. Or least as sure as I can be about anything anymore. No tellin' where this is headed if someone doesn't take a chance somewhere.

Might as well be me. I'll walk out first. Grogan, Devonshire, Cunningham, you stay behind. Red, Doc and I will walk up to the top of the bluff."

"What makes you think we'll even get that far, you crazy pale face?" Redfeather scowled. "I ain't quite of that frame of mind at the moment."

"Your choice. You know why I asked you here."

"Yeah, but I ain't figured on facing down rifles pointed at me by a bunch of pissed off Indians bent on gettin' some more decorations for their teepees. I don't remember that part bein' in the bargain."

"It wasn't. There aren't any more bargains. Now let's go."

Grogan dismounted and stepped forward. "Sheriff, I'll come with you if you want me to. If I'm going to be a deputy here, seems I'd better do what I can. I don't know the Cheyenne tongue, but I'm sure willin' to walk up there with you. Just to show we're not scared."

"Grogan, that's brave of you, and I appreciate the offer, but I want you to stay with Cunningham and Devonshire. In case I don't come back, you're in charge. Just stay with them and the horses."

"You sure, Sheriff?"

"I'm sure, Grogan. Doc, Johnny, let's go."

First Talbot, then Redfeather and Johnson began walking slowly toward the top of Sandy Bluff, keeping their eyes steadily on Running Bear and his men. After they had walked within about ten yards of the Indians, Jim saw Running Bear lower his right hand, and his three warriors lowered their rifles. The Indians then dismounted and stood silently in front of their horses, holding their rifles and watching the three white men cautiously move closer toward them. When they were within just a few yards of Running Bear, he held out his hand, snapped "Stop," and the visitors halted.

"Sheriff, white man, what you want? This our land, not yours."

"I know that, Chief. We're here about the raid on Tompkin's cabin. White man nearly killed, horses stolen, one of your braves dead. This must stop! We must make peace in these mountains, these canyons, before more men die. Before no peace is possible."

"Many white men, cattle, fire-wagon on our land. Kill many buffalo, break promise. White men lie."

"Chief, I know this, but we need some law between us. You know Doc Johnson here. Talk to him and Johnny Redfeather. They promise no forked tongues." Talbot turned to Redfeather and Johnson. "Right?"

"Right," said Doc, glancing sideways at Redfeather.

"Right," Red grumbled, eyes still fixed on the four Indians just ten yards away cradling their rifles.

Running Bear nodded, and motioned Redfeather and Doc to come forward and follow him. The three men walked together beyond the Indians and their horses to a spot further up and along the ridge out of sight from below. Talbot retreated to his deputies who sat upright in their saddles with their rifles slung over their forearms and pointed down. For the duration of the meeting occurring above, the two groups nervously eyed each other, each expecting the other to fire first and barely resisting the urge to do so.

Forty-five minutes later Redfeather, Johnson, and Running Bear walked down from the top of Sandy Bluff. The Chief stopped by his men, and Doc and Redfeather walked several yards further down. Red motioned for Talbot to join them.

"Well?" asked Talbot when he reached them.

Doc frowned, shook his head, and turned to Redfeather.

"Johnny, what's up?" Talbot asked. "What happened up there? You were up there longer than I expected."

"Running Bear ain't givin' up no men and no rifles. You'd have to come and take 'em. There's no deal."

Talbot looked up at Running Bear a few yards away and scowled. "Chief, a white man, Bridges, was killed, his rifles taken. Horses stolen. A brave died at Doc's cabin. You know that!"

"Many braves die, buffalo. Long time now!"

"Chief, this must end! For everyone, not just the white man."

"Sheriff," Redfeather interjected, "Running Bear won't give up any men, that's flat. Don't go there. And he wants cattle off all lands he's claimed for hunting and what he says are sacred to the Cheyenne, plus now more."

"What more?"

"Most of the flats leading to Reiser Canyon. Especially he says around Eagle Canyon, that's real special for the Southern Cheyenne. Always been sacred to Indian people, since forever. Ever see it you'd know why. And west and north of the river, out along Greasewood Canyon."

"Red, Tompkin will never concede that much extra land! He's got near three hundred head in the spring and summer, and he's fixin' to grow that herd. That's impossible!"

"Sheriff, Running Bear's in no mood for makin' more deals with white men. Says they ain't worth shit, and I'd have to say, speakin' for whatever Indian is left somewhere inside me, I'd have to agree."

"Talbot," Devonshire yelled from below, "how much longer we gonna stand here holding our asses while you and this half-breed discuss the future of these canyons? What the hell'd we come out here for anyway? This some sort of dumb shit pow-wow we got goin' here?"

Talbot whirled toward Devonshire. "I brought you out here, Devonshire," he yelled, "for your gun, not your politics. Just hold on, we're almost done."

Talbot turned to Redfeather. "Listen Johnny, tell Running Bear that Doc and I will go see Tompkin again and talk further. Ask him meanwhile to reign in his braves, and to leave Tompkin and his horses and cattle alone for now. We're not done here, not by a long shot. You tell the Chief that, and we'll go back peacefully. Just tell him to keep the guns lowered. We didn't come here to shoot anyone, or to get shot at for that matter either."

"Then why the fuck...?" roared Devonshire from below.

"To try to stop the killin' and make sure nobody gets hurt, that's why!" Talbot yelled back, looking squarely at the three men below him. "Now put those rifles back in your saddle holsters and let's head back to town. It's gettin' cold and we got a ways to go before sundown. Don't want to be up here at night. Johnny, speak to Running Bear, tell him we'll leave peacefully now. We'll go further down and wait for you."

Sheriff Talbot and Doc Johnson walked to their horses, mounted, and with Grogan, Devonshire and Cunningham rode a short way down, then stopped. Johnny Redfeather spoke to Running Bear for several minutes, then returned, mounted, and joined the others.

"Well?" Talbot asked when Red joined them.

"Well, Sheriff, I ain't sure this was worth riskin' getting' shot in cold blood up here. You sometimes got a right strange way of tryin' to fix up somethin' that already seems too damn big to fix no matter how ya look at it. Running Bear ain't up for no more pow-wows with white men. I see what you're tryin' all right, but I can't rightly say I see it workin' no how."

"Well, Johnny, I appreciate you tryin'. I truly do. Seems like I maybe got to try with Tompkin one more time."

"Sheriff," Grogan said, "since there don't seem to be simple solutions in these canyons any more, seems like you want to have me along from now on when you go visiting. Think maybe you asked for help just in time."

"Talbot," Devonshire added, "you bring us back up here next time you better have a better idea of what you're doin'. Me and Cunningham don't mind helpin' out, but we ain't exactly hired to be killed with our guns in our holsters. That's not what deputes are for."

"Devonshire, I know that. I'm just tryin to save this territory from more bloodshed any way I can. Now let's ride. It's gettin' damn cold up here!"

The small party headed back down Sandy Bluff toward Green River. Chief Running Bear and his men watched them descend, then headed down toward their encampment in Greens Canyon. The two parties rode swiftly, fearing being swallowed by the setting sun.

16
Tompkin's Revenge

Running Bear's band of some thirty-five Southern Cheyenne, including "dog soldiers," women and children, was camped about six miles north of town near Greens Canyon, a long, narrow canyon cut millennia ago by a stream that rushed down from a 6,800 foot peak at the north-east end of the valley. Indians had settled and hunted in the Greens and Greasewood Canyon complex for thousands of years. As these lands provided water and grasslands for buffalo, so they did for Tompkin's cattle, and here lay the land that he was determined to command.

Tompkin, Williams, Curly, Benedict, and Jeremiah sat around the roaring stove in his older bunkhouse on a cold, damp afternoon the second week of November. Leaning against the door of the bunkhouse nearest the pot-belly stove, Benedict spoke. "The Indians been rippin' up rails and burning ties for more than a year now. Get the railway men! Spring comes them graders be back to layin' track and won't have no time. So get 'em now."

"Yeah, but what are they willin' to do?" asked Curly. "I figure we got to kill them Indian bastards now, not just drive em' out or scare 'em. Kill all of them no-good redskins. Look what they did at Staggart's cabin. Stole horses, damn near killed him, scalped Bridges, stole them rifles he was bringin'. This is war, no use callin' it somethin' else, like a little skirmish over a few acres of land or a few puddles of water. It's war, plain and simple. Listen Tompkin, you've talked to this Sheriff Talbot, right? What's his take on all this? He some kind of god-damn do gooder, like I think this Doc Johnson is? I hear he treats Indians, even helps them women havin' babies sometimes. You know what that says about him. Talbot don't have no posse out here yet, but that don't mean he couldn't get one quick. What he ever do about the raid?"

"As far as I know...." A knock on the door interrupted Tompkin. "Oh for chrissake, now what? Curly, see who's there."

Curly opened the door to Sheriff Talbot, Deputy Grogan, and Devonshire and Cunningham, all carrying rifles aimed straight ahead. "Tompkin, it's the fuckin' sheriff! And looks like he got him that posse you said he hadn't have."

Tompkin sprang for the door, pistol in hand. “Drop it, Tompkin!” Talbot ordered. “We came here to talk, not to shoot. But we’ll shoot if we have to! Now put that gun away.”

“Oh yeah, so you can shoot us all in cold blood? That your new idea?”

“We’re not planning to shoot anybody. We’ll leave the rifles outside here. Just put the pistol down, and tell your men to do the same.”

Tompkin stepped back from the door, then turned to see that everyone in the bunkhouse, except Jeremiah, had drawn their guns. He looked back at Talbot, then slowly back at his men. “All right, put ‘em down. Come on in, Talbot. I’ll take you at your word.”

“Thank you, Tompkin. That’s right civil of you.”

“Yeah, but you better have somethin’ positive to tell me about your little visit with this Indian chief. I ain’t fixin’ to wait any longer to settle this mess myself.”

Talbot and his men walked nervously into the bunkhouse. They noticed the rows of rifles and all the boxes of ammunition propped against the cabin walls, and paused before sitting down silently on the edges of two bunks facing Tompkin’s men, who sat down on chairs in a half circle near the stove. For several seconds the men stared at each other across the silent chasm.

“All right, now what you got to tell me?”

“I visited Running Bear three days ago. He won’t surrender any of his warriors. Insists he is only defending his territory and sacred sites, which I have told you about many times before. There’s no damn reason for you to be runnin’ your cattle anywhere near Eagle Canyon, and you know that.”

“Well, is that right? His sacred this and his sacred that! Won’t give up any of his warriors! So, you gonna arrest any of ‘em? Take this little posse of three up into them canyons and arrest all them savages? Uh, you gonna do any of those things? ‘Cause if you and your deputies here won’t do it, we will. There’s no talkin or negotiatin’ with savages. If they want war, they’ll get war, and believe me I can get any number of railroad men out here too. They got no damn use for Indians ripping up rails and attacking road gangs. So be careful, if you know what’s good for you!”

“Now hold on Tompkin, just hold on a damn minute! You threatening me? Cause if you are, you’re asking for more trouble than you bargained for. I’m not sheriff out here just so I can wear this piece of silver on my vest. It’s a whole lot more than that. I’ve told you before that taking the law into your own hands, your idea of some kind of vigilante justice, will just make things worse for everybody in this territory. All you’ll do is get more people killed, yours and the Cheyenne. That what you want?”

“Well, what exactly do you want, Mister Sheriff ? More white men scalped? Horses run off? Indians running all Dakota Territory? Railroads dug up? You think they won't kill you and that doctor Johnson if they get a chance? You know what? I think you're plum scared of them redskins. You come in here wearing that tin badge that you think protects you, but you're too scared to arrest any of them that killed Bridges. You're a joke, you know that? Running Bear just pisses all over you, doesn't he?"

Talbot stood immediately. Grogan also rose and reached for his gun,Talbot motioned for him to hold his fire, and turned immediately to Devonshire and Cunningham, who also stood with their guns drawn. Benedict and Curly sprang to their feet and immediately grabbed their pistols. "No!" Talbot screamed, "hold your fire! All of you!" Talbot turned to Tompkin, his hands still at his sides, and walked slowly toward him. Benedict and Curly inched closer to Tompkin, while Williams and Jeremiah stood several feet behind them. Surrounded by their men, their pistols cocked, Talbot and Tompkin glared at each other. After a few seconds Sheriff Talbot turned back to his men.

"All right, that's enough. Put 'em away! I got one more thing to say to Mister Tompkin, then we're all gonna walk out of here peacefully and nobody's gonna get hurt." The men slipped their pistols back into their holsters and dropped their hands to their sides. Tompkin stood erect as Talbot approached him.

"Okay, you've had your filthy say, Tompkin. Now hear me, and this is the last time I'll say this. We can try to make these mountains and canyons peaceful for all concerned, white men and red men, or we can all die in a futile effort to have our own way. If you think I don't care about the man you lost, you're wrong. If you think I care only for the Indians' welfare, or their way of life, or their territory or rights, you are wrong. And if you think I cannot get a larger posse up here quickly, or won't, you are wrong again. I'm making one last effort to resolve these disputes peacefully with no more raids or gunfights or dead men, and if that doesn't work, hell only knows how much blood will finally be spilled. I don't want that. I've been in war, real war, and it's the ugliest god damn thing you can imagine. There are men in this room who know first hand exactly what I am talking about. And you don't want that here. Trust me, you do not. You might think you do, but you do not."

"You through lecturing me?"

"Yeah, I'm through. But mark my words. One last try. Stay off Indian land this winter and next spring with your damn cattle. You hear? Off!"

Talbot turned back to his deputies, motioned them to follow, then headed out the door. "We'll see ourselves out, thank you just the same." Sheriff Talbot and his posse picked up their rifles, mounted their horses, and rode swiftly back toward Green River.

"Fuckin' christ," screamed Curly as Talbot's men rode away. "Why didn't we just shoot the bastards?"

"Bide your time, Curly! Bide your time. It will come, trust me."

"It sure will, y'all," Jeremiah murmured as he walked out the door, mounted his horse, and began riding the two miles back to his solitary cabin.

Williams watched Staggart walk out of the bunkhouse, then turned back and glared at Curly and Tompkin. "And what exactly does 'bide your time' mean, if you don't mind me askin'?"

"Right now, Williams, whatever you think it means," Tompkin replied. "Don't need to know nothin' more than that. We'll just have to see what it means from here on, how things develop. If that damn sheriff won't take care of these Indians, maybe we'll have to do it ourselves. Maybe you're not exactly up for more fightin', like this soft-headed sheriff tryin' to make peace with savages. Well, I'm just not sure that's possible anymore, and every man here got to accept that or get out. Understood?"

"Yeah, I get it. I'll fight if I have to. But I'm not fixin' like Curly here to shoot people visiting this bunkhouse just 'cause we disagree with 'em. Especially a sheriff! That don't make no sense!"

"I ain't fixin' to shoot nobody in cold blood!' Curly snapped. "I'm just sayin', like Brent here, we might'n have to take this all on ourselves. That's all. And be god damn prepared if'n it comes to that!"

"We'll see," muttered Williams. "We'll see."

17
Winter Darkness

Through November and into December winter descended rapidly on south western Wyoming. Frost decorated the ground, and the skeletons of the deciduous trees that line Green River and its tributaries emerged almost overnight from beneath their leafy covers. Snow covered peaks of the high mountains merged with low, billowing clouds until the horizon seemed a vast, endless panorama of white velvet. Only the occasional shaft of light from the declining sun marked the illusionary boundary between mountain peaks and sky.

Tompkin's herders continued to drive his cattle over much of the high desert plains and valleys in the canyon country. When late autumn rains came they often left their animals to graze where significant amounts of water accumulated in rock formations and arroyos. Tompkin deliberately ignored Sheriff Talbot's warnings about trespassing on lands he assumed were sacred to Running Bear's Southern Cheyenne. He sent large groups of men out with his growing herds, with instructions to avoid conflicts if at all possible, but also to defend themselves and the herds if attacked. With winter and holiday seasons coming, he knew that the demand for meat in the saloons and restaurants in Green River and other settlements in the territory would increase. He also anticipated that demands for beef further east would increase, even if work on the railroads might slow. Tompkin believed himself master of the territory surrounding Green River, and nothing, not rebellious Indian tribes with their talk of hunting grounds and sacred sites, nor the annoying intrusions of a sheriff fantasying about goodwill and justice, was going to interfere with his expansive plans. He decided to make the area around Jeremiah's cabin rather than his own place his headquarters, and so hired gangs of Mexican and Chinese laborers from the railroad to build a second, separate bunkhouse with room for several more men in a clearing thirty yards from the cabin. He ordered a pot belly stove that came mostly by rail from Kansas City, and hired a Chinese cook to prepare meals for the herders. He also expanded the corral to keep up to fifteen horses.

Convinced that Sheriff Talbot was unwilling, and probably unable, to defend his cattle operation against Running Bear's warriors, Tompkin finally decided to raise his own army to destroy the Indian encampment.

He knew that many of the railroad workers in the territory, including many burly graders clearing land ahead of the planned route, were furious about the continued attacks of the Cheyenne, who tore up rails and occasionally killed workers during their raids on the road gangs. He suspected too that he would be able to recruit miners and loggers who were often harassed as they worked in the mountains and forests outside of Green River. Believing fully in his right to control as much of the Dakota Territory as he desired, Brent Tompkin schemed alone, night after night in his cabin, while his herders slept together in the new bunkhouse two miles away.

Meanwhile, as work days shortened and temperatures fell, Madame Milly Waters and her employees at the Green River Saloon thrived in her cathedral of a cathouse. Its unusual configuration had been modeled on an old riverboat design. The first floor was mostly taken up by the bar that spanned three-quarters of the length of the building. There wouldn't have been enough structural support for a second floor were it not for the four huge Doric columns, two at each end of the building, supporting an open walkway on the second floor. Along the walkway were ten evenly spaced doorways which opened into the upper rooms. Against the wall next to each room stood a small couch or a battered, over-stuffed chair. At both ends of the second floor walkway, overlooking the bar and gambling tables below, rested a very long "fainting couch" that provided a place for girls and their customers to sit or lie down while waiting for access to a room. The design made for a surprisingly stout foundation for a place that size, while offering the maximum amount of uninterrupted space within. A massive roof, sanctifying all within, enclosed the entire structure.

Sam was busy serving whiskey to ever-increasing hordes from the logging, mining, and railroad camps who converged on the place till midnight ("Damn near seven nights a week now!" he complained) demanding and paying generously for all the services that Milly's had to offer. The couches on the second floor were occupied constantly by waiting pairs of Green River's fairest "ladies of the evening" and their often inebriated escorts. After way too much drinking downstairs, they nonetheless assured themselves that they could sufficiently rouse their sexual powers. Never mind Milly's subtle hints that their "fire hoses," as she labeled the male apparatus, might not have enough water pressure after several hours at the bar. When some of Milly's girls complained the next morning about their "floozie," stark naked customers who fell asleep even before proper introductions had been made and who had to be dragged out of the room with their smelly clothes and boots tossed out after them, Milly just groaned and asked them if they would prefer walking the streets at midnight. "Here," she insisted, "you at least have a warm bed once the drunks are gone and I close up."

With the cooler nights Old Willie, the bedraggled guitar player, now played indoors whenever Charley the piano player wasn't banging out honky-tonk tunes in the far corner of the saloon. Old Willie's past, like that of many in Green River, including most of Milly's patrons, was as murky as his present, and he liked to keep both that way. He had wandered into the saloon one rainy night in early July, and had asked about providing, as he called it, "some real nice entertainment" for her customers. Milly had agreed to let him play outside on the boardwalk during decent weather, and inside near the end of the bar once winter descended. For this privilege Milly asked only that he split logs out behind the saloon and use them to stoke the three cast iron stoves she used to heat the saloon during the long, bitterly cold nights. On those nights when Willie was sober enough to show up and play he rode to the saloon on a rickety wagon drawn by a decrepit, mangy horse that could barely move, much less pull his wagon. No one knew, nor much cared, where he had been staying before he showed up at the swinging doors of the saloon. But as his playing was considered downright pleasant by most of the patrons, especially Milly's girls, he became a nightly fixture of the establishment. He claimed to know some of what he called "Negro music," and delighted to play some of those tunes for Johnny Redfeather and Sheriff Talbot, who both found his strumming enjoyable. Most winter nights he slept in the saloon on one of the couches outside the upstairs rooms, assuming he had not been offered a preferable alternative by a private party during the evening.

Old Willie was especially fond of Snuffy. From the moment he met her Willie was sure that he saw in her the facial features of a Mexican woman he had briefly lived with. "Milly," he asked one night shortly after he arrived, "where'd that kid come from? Her mother around here? How long she been here? I spent a while with a Mexican woman named Amanda a while back in Denver till she high tailed it out of town, sometime in eighteen fifty-three as I recall. Ain't seen her since, but even with all that wild hair on her head that Snuffy's 'bout as close to lookin' like Amanda as a little sprout could be."

"Willie, now you listen to me," Milly replied firmly, staring straight into his old, worn eyes as she wrung out a bar cloth and slapped it on the counter. "You can play here most nights if you wish, but my girls' private lives is just that: private. And as I like to say around here, 'You can fry bacon on that.' Ain't that right, Sam?" she hollered to him at the opposite end of the bar.

"Sure is, Miss Milly. That rule's good as golden around here. Has been ever since I been here anyway."

"That's right, and as long as I own this saloon it ain't never gonna change. I give my girls my word on that, and that's flat! And don't let me catch you pesterin' Snuffy 'bout all this, Willie. You just chop that wood and play your whadda ya call it 'Negro music,' and don't mind nothin' more. Snuffy don't need to know nothin' more than what she knows right now. And that's flat!"

"Well, all right Miss Milly. Whatever you say."

Nonetheless, when he wasn't playing mournful tunes on his battered guitar Willie and Snuffy would sit together talking at a table in a back room, obviously enjoying each other's company. Snuffy liked the old man, who regaled her with stories of his travels and his music playing. He kept Snuffy occupied when Johnny Redfeather wasn't around to let her practice the two-handed cross-draw with his pistols that he had showed her after the shoot-up in September. For her part Snuffy provided good company for the lonely and rather pathetic old man who seemed as rootless as the tumbleweed that the winter winds drove down and around the streets of Green River.

By early December Sunday had become the most entertaining night of the week. On the afternoon of the second Sunday of November, the Reverend Bartholomew Aloysius Simpson had decided to undertake a radical new approach to saving the souls of Milly and Frank Waters. Merely appealing to them at the ten o'clock service had obviously not worked, so the Reverend decided that he would attack the Waters' den of inequity itself, as it was the most popular saloon and bordello in town. So Reverend Simpson assembled an "Army of the Righteous," as he called his followers, including several lady parishioners from his Presbyterian Church, most noteworthy among them the fiery Miss Madeline St. Clair, the local school teacher and fervent teetotaler. Beginning that first Sunday of December and every Sunday thereafter at 7:00 PM sharp they would barge into the Green River Saloon and regale the entire establishment about the evils of whiskey and fornication and accuse Frank and Milly of leading young women and men into the "devil's cellar," Miss St. Clair's favorite term for hell. Reverend Simpson would push open the saloon's swinging doors and begin his impromptu revival by reading Bible verses about the woman taken in adultery, the seven deadly sins, and the ten commandments. Being a realist, Milly Waters was convinced of the economic benefits of providing "services" to the men of Green River and its environs, and embraced the wisdom of "keeping her girls off the street" in a respectable bordello where most nights there was a fine sheriff in attendance just in case someone got too drunk or tried to "take advantage" of one of her girls. She thus stood firmly behind the bar with Frank and Sam and paid scant attention to these weekly raids of the righteous.

Snuffy and Old Willie relished them. Knowing the Reverend's penchant for the virtue of punctuality, at 6:55 every Sunday evening Snuffy positioned herself half way between the doors of the saloon and the bar, and Old Willie sat on a stool near the end of the bar just waiting to cheer her on. As the doors swung open and Simpson's contingent invaded the anteroom of the devil's cellar the place went quiet, everyone waiting to hear the latest confrontation between the Lord's avengers and the pint-sized "defender" of the Green River Saloon. The preacher and Miss St. Clair were determined to prevent anyone from leaving during their revival and so always arranged their followers in a straight line just inside the doors. After Rev. Bartholomew Aloysius Simpson, who always insisted on being called by all of his "God-given names," there being, he asserted, strength and sanctity in the number three, completed his reading of appropriate Biblical verses he launched into his script of sins and broken commandments that plagued Milly's Saloon:

"Thou hast not, Madame Waters, kept holy the Lord's Day.

Thou hast cast false gods before both women and men.

Thou hast created in this establishment a temple to Mammon.

Thou hast opened the door to the devil's cellar and tempted men and women thither.

Thou and thy courtesans have led men to commit adultery and thus to break the bonds of holy matrimony.

Thou hast offered injurious spirits to be drunk beyond all measure and allowed devilish words to be spoken.

Thou hast encouraged gambling and violence to ensue, thus endangering the decent citizens of Green River beyond all bounds.

And thou hast forgotten: 'Blessed are they which do hunger and thirst after righteousness, for they shall be filled.'

And thou hast also corrupted the soul of this filthy child who shall burn in hell if she is not there already."

Or some such. The Reverend's script seldom varied. His knowledge of the sins committed daily in Milly's was firmly established. After he had finished his incantation, but before his forces could actually advance on the enemy and begin to instruct them about the perils of their souls, Snuffy always challenged the whole sanctimonious operation by launching a wad of her favorite apple-cured baccy at the Reverend's feet, a tactic that horrified Miss St. Clair and infuriated the good preacher. As Snuffy used to practice spitting every Sunday afternoon out back of the saloon, by the time the Lord's Army arrived she could launch a wad a good three to four feet, thus keeping the interlopers from getting too close to the bar. The further Snuffy spat the louder the cheer went up from Milly's patrons around the saloon, especially Old Willie, who strummed a few chaotic chords to accompany the cheering.

"How dare you spit that scum at me, young lady, if that's what you insist you are! We're here to do the Lord's work, and your filthy manners are not going to deter us! Not one bit!" roared Rev. Simpson every Sunday as he furiously made the sign of the cross and Miss St. Clair and the other ladies shuttered and covered their noses with silk hankies. "You think you can deter us with that, that, whatever filth that comes out of your mouth. You're the devil's daughter, that's who you are! You are thoroughly ruined, your soul may already be lost. There is no way to know how much confessing and praying you will need to find righteousness before it is too late! And Milly and these other wretched women here are to blame, and we are going to save you and them and close this beastly house of sin. Now!"

"Nah ya ain't," was always Snuffy's loud, proud response, uttered after she launched another missile at the feet of the assembled ladies. "This here ain't filth, it's grade A apple-wood cured baccy, and I ain't no damn lady neither, and like I told you before this ain't no damn church. Ain't gonna be neither, so's you might as well go preach to them horses outside. We're just goin' 'bout our own business here, ain't that right, Sam and Milly?"

With that Snuffy would turn for approval to the unholy ones watching all this from behind the bar, just waiting to see whether the sanctified Reverend Bartholomew Aloysius Simpson and Miss St. Clair would begin preaching from where they stood or cross the baccy line to minister directly to the sinners arrayed before them. The ladies always carried vials of what Miss St. Clair insisted was holy water and fresh white cloths with which they planned to baptize all the lost souls of Green River and wipe clean from their brows the signs of wretched sinfulness. However, the denizens of Milly's generally ignored the ladies' pleading and returned to their card games, whiskey, and other entertainments as might characterize any festive evening in a frontier saloon. As befit their solemn station in life Reverend Simpson, Miss St. Clair, and their pious ladies, frustrated at yet another failure to rescue souls and recruit soldiers for the Lord's Army, nonetheless strode elegantly out of the saloon determined to return next Sunday promptly at 7:00 PM fortified with a rearranged list of sins and commandments that might finally arouse the consciences of Milly, Frank, Sam, and their customers. Old Willie always serenaded their exit, pounding yet more chaotic chords from his guitar accompanied, sort of, by Charley on the piano. Sheriff Talbot, who generally enjoyed the show, obliged Milly by staying on Sunday nights, just to ensure that the confrontation remained peaceful, even if tempers did seem to rise on those winter nights between the hopeless sinners of the Green River Saloon and their aspiring saviors.

"I don't know why those crazy church people can't just leave others alone," Milly would fume to Sam once they came out from behind the bar. "Every damn Sunday night they're in here, tryin' to change what they know they can't. Frank and I go to church on Sunday and I tell that preacher fellow I'm just runnin' my business and providin' for the folks in town and them men from the camps, and that this is a respectable establishment. I take care of my girls, including Snuffy. Nobody goes hungry, and they sure as hell don't go thirsty. Me and Frank just provide what men want. Lord knows this damn town is wild enough as it is, what with Tompkin and the herders and railroad men. Take away a few pleasures and what do you think will happen next? Don't make no damn sense, all this preachin'. I got the law in here most nights, either the sheriff or his deputy, if he's got one. We go to church on Sunday morning, why ain't that enough?"

"It sure as hell oughta be," Sam would agree. "It sure should." And to the tunes of Old Willie's guitar or Charley's piano in the far corner of the saloon Milly's patrons would return to their pleasures. After most such Sunday escapades, and increasingly as winter approached, Sheriff Talbot would retire to his office rather than ride the two miles to his cabin, which had become intolerably lonely. The Reverend's and Miss St. Clair's words about "lost souls" struck him in ways more painful than any preacher in that gritty saloon could ever comprehend. "Why is it," he asked the winter silence as he walked toward the round-about, "that since Abigail died I spend more nights in my damn little office next to that stinking jail than I do back at our cabin? Doesn't seem right somehow."

***

Through early winter Jeremiah Staggart remained isolated in his cabin, preferring to remain there rather than stay with the other men in the new bunkhouse. Benedict told Curly and Williams that Tompkin had asked them to be sure Staggart did as he was told, and to report to Tompkin if they thought he was behaving oddly. Even though Tompkin had moved all of his herders into the new bunkhouse barely thirty yards from Jeremiah's cabin, he still spent most nights alone, though he continued to tend the horses and the arms stash. As winter descended Tompkin's men rode out less, so Jeremiah spoke with them only when they occasionally came for horses and supplies, and he seldom joined them for drinking and cards in the bunkhouse. Ever wary, he often lay awake late into the night on his cot near the cast iron stove, huddled under layers of clothing and wool blankets he had bought in town. He feared another Indian attack even though now many more men were close. He began to fear that Tompkin, and men like Benedict and Curly, could become uncontrollably violent, and that Sheriff Talbot would ultimately fail to prevent more bloodshed. He desperately wanted to avoid more of the unrelenting insanity of conflict. Many nights his sleep was invaded by images of his burned homestead. The charred bodies of his wife and son competed nightly with horrid memories of Chickamauga and Chattanooga. Skeletons of soldiers and children, holding hands, hobbled in a blazing circle.

On a ride into town on December 5th he stopped at the post office and picked up a copy of the King James Bible he had ordered a month earlier from a church in Virginia. At night he took to reading by a kerosene lamp many of the Old Testament passages he remembered his father reading to him as a boy. He recalled especially the words of the prophets, their searing warnings to the people of Judah for abandoning the worship of the one true God and the famine and deprivation that would follow. In Isaiah 34 he read: "The sword of the Lord is filled with blood, it is made fat with fatness, and with the blood of lambs and goats, with the fat of the kidneys of rams." And he read too in Isaiah of prophecies of salvation and renewal: "The wilderness and the solitary place shall be glad for them: and the desert shall rejoice, and blossom as the rose. Say to them that are of a fearful heart, Be strong, fear not: behold, your God will come with vengeance, even God with a recompense; he will come and save you."

How, he wondered, was this transformation to be? If the wilderness will fill with slaughtered rams and goats, what or who shall save its inhabitants, its suffering people? Surely as in times past a savior must emerge in such a bleak place where God has been abandoned and His vengeance is therefore imminent. He turned to his namesake Jeremiah and found what seemed to him truly prophetic words: "Before I formed thee in the belly I knew thee: and before thou camest forth out of the womb I sanctified thee, and I ordained thee a prophet unto the nations." And he read in Chapter 26, verse 8 that for prophesying "the priests and the prophets and all the people took him, saying, Thou shalt surely die." But he also read in Chapter 25 God's command to "Take the wine cup of this fury at my hand, and cause all the nations, to whom I send thee, to drink it. And they shall drink, and be moved, and be mad, because of the sword that I will send among them."

Many nights, wrapped head to foot in woolen blankets, Jeremiah stumbled to the door of his solitary cabin and wailed unto his God of his loss and cursed the fires that had consumed his wife and son. He hurled their names to the snow and the cold and demanded vengeance on those who dared to slaughter the innocent. On a clear night an Indian woman and child appeared to him, and in her right hand she carried a sword that glistened in the moonlight. "Surely thou art innocent! Surely thou must be saved from the fires!" he cried. "But who shall wield the sword? Who shall be justified? Who shall be worthy?"

Three nights later the Indian woman and her son pleaded before him with out-stretched arms.

18
Tompkin's Army

In late December Tompkin sat around a small table next to a roaring stove in a small office adjacent to a bunkhouse near the rail yards on the far side of Green River. Across from him, barely able to fit into his chair, sat Luke O'Sullivan, a huge, brawling, mountain of a man, head of a grading and track-laying gang for the Union Pacific Railroad and known to have killed a Chinese worker in a fight.

"Guns! That all you need? Hell, we got lots of 'em stashed in sheds along the tracks and in the work houses. Need 'em all the time. Damn Indians come at us all times of the day, sometimes at night too. Seem to like raids under a full moon, ridin' and screamin' like maniacs."

"How many men you got that's willing to fight?"

"Hmmm. Fight you say? Can't rightly say now. Have to talk to them first. Right now they're bored all right, but signin' up for a full-fledged shootin' war might be too much for some of 'em. Have to see is all. You talk to Talbot 'bout all this lately? I hear he's got a small posse in town now, seen a deputy in some of the saloons too. You figure he won't do nothin, is that what I'm hearing now?"

"Pretty much, yeah. He ain't done nothin' so far 'bout what happened up at my corral, or the killin' of my man Bridges and stealin' of my rifles I gave him to get to my cabin. Sheriff ain't worth shit in my book, not any more."

"Yeah, well maybe that's your view, but goin' after a whole bunch of warriors up in them canyons somewhere ain't exactly soundin' like a good idea either. You even know where they's camped out?"

"I reckon somewhere around Greens Canyon. I'll send some of my men up there soon as I can spare them. Maybe when the snow melts a little. I'll find out for sure and then plan a surprise for 'em they won't never forget, every god damn last one of them savages."

"Well, all right, I'll see what I can do. But no promises, ya hear?"

"Yeah, I hear. I'll ride back in a few weeks. See how many men you can get that will commit and for sure be willing to fight. I'm fixin' on a surprise move, maybe late winter or early spring, dependin' on snow levels up in the passes. Give the red savages a taste of their own kinda warfare. Like

I said they raided my place at night, run off horses, and I figure it's their turn for a little surprise. God damn sheriff ain't doin' nothin' to stop them, so we got to do it ourselves. Understand that?"

"Yeah, I hear ya. Some of our boys were with that gang that shot up Milly's back in town last September. Most just for fun but also they was pissed 'cause they didn't think Talbot and that so called little posse he called up back then, couple of pretty good shots I hear, was doin' enough about the Indian raids east of here. Hell, they seem to like just shootin' up places. Kinda dumb if you ask me but they get mad enough and all liquored up and they just go gun crazy I guess. Hear tell one of our boys, this crazy Kraut named Rensfeld, got his big fat ass kicked out of Hal's Saloon for fightin' one night back in July and flew out the door firin' like a mad man. Thinks he hit some dame in a buggy 'fore he run off. Says he didn't mean to hurt nobody. Says the driver turned around and sped out of town. Figured he was damn lucky the guy didn't come after him."

Tompkin stared at O'Sullivan. "July you say, in town? A guy named Rensfeld?"

"Yeah, like I say big dumb Kraut. God damn animal when he's drinkin', which is most of the time. But a damn hell of a worker when he's sober."

"Yeah, I got a few herders like that. Benedict for one. Likes his liquor all right, but damn good with horses and the herd. So, whadda ya think? You in?"

"Let me know more. How many warriors, where they's camped. When you plan on doin' this raid. Have to see about getting horses, since we ain't got many in camp here. I gotta know more 'fore I commit any men. Don't sound exactly doable right now. I might could get you ten, maybe fifteen men with rifles, plus ammunition. Not sure, but I could try. Don't rightly know how many's willing to actually fight Indians. But I gotta ask again, how you figure Talbot's gonna react? He ain't done much for us, but we go killin' a whole tribe of redskins and that's a different story altogether. He'll be all over our ass with a bigger posse, and maybe federal marshals, in no time if we're not careful."

"Talbot can't arrest if he don't know nothin'. We'll make it look like we're just fightin' back, just doin' what the Indians been doin' to us out here for months. If he can't get a bigger posse fast enough he can't stop us and can't arrest twenty five men at a time. Won't be no proof who did what any way you figure. Not if we're smart about it. If Talbot won't call in the cavalry 'cause he thinks he can play good guy and doesn't want a war out here, then we got to act quick and take the law into our own hands. And that's just what we're fixin' to do. I've waited long enough!"

"Yeah, well, maybe, maybe not. These railroad guys are tough, but, 'cept maybe for Rensfeld, not stupid you know. One's not the other, not by a long shot. You got to give me some time, like you say a week, maybe a little more. Say two, maybe three weeks. That suit you?"

"Yeah, that suits me fine. I got to get some of my own men out scouting the canyons soon as we can, and I don't rightly know when that'll be. I still got herdin' to do, got to get cows ready for market. And we got to know the best place to attack. This gonna be one shot and I ain't plannin' on no mistakes. Not this time. Maybe attack by late February, or early March, a little warmer then."

"All right, I'll see what I can do. But no promises, ya hear?"

"Yeah, I hear. That's good enough for now. Let's say three, maybe four weeks, give us both more time. I'll come back then. And I'll see about more horses."

"Good, I'll be looking out for you. See you then."

"One other thing. This Rensfeld guy. He still around here? Know where I can find him?"

"Hell, yeah! Hal's! Damn near every night. Don't go to Milly's no more since Talbot knocked him down and planted his boot on his neck. Says the scar's still there. Big guy, bigger than me almost. Fat face and fat belly, red hair. Almost looks Irish if you ask me. But he's a genuine Kraut all right. Nasty when he's drunk, which he mostly is now, and always tryin' to play cards to win whiskey money. That's what got him got kicked out of Milly's. Sheriff claimed he caught him cheatin' on a couple guys so threw him out and told him him he weren't welcome no more. Pissed him off real good I'd say. If there's one man Rensfeld hates more'n any other in this town it's the sheriff. Says he 'hates his stinkin' fuckin guts' when he comes back drunk as a skunk damn near every night."

"That so. Well, thanks. I just might have to meet this guy. Might have some business with him later on."

"Yeah, well, good luck catchin' him sober enough to talk sense 'bout anythin' 'cept Talbot."

"I'll try my luck. See ya later."

"Sure, see ya later."

Tompkin rode slowly through the early winter gloom back toward his cabin. "So Talbot's story about his wife's death was true," he mused. "And now I know who shot her. Just might be this Rensfeld Kraut could prove useful," he thought. Gazing at the mammoth cloud formations heavy with an approaching storm scudding across the heavens before him, he wondered: "Since these mountains do not care how a man dies, why should I?"

19
New Year's Eve, 1866

"O'Sullivan says his name's Rensfeld. Big red-headed Kraut, the guy who shot Talbot's wife in their buggy that night back in July. So drunk he didn't know who he shot and sure as shit didn't care. Talbot doesn't know he did it, but O'Sullivan says Rensfeld hates him on account of throwin' him outta' Milly's one night last August. Told him to keep his fat ass outta the saloon for good. So Rensfeld's no friend of his, and since he killed his wife maybe we can persuade him to finish the job."

"Makes sense," Curly responded, downing a bottled beer and resting his feet on a chair in Tompkin's cabin. "No sense havin' half a useless family around. Get him outta the way and what then?"

"I been to see O'Sullivan in the railway bunkhouse. Told him I'm fixin' to take out these Indians once and for all, probably late February or early March, once the passes open and we can get in there quick and easy. Greens Canyon is about five, six miles northeast from town, ain't just too far, but we got to be sure we know the area good and have a plan for attacking. O'Sullivan says he's got plenty of rifles, and he's tryin' to round up some of his railroad men to fight. They hate the Cheyenne as much as we do, so I hope he can convince some of his men to join us. We'll need more than just our herders. We ain't got more'n six or seven, and them Indians got more than that I figure. Probably way more."

"Yeah, and I hear them 'dog soldiers,' or whatever they call themselves, fight like animals."

"Yeah, but I ain't worried. We surprise 'em, gun 'em down before they know what hit 'em."

"Good. Now, what about Rensfeld and Talbot? What's up with them?"

"Rensfeld spends most nights at Hal's. He needs money for whiskey, and he plays cards so's he can drink. Go to Hal's, find him, tell him we're offering him money to kill Talbot, plain and simple. He just has to be sober long enough to get off one good shot. Set it up for New Year's Eve. Milly always has a big party at her saloon, and Talbot will be there. His deputies will be elsewhere in town. Tell Rensfeld to be near the saloon when Milly closes, and we'll get Benny to back him. Point is to use this guy to take out

Talbot if we can. He don't mean nothin' to us or anyone else, just a big dumb drunk. Tell him it's his chance for revenge against the god damn sheriff. He'll love that!"

"Yeah, him and me both!"

***

On Sunday, December 30th Milly foiled the Reverend Simpson's attempt to begin evangelizing her establishment by closing at 6:00 PM in order to prepare for her grand New Year's Eve party. Reverend Simpson had found in the Book of Joel, Chapter one, verse three, a call to action which he convinced himself would propel his Army of the Lord to spiritual victory if they could just get inside the swinging doors of the saloon: "Awake, ye drunkards, and weep; and howl, all ye drinkers of wine, because of the new wine: for it is cut off from your mouth." He had also consulted a horoscope and convinced himself that 1867, aided by the proper alignment of the planets, would be the year that he and his recruits would finally conquer the forces of evil inhabiting every nook and cranny of Milly's saloon and indeed all of Green River. Thus fortified by their assured victory and chanting the words of Joel they arrived at the Green River Saloon promptly at 6:55 PM only to find it closed and the large swinging doors locked from within.

They saw through the windows Milly and Frank, her girls, Johnny Redfeather, Snuffy, Charley, and Old Willie stringing up decorations and placing fancy table cloths and candles on tables and cleaning glasses and plates. Sam was busy unloading crates of whiskey and beer bottles behind the bar. Horrified by the fervid preparations for exactly what they had come to prevent, Reverend Simpson and Miss St. Clair pounded on the locked doors and frosted windows while Simpson pointed to the verses from Joel that he was convinced would be the salvation of all inside. Once or twice Snuffy approached the windows and shooed them away, further enraging Miss St. Clair, who was absolutely convinced that the soul of the arrogant little baccy-spiting monster was already dwelling in the "devil's cellar" and beyond salvation. After nearly fifteen minutes of pleading with Milly and her staff, getting chilled by the wintry air and falling snow, and being pushed aside by the crowds eager to enter, Reverend Simpson and his army withdrew from this skirmish, determined to return for yet another battle in their quest to drive Satan's minions from the Green River Saloon.

Light snow fell most of December 31st, and by 7:30 on a very cold New Year's Eve when Milly opened her saloon the town was blanketed by a lovely white covering. Light from flickering candles and kerosene lamps shining from windows of cafes and restaurants and hanging from poles all along the main street shimmered off the falling snow. People rode horses or drove their buggies from one end of town to the other, or walking to various celebrations crunched the crisp snow beneath their boots. The whole town was out and about on this festive occasion, and by nine o'clock Milly's was packed. There were wreaths on the swinging doors and above the bar, and between the timbers on the first and second floors hung paper snowflakes and an Old St. Nick and angel figures supposedly imported from Germany that Frank had purchased at the General Store. While most of the railroad men, miners, loggers, and herders preferred Hal's more raucous bash, many of the more respectable men and women of Green River society sat at tables consuming inordinate amounts of food and every whiskey and bottled beer Milly could produce. Sam needed a third hand to keep up with the orders at the bar, and the barmaids were nearly run off their feet dashing from table to table fulfilling their customers' increasingly vocal orders for both dinner and alcohol. Reginald, the second cook Milly had hired just for this evening, said he had never seen so many orders for beef and potatoes in one night in his life. Single men, mostly local shop owners and their employees, who were planning on late night entertainment, stuffed dollar bills in ladies' blouses and asked for room numbers. The women laughed each time another greenback was thrust into their bosom, knowing damn well that the fires of passion would probably be mere embers well before their prospective customers could even mount the stairs to the rooms above. Old Willie, when he wasn't out back chopping fire wood for the three roaring pot-belly stoves, collapsed in a stuffed chair in his usual corner strumming his guitar to whatever half-remembered tunes tumbled in his head. Charley, well oiled himself on this jolly evening, contented himself with banging out a few stale chords on his decrepit piano. No one seemed to notice.

Johnny Redfeather sat at a table entertaining himself telling whiskey fueled tall tales about his exploits for both the Union and Confederate armies to some of the girls. Courtney Dillard perched herself on his lap for most of the evening. Snuffy sat next to him savoring her apple-cured baccy and whacking his shins every time she knew he was stretching the truth. She had been around Red long enough and heard enough of his tales to recognize when he was reaching way beyond what even naïve courtesans could believe.

Around 8:00 PM Doctor Johnson and Sheriff Talbot and his deputy Butch Grogan, accompanied by Maggie and her husband Jim, walked into the party and sat down at a large, round table. Marilee, the most seriously wounded during the attack on the saloon in September, hurried to their table when she saw them sit down and remove their heavy coats. Talbot rested his Stetson carefully on the back of his chair.

"Doc," she exclaimed, "and you too Sheriff and Maggie, I don't recall that I ever thanked you proper for tending to me especially and the other girls when we were attacked. We all were scared right out of our wits, and them shots hurt real bad, and I thought I was goin' to die for sure. Milly says Doc you and Maggie and that Mexican woman stayed with us and took out those bullets and fixed us up real good. And I sure am grateful. And Milly says the drinks won't cost you all nothin' tonight. On the house, she told us. She's just grateful you all and that Johnny Redfeather saved us that night. Don't rightly know where we'd be right now without you. So what can I get for you all?"

"Well," sighed Sheriff Talbot, "that's right sweet, Marilee. Oh, and before I forget, this is my new permanent deputy, Butch Grogan. He's here from Fort Collins. He's been out and about since he arrived, learning the town and the territory, but not sure you two have met. He'll be with me tonight. I sent some others down to Hal's and a few other places in town. I told Butch he had to experience Milly's on a night like this. I know she wanted us here. So, shall we say a round of good bourbon? Think that would be fine indeed, right friends?"

"That sur nuff sound good to me, if'n y'all agree," said Jim, smiling under his broad-rimmed hat and glancing sideways at Maggie. "Course I don' spose tonight I got to check on that, it bein' New Year's Eve and all, now do I?"

"Y'all ain't got to check on nothin' tonight long as you don' git all up wid that Red fella. He can drink yer black ass blind, and y'all knows that. That's all I got to say tonight! Now jus' stop fussin' and enjoy yerself some. Lawd almighty!"

"Yessum!"

When they all stopped laughing they raised a glass to the new year and to Jim's new found freedom, then turned their attention to the steaks they had ordered and a second round of whiskey. As Milly had requested, Sheriff Talbot and his deputy spent most of the evening roving around the saloon checking on card games and whiskey consumption, trying to stay out of the way of impromptu dancers who occasionally bumped into tables or other patrons swirling to dance tunes only they could hear. They had to settle a few conflicts about promised "engagements," especially among potential "customers" whose memories about names, times, and room numbers were helplessly scrambled. To say nothing of what Milly called their incapacitated "fire power."

Near 11:30 Johnny Redfeather assured Sheriff Talbot that he had made secure arrangements for the night. Ms. Courtney Dillard, aka Darla, vowed that she would share her bed this festive night with the fabled warrior who single handed, she insisted, had saved the Green River Saloon that fateful and dangerous night in September.

"Sheriff, I'll be all go to hell but I sure am glad I ain't goin' out again in that snow. Too damn cold! Ain't nothin' works too good in that cold."

"Yeah, guess you're right on that score. Well, kiss the little darlin' for me."

"I sure will. Say man, what about you? Where you bunkin' tonight? Your cabin nearby?"

"Not too far, but tonight my deputy and I'll be stayin' in my office near the jail. Easier that way. Got some bunks and blankets there. Doc offered to take me to his place, so did Maggie and Jim, but I got to be here in the morning. Best this way."

"Well, whatever you say Sheriff. Seems like you got to get you a nice, warm woman."

Talbot winced and turned from Red, who reached for a whiskey glass on his table and called out to Courtney Dillard who had ascended to a couch at the top of the stairs. "You 'bout ready up there? Seems you been prettyin' up a damn long time now. Last time I looked at you there wasn't that much more left to fix up!"

"You lousy rascal! Get your red ass up here! I'll show you what needs fixin' up!"

Walking back toward the center of the saloon Talbot spotted Jeremiah leaning against the bar talking with Roxy and two other girls. Talbot was surprised to see him in Milly's but not entirely displeased.

"Well Jeremiah, fancy seeing you in here tonight! I did not see you come in earlier. I don't think I recognized any of Tompkin's men in here tonight. You here alone then?"

"Yes, Sheriff. A bunch of us rode into town earlier and his men went up to Hal's I guess. I told Williams I'd just as soon stop off here, see what the place looks like now. I figured you might be here too. Kinda hopin' I might see you again after our talk at my cabin."

"Well, you're right on that score. Hey, just about time for the new year I guess. Order a whiskey and get ready for the big moment. I'll see about joining you in a bit."

"That'd be just fine I reckon. Here's to you, Sheriff."

Talbot nodded and was about to order himself a whiskey when he felt a tug on his right sleeve. "Sheriff," Marilee said softly, trying to keep her voice down amid the growing jubilation as midnight approached, "you got a minute? Come with me over near the corner behind the bar. Won't take but a minute."

They stood close together in a small nook behind the bar and out of sight of most of the patrons. Marilee gingerly placed her hands on Talbot's vest, then shyly looked up at him. "Sheriff Jim, I don't know quite how to say this," she began shyly, "and maybe I shouldn't. And maybe you don't want to hear this. But, here goes anyway. I know you miss your dear Abigail somethin' terrible. She was a fine and upright lady, and Lord knows I sure ain't no saint. I know she called you 'Gentleman Jim,' and I sure know why. You could have any one of these girls in this saloon any night of the week, and you never even ask. And I guess we understand that, and respect you for that. None of us will ever measure up to your Abigail, and we all know that for sure. But, well, you, you just don't have to sleep back in that cold office on New Year's."

Jim Talbot sighed deeply, and tried to step back, but Marilee held his vest tightly. She began to choke as she continued. "Ain't one of these girls in here wouldn't give up this life for a man like you, and I figure I'm just the first one to come right out and say it. This ain't no real life for a woman. Ask Milly or Frank, or Sam, or Maggie, they'll tell you. I guess tonight I just got the courage to say all his, what with the holiday celebration and all. And I don't have no appointments tonight either. I told everyone of these men in here no, not tonight. You want to share my bed, you sure are welcome. It'd be like a new year's present I figure. Just for you." Marilee rested her head on Talbot's chest. She was crying.

Jim Talbot placed his hands on her elbows, then moved them up to her shoulders. He drew her closer to him. For several seconds they stood together. Marilee sobbed into his chest, and he felt her warmth. Talbot moved his hands down and took her trembling hands in his.

"Marilee, no, not tonight. I ... I, Abigail was everything to me. I can't forget her touch, her kisses, her soft sweet body in my arms. After all that killing in the war, all I wanted was to make a totally new life with her, and now since that's gone I can't trust happiness ever again. No point in pretending with you or anyone else. You need to understand that about me now. I hope you can accept it."

Marilee sighed deeply and clung to him, then reached up and pulled his face down and kissed him. He gently pulled away and held her at arm's length. "We'd best go. Must be almost midnight by now. Don't want to miss the magic moment, and I need to keep the peace for Milly."

"Sure, there's always duty, isn't there?"

"Seems now that's all I got left. That and memories."

"I could care a whole lot for you. You change your mind, you be sure to let me know."

"Not likely, not for a spell anyway."

He kissed her forehead, then squeezed her hands and slowly walked away. He reached the front of the bar just before midnight, and as Sam and

Milly counted down the final seconds Talbot raised his glass to Marilee as she joined Roxy and several of the other girls shouting "Happy New Year" at midnight with the celebrating patrons of the Green River Saloon. After downing her drink Marilee blew Talbot a kiss, and he smiled and blew it back to her.

Around 12:30, after one final round, amid grand rejoicing and shouting, Milly proclaimed "Bottoms up!" which was her way of announcing closing time. The girls and their patrons for the night, those still up to the task, ambled slowly upstairs. Talbot noticed that Marilee did indeed walk upstairs alone. He sighed, shook his head, then noticed Jeremiah still standing where he had left him earlier.

"Jeremiah, I never did come back to have that whiskey with you. Plum sorry for that. Little lady had something she wanted to say to me."

"So I see. Well, that's all right. Ladies want to talk, we men sure should listen."

"I reckon yes. I don't do much of that in here. Not since Abigail died."

"I understand that all right. I sure do."

"Say, you headin' back to that cabin this late? Me and Butch, that's my new deputy, we're fixin' to stay at my office. Probably got room for a third, place to tie up your horse. It'd be alright for a night I figure. Damn cold to be out ridin' alone by now. The others gone back?"

"Some maybe. Most I figure shacked up with some gal from Hal's. Pretty sure they's all liquor'd up real good by now, not fit to ride a horse or drive a buggy even if they wanted to. You might have some customers for that jail 'fore the night's over. I'd just as soon not ride back tonight, so yeah, I'd sure 'appreciate a place closer in for the night."

"Sure nough. Well, let's see if Milly and Frank need any help, say good night, and head out. We got to set up a bunk and some blankets for Old Willie by one of those stoves."

Talbot, Grogan, and Jeremiah began returning tables to the center of the saloon where they had been before being moved for the impromptu dancing earlier in the evening. They began to carry plates and whiskey glasses back behind the bar.

"Just leave 'em, Sheriff. We'll get all that tomorrow," Milly insisted. "Old Willie's asleep or passed out. His bunk's over at the other end of the building, near the piano. Sure appreciate it if you could set it up for him. Charley's gone upstairs already."

Milly, Frank and Sam wiped down the bar and put away a few half-empty whiskey bottles.

"Damn fine party, Sam! Don't you think?"

"Sure was, Miss Milly. Weren't no trouble neither. Sheriff and his new young deputy, what's his name, Grogan, got here just in time. Not a minute too late. Some of them card games were gettin' pretty loud, but Sheriff calmed 'em down. We sure did sell a lot of whiskey. And Reginald said he ain't never seen so much food ordered. So all around we did right good I figure."

"We did." And lowering her voice, she said to Sam, "Just before midnight I saw Marilee over in that little nook behind the end of the bar talkin' to Sheriff Talbot, and you and I both know what's on her mind. She got a crush on that man big as one of them mountains out there ever since that damn shoot up in September. But that poor man been lost since his Abigail died, and ain't he as good a man as come through here in years? I figure his insides is still all tore up and ain't no way to fix that. They was just so sweet together!"

"Now Milly," Frank suddenly chimed in, "best leave Sheriff Talbot and his insides all to himself. You don't rightly know what's goin' on in him. His hurt is bad, and he don't need us interfering in his personal life. Just leave him alone now."

"Yeah, Frank, I know that. Just seems not right him bein' so alone still. Lord almighty! But let's finish now and close this place. I'm tired!"

The respectable ladies and gentlemen bundled up and headed outdoors to walk or to ride home in their waiting buggies through the still falling and drifting snow blown around town by wind coming off the western mountains. Maggie, Jim and Doc Johnson, who assured Sheriff Talbot that they would get to Maggie's place all right, despite Jim's considerable whiskey consumption, waved good night to no one in particular as they stumbled warily out of the saloon to Doc's "carriage," as he always called it. Several people noticed a large, solitary figure, dressed shabbily and obviously shivering in the cold, lurking among the shadows created by the kerosene lamp at the far end of the building. "Poor man looks awful," a woman remarked as her husband helped her into their buggy.

"I've seen much worse," her husband replied.

"Good night Sam, Milly, Frank," Talbot called out as he, Jeremiah, and Grogan exited the saloon. "Fine party, I must say. Old Willie's fast asleep under his blankets. He'll survive all right."

"'Night, Sheriff. Thanks for being here. Stay warm."

Around one o'clock Milly, Frank and Sam followed them outside, closed the saloon, then stepped into their buggy and drove their horses toward the far end of town. Talbot, Grogan, and Jeremiah huddled under their coats and began walking on the boardwalk in the opposite direction toward the round-about half a mile away. The shadowy figure, his hands shivering, ducked back along the side of the building, then watched them walk past the corner. When they were several paces past him he stepped forward onto the boardwalk and drunkenly hobbled after them. After several steps he stopped, raised a gun with shaking hands, and yelled, "Talbot, you fuckin' son of a bitch, you done for now!"

Before the man could fire Grogan whirled, shoved Talbot aside, and shot the man in the chest.

"Christ almighty," Talbot yelled, "Who the hell is that? Grogan, you were fast!"

"I thought I heard extra steps coming behind us crunching in the snow."

"Oh Jesus! Jeremiah, you all right?"

"Yes, I'm fine. Just scared is all. No tellin' who that is."

"Best see if he's still breathing."

Grogan kept his gun drawn as they walked quickly back toward the man writhing in the snow, a large pool of blood quickly freezing on the boardwalk. When Talbot was sure the man was no longer holding his gun, he bent down close to his face.

"Rensfeld! Rensfeld! What the hell? Trying to kill a sheriff?"

"Throw'd me out will ya?" he gasped. "Got ya both...."

"Rensfeld, whadda you mean both? Both who? Who? Who?"

"Sheriff, he's dead," Grogan said, leaning next to Talbot. "Let him be."

Jeremiah joined them leaning over the body. "Sheriff, isn't this the guy you threw out of Milly's that night we met? Drunk and cheatin' at cards?" he asked.

"Yeah Jeremiah, this is him. I'd recognize this ugly face anywhere, dead or alive. But I just can't see him wanting to shoot me just cause of that. There's plenty of other places in town he can play cards. Hal's for one. I suspect that's where he's been most of tonight. Even dead he stinks terrible of whiskey. I just wonder, maybe Tompkin.... You ever hear Tompkin's men mention Rensfeld around the bunkhouse or on the trail?"

"No Sheriff, never heard his name anywhere. Sorry."

"Well, we best get his body up to the jail. We'll deal with it in the morning. Plenty of time then. Maybe warmer too. Grogan, I sure am grateful. You earned that badge tonight!"

"I'm just glad I was here."

Talbot lifted the body by the shoulders and Grogan and Staggart each held one leg. They shuffled slowly toward the round-about, then rested there for a moment. Sheriff Talbot looked at the statue of the Indian chief and white man clasping forearms.

"Always like to stop and look at that. It gives me some hope for peace in Green River and Dakota Territory. Real nice idea I think."

"I agree, Sheriff," Jeremiah added.

Walking toward the jail with their carcass on this first day of the New Year, Sheriff Talbot feared that his near escape portended more violence. He knew why Rensfeld hated him, but he wondered too: could Brent Tompkin be linked in any way to the depraved assassin whose bloody body he was now dragging behind him in the gently falling snow?

20
Reckonings

Around eleven New Year's morning Talbot, Grogan, and Jeremiah sat around the stove in the sheriff's office. The morning sunlight glistened brightly off the fresh snow that had fallen during the night. Talbot produced three cups of coffee along with bacon and eggs he prepared on a small wood stove in the corner of the room.

"So, Jeremiah, you've heard nothing from Tompkin or any of his herders about this Rensfeld thug we need to bury this morning. Not from Curly, Benedict, Williams, any of them? I sure remember him from that night in Milly's last August, and that wasn't the first time I'd had to throw him out of there, or arrest him out front of Hal's for brawlin' with some guy over a dame. Just seems most nights, and even some days, he's plum out of control, but I didn't expect him to try to shoot me in the back. Guess I still got a lot to learn 'bout bein' a sheriff here. Butch, take note. Might pay to be more suspicious and more careful out walkin' at midnight around these parts."

"Yes Sheriff, you've told me about the conflicts out here: the railroad's comin' this way fast, miners prospectin', and I can see why Tompkin and his herders would want Running Bear gone. I'm bettin' last night was more than just an old drunk tryin' to get back at you for slammin' him in a cell over and over."

"Maybe, Butch, maybe. Jeremiah, where you sittin' on this now? You still work for Tompkin, but you were at Milly's last night, not with the other herders who I guess were mostly at Hal's, right? You plan to stay in Tompkin's cabin, or are you making other plans? You know how my Abigail died, and I told Butch here too, and this Benedict maybe knows who came shootin' out of Hal's that night, and if so then Tompkin's maybe got men willin' to hire drunken killers. And who knows what else, you see?"

Waiting for Jeremiah's answer, Talbot looked away, and the face he turned back to the two men was grim.

"Jim, like I said, I've never heard of Rensfeld from anyone up at Tompkin's. But I got to go back there, least ways for a while. I stay mostly in that small cabin you visited, and I don't mess too much with the other herders. But if'n I hear anything 'bout him or your Abigail I'll sure let you know."

"That's right good of you, Jeremiah. You know where to find me."

"Sheriff," Butch said, leaning forward in his chair, "seems like we owe this Tompkin another visit, seein' as how I'm likely to have more contact with him in the future, 'specially if this Indian business gets worse. I'm bettin' no one should put anything past him."

"Well, yes, you're probably right about another visit, but I guarantee you we will not be welcome. Jeremiah, when you get back, tell Tompkin to expect us for a little chat about two o'clock today. Tell him it'll be right peaceful, though I might wonder how surprised he'll be to hear I'll be visiting again after the last time. Butch, pack your Remington just in case."

"Right, Sheriff."

"And keep your wits about you, just like last night."

Riding back toward Tompkin's new bunkhouse through the freshly fallen snow and the brilliant sunshine shortly after noon, Jeremiah sensed the hand of the Lord in winter's solemn, glistening silence. Though the air was cold the sun warmed him as he rode west into its beams still shining just high enough above the distant mountains to grace this first day of the year of our Lord 1867. Jeremiah felt strangely in his bones that this day would be auspicious for him. The events of last night notwithstanding, he believed he was moving closer in this still alien land to a time when the fiery visions and frantic screams that had wracked his dreams for years would cease. Even in this seemingly indifferent wilderness now gloriously shrouded in white he began to believe that he could fulfill the redeeming mission his father believed awaited him. He knew that he must now face the coming time alone, and though he believed that the Lord might now be calling him to the destiny envisioned in his naming, he also realized that he must tread cautiously the treacherous path before him.

When Jeremiah opened the door to the bunkhouse, which he noticed reeked of stale whiskey, Curly and Tompkin immediately confronted him just inside the doorway.

"Staggart, god damnit, where the hell'd you go last night? Curly told me you wasn't at Hal's, or that other place either!" Tompkin raged. "Where the devil you been anyway?"

"I stopped at Milly's, spent the night there with Talbot and his new deputy Butch Grogan at their office in town. Guy's a hell of a shot it turns out. Killed a big German named Rensfeld who tried to shoot the sheriff in the back. Needless to say, Talbot ain't too happy 'bout all these goings on last night. Wanted me to tell you he and his deputy fixin' to be here 'bout two o'clock."

"Talbot! Talbot! With a deputy! What the fuck you talkin' about? I thought...."

"You thought what, Tompkin? Mind tellin' me before Talbot gets here?"

"I...I thought he wouldn't come back, is all. Told him not to last time he was here. Ain't nothin' more'n that."

"You sure 'bout that?"

"Yeah, I'm sure 'bout that! Mind your own god damn business around here, Staggart. What's he want with us now?"

"Well, he says it's for a friendly visit, seein' as how he's wonderin' 'bout this big Kraut his deputy killed. Wants to know if'n y'all know anythin' 'bout him. I told him I ain't never heard of him here, but I guess he's wantin' to find out for his self."

"Staggart, you talk too god damn much for your own good. Just shut up about other men around here, if you know what's good for you. Think Curly told you that at least once before now."

"Yeah, I heard him. Just that tryin' to shoot a sheriff in the back ain't no small thing. I ain't sayin' you got somethin' to do with that, cause I saw Talbot throw this Rensfeld guy outta Milly's saloon first night I was here. Real impressive! But still, try to kill a man that way, no way that's right!"

"Well, Staggart, don't bother your mind 'bout it none. Just leave it be and go back to your cabin. Me and Curly got to talk before Talbot and his deputy get here.Where's he from anyway?"

"Don't rightly know. All's I know is he sure can shoot straight. Fast too!" Jeremiah turned from the doorway and walked back to his cabin, where he reignited the fire in his stove then lay down on his bunk and began re-reading the pages he had marked in Job and Jeremiah.

Tompkin and Curly stepped outside the bunkhouse and moved several yards away from the front door. "So, you took care of this, Curly? Really! You dumb shit! Can't you do nothin' right 'cept shoot your mouth off and drink whiskey? I got to do everythin'? What you'd tell Rensfeld 'bout back up anyway? Wasn't Benny supposed to be with him? What happened?"

"I gave Rensfeld two pistols and showed him where to wait. I know'd where Talbot's office was and where he'd be walkin' to after Milly's closed, but I didn't know his deputy'd be with him. I got back to Hal's 'bout eleven-thirty and couldn't find Benny. Figured he was drunk or hold up with some whore. Ain't seen him since. We left Hal's just after midnight, like we planned, and we all went to the cat house."

"Well, when Talbot and that deputy get here you keep your fuckin' mouth shut. All's you need to say is that you and the boys was at Hal's last night, and then went with some whores. That's all, ya hear?"

"Yeah, I hear," Curly snarled, and stormed back into the bunkhouse.

***

A few minutes after two o'clock, Sheriff Talbot and Butch Grogan cautiously approached the bunkhouse, halting their horses ten yards from the front door. Tompkin and Curly stepped onto the porch and closed the door behind them. Curly reached for his holster, but before he could touch his gun, Grogan pulled his from his holster and pointed it squarely at Curly's chest.

"Drop it, mister! We didn't come here to get shot at."

"Better do as he says, Curly," Talbot snapped. "My deputy Grogan here got you beat already. Besides, it's too damn cold for a shoot-out."

Curly looked at Tompkin, then lowered his right hand and scowled at the visitors. "All right. This time."

Talbot dismounted and stood in front of his horse. Grogan remained mounted and kept his pistol drawn.

"Talbot, I seem to recall sayin' you wasn't welcome here no more!" Tompkin shouted. "You forget that already?"

"Listen to me, Tompkin, this will be real quick! A Kraut named Rensfeld tried to shoot me in the back last night as we were walkin' back from Milly's. Lucky for me Deputy Grogan here heard him and killed him with one shot. Now I'm just a mite bit curious. You, or maybe Benny, know anything 'bout this big lug? I've jailed him several times for causin' all kinds of trouble in town, and seems he used to like to go around town shootin' up places. Like Hal's. Someday, one way or another, I'll find out who killed my Abigail, and when I do Lord help that man. Last night Rensfeld muttered something about 'Got ya both' just before he died. You got any idea what that might mean? That mean Abigail, maybe? He the one Benny talked about out on the trail comin' out of Hal's firin' guns last July?"

"Talbot, I told you once before I am right sorry 'bout your wife's death, but I know nothin' 'bout what Benny's been blabbin' about. That's his business. What them miners or railroad men or my herders do in town is their business, not mine. I told you I got cattle to run and Indians to deal with, and I ain't about to worry about a bunch of god damn drunks at saloons in town. I know nothin' about this Rensfeld or Hal's or somebody tryin' to kill you or anything else last night. I was up in my cabin, not in town. You ain't exactly my favorite person around this territory, but I'm no killer."

"No, maybe not yet, but men who work for you, or men you pay with money and liquor, could be. And don't think I don't know that. We'll be goin' now, and you remind this hot-head here to keep his hands at his side. Grogan practically got eyes in the back of his head, and like you just saw, he's real fast. So don't try anything stupid. Real bad way to start the new year I'd say."

Talbot backed up, then mounted his horse. Grogan sheathed his pistol, and he and Talbot turned their horses around and slowly began riding away. Five seconds later Grogan spun in his saddle, his gun out, and looked back at the two men. His stare froze Curly's right hand moving toward his holster. "Slow learner, aren't you?" Grogan quipped, then turned and with Sheriff Talbot galloped away. The slender sun was already slipping behind Jones Ridge and the cold was crunching their bones.

"Curly, you fucking no good fool! You absolutely no good fool! Find Benny. Kill him! See if you can do that! Now get back inside that bunkhouse!"

21
Jeremiah's Wound

Late the following afternoon Curly rushed into Tompkin's bunkhouse.

"Benny's dead! Froze to death in a snow bank by a whore house near the railroad bunkhouse last night. One of them train workers told me. Found his frozen ass stiffer'n ice! Guess he ain't squealed to nobody."

"God damnit Curly! Yeah, he ain't squealed to nobody, but Talbot ain't dead either. Why'd you let Benny get so boozed up when he was supposed to be backin' Rensfeld? You told me he'd be at Milly's when it closed!"

"I lost track of him at Hal's. Think he and some whore probably got drinkin' real heavy and she took him somewhere, maybe to her joint, and she got him more liquored and probably just took his money and kicked him out. Poor dumb bastard musta fell tryin' to get back to Hal's. I went lookin' for him but couldn't find him nowhere. But at least he's ain't talkin now."

"Yeah, no thanks to you! I hear the men. No more on this now."

Several men, including Williams, Staggart, a veteran herder named Mitchell, and five or six others entered the bunkhouse and gathered around the stove. As they gradually moved to chairs around the big central table Tompkin told them to sit down and listen carefully to what he had to say.

"Okay, listen up, all of you. First off, you got to know, Benny's dead. Froze to death last night after chasin' a whore out to some cat house. Never made it back to Hal's. Second, you all know Talbot was here yesterday with his new deputy, Grogan I think his name is, and a while back with two other men. So I figure he's expectin' more help around here. Running what's his name ain't giving up his warriors or our rifles, and I ain't about to lay down and retreat on grazin' land and water out here neither. So looks like we got us a little confrontation goin' on. No tellin' where it's all headed, but I told Talbot again I'm not waitin' too much longer for him or his little posse to drive out them Indians. Just so's you know. If we got to defend ourselves, we will."

"So that's what happened to old Benny," Williams said. "I wondered why he never came back. Curly you was lookin' for him like your life depended on it, so I figured you and he had some serious business to discuss. Am I right?"

"T'weren't nothing all that serious. Nothin' you got to worry 'bout, Williams."

"Well, seemed kinda odd you lookin' so hard just for him near midnight, middle of all them drunks and them damn women hanging on to any man they could find who could stand upright. Didn't see what was suddenly so special 'bout big ole Benny."

"Just didn't want anyone, you know, left behind when we headed for the cat houses, that's all. Benny weren't real bright, figured he might get lost or somethin'. Ain't nothin' more than that, Williams. Let it be."

"We got more important things to talk about," Tompkin interrupted. "Benny's gone. Like Curly said, let him be now."

Mitchell spoke up immediately. "Tompkin, what you fixin' on doin' this winter, if you don't mind my askin'? We gonna have a cattle business this spring when the calves are born, or not? Just who's gonna run these valleys, us or the Indians? And what's this I hear about the sheriff comin' back? What the hell for? He still tryin' to tell us where to run our animals?"

"What I'm fixin' to do, Mitchell, is see to it that we have a cattle business next spring all right, and I'll do whatever it takes to make damn sure nothin' stands in our way. Not a bunch of redskins or a lame sheriff tryin' to tell us we gotta smoke a peace pipe with these savages up in them canyons. If we have to take 'em out ourselves, then we will. I'm here to ask every man where's he's at right now. I'm outta patience, sick of waiting. So, what you all got to say?"

"We ain't got no where's near enough herders to attack them, if that's what you're proposing," said Mitchell. "They got rifles and lots more men than we do. We all know that."

"True enough," agreed Williams "Besides, you do that and you know damn well what's gonna happen next. Sheriff will get a real posse and a federal marshall and soldiers out here in no time, and they'll be all over us. That don't sound real smart to me, Tompkin."

"Who was it shot up Milly's place last September?" Curly asked. "Bunch of drunk railroad men, loggers, miners, whatever? Tried to warn Talbot I guess, or just scare him. Gather it didn't work too good, seein' as how he's been visitin' out here. But if we need men we know where to find them. 'Specially in winter."

"Curly," said Williams, "you keep thinkin' that way and you're gonna meet up with a sheriff's bullet some day. I still say there's no point in startin' something we can't finish. This territory's crawlin' with former soldiers just lookin' for somethin' to do, and you may not like it but Talbot can get them out here quicker than you think. No point bein' stupid just 'cause you're mad as hell soon as you get outta your bunk in the morning."

"Williams, you mind your business and I'll mind mine! I'm just tellin' everybody here what I think, and I agree with Brent that we might just have to clear out them Indians ourselves. Talbot won't do it. Why ain't that clear by now?"

"Look," added Tompkin, "Curly's right. Talbot ain't fixin' to kill no Indians if he can help it. Keeps goin' on about sacred places and hunting grounds and all sorts of god damn crap. Keeps talkin' like they're supposed to be just like us and not some savage breed from hell!"

Jeremiah looked up from his chair. "Ain't no people from hell 'cept those what will tie up a woman and boy and burn down a house and leave them to die inside the fire. Them's from hell!"

In stunned silence the men stared at Jeremiah, then at each other, as if begging for something to say. Tompkin cleared his throat and looked around, then squarely at Jeremiah.

"Jeremiah, I knew about this from Talbot a while back, though he asked me not to let on. But seein' as how you've told us, guess that don't matter now. Want to explain what happened?"

"Don't need no explainin'. Got back from battle for a few days, our nice little place with a house and barn and creeks, found all burnt down and skeletons of my missus and little boy inside the ruins. Yanks I figure, killed my family and fire and vermin ate 'em. I'd say others may be lost, violent, seekin' revenge, but they ain't necessarily from hell. Can maybe still be saved. You don't know."

Stuart, one of the herders, stood up behind Tompkin. "You a rebel then? Well I reckon that's all right. Too late now anyway. But what exactly you doin' here, if you don't mind sayin'?"

"Just tryin' to put that behind me, move on you might say. Find a new life, maybe try to settle down again. I didn't reckon to find no more fightin' and killin' when I boarded that train out here. Just lookin' to git away, that's all. Just away."

Tompkin sensed the rising tension in the room. He took off his hat and held it in his hands for a few seconds, then looked up at Staggart.

"Look here, Jeremiah. Ain't no man here isn't right sorry for your terrible loss. Your wound is deep, and no one of us here can understand what you must feel. But if you're fixin' to work for me out here from now on, you got to understand what we're facin' with these damn Indians. I told Talbot I got a legit cattle business here and I got markets and a railroad to take my meat back east, and I sure ain't about to let this bullshit about sacred lands mess up everything I put into this. Right now I don't give a damn about no sheriff nor no treaties either. So you got to decide. If you work for me you got to cooperate to defend this herd. No tellin' how this gonna end, but if it comes to a shootin' war, I guarantee you we ain't gonna lose. You got that?"

"Yeah, I got that. Ain't quite that simple to me, but I see your point well enough. Y'all plan what you think you wanna do. Just let me be a spell. I'll go on back to my cabin for now."

"Jeremiah, just remember what I said. Me and the men expect you'll do that when the time comes. You ain't got too many choices now."

"Like I said, I get your point. Can't say no more now."

Back in his cabin away from the bunkhouse Jeremiah lit a kerosene lamp and then knelt to open the door of the small stove. He stirred the embers, threw on kindling, and struck matches at the base of the small pyramid of paper and wood. From the rapidly growing flames the faces of a woman and child gradually emerged before him, and the crackling tongues of fire called "Jeremiah! Jeremiah!" "No! No! No!" he mumbled over and over as the flames became a pyre inside the small stove. He rose, and lurching to the shelf above his bed reached for his Bible. In the dim light he turned pages frantically until he came to the Book of Jeremiah, where he read aloud once again, "Before thou camest forth out of the womb I sanctified thee." He read again the prophet's calling on the Lord for vengeance: "But, O Lord of hosts, that judgest righteously, that triest the reins and the heart, let me see thy vengeance on them; for unto thee have I revealed my cause." Jeremiah fell to his knees, clasped his hands together, and lifting his head cried loudly so that his anguish might be heard: "Righteous art thou, O Lord, when I plead with thee: yet let me talk with thee of thy judgments:. Wherefore doth the way of the wicked prosper? wherefore are all they happy that deal very treacherously?"

An hour later Jeremiah awoke, cold and trembling, sprawled on the floor. He stumbled to his bunk, and lay back in the comfort of the dwindling fire and blankets and, he believed, his plea to the Lord.

22
Jeremiah's February Ride

The weeks after the New Year's meeting in Tompkin's bunkhouse, Jeremiah took to himself. He slept alone in the small cabin, away from the others, and always with a loaded rifle and pistol by his side. He seldom went with the other herders now, preferring to stay behind and, as he told Tompkin, guard the cabin and bunkhouse and the few horses left in the corral that Tompkin's men weren't riding. Some of the men, especially Williams, expressed concern to Tompkin about Jeremiah's withdrawal, and worried about having among them a man they knew was deeply wounded in ways none of them could understand. But, knowing about his loss, they mostly left Jeremiah to his solitude, and even during shared meals in the bunkhouse most of the men didn't make much effort to speak with him. Jeremiah often sat apart from the others, and even when he sat with a few men he spoke very little beyond polite greetings during a meal.

After supper on a bitterly cold Sunday in the middle of the month, Williams sat down next to Jeremiah who lingered alone at the far end of one of the long benches near the roaring stove.

"You doin' all right then, Jeremiah? Seems we don't see you much any more. Keepin' all cooped up in that little cabin down a ways. Must be awful cold in there at night. Pretty sure it's a damn sight warmer in the bunkhouse here, what with the two stoves that Curly keeps fired up. There's sure room in here for you if you want it."

"I'm keepin' the stove goin' all right I guess. Thanks for askin' just the same. I keep the little kerosene lamp goin' too cause I like to read at night, so I'm mostly doin' all right by myself in there. Right cold when I wake up for sure, but I can get the fire started up darn quick most mornings. Ain't just too hard."

"Readin' uh? Yeah, sure ain't much of that in this bunkhouse. Mostly whiskey drinkin' and card games and cussin' 'bout Indians and that sheriff fella. So what you readin' mostly, if you don't mind my askin'"?

"I got me a Bible a while back in town."

"Bible? Where exactly you learn to read that?"

"My daddy taught me back in Tennessee when I was young. Said it was real important that I knowed the good book like he called it, 'specially the Old Testament, seein' as how he done give me a prophet's name. So I been studyin' it real hard here of late."

"You got favorite stories? I think I heard a few of 'em somewhere."

"Yeah. Job, Isaiah, and like I said especially Jeremiah, 'cause of my name. I like readin' them and ponderin' what they all mean, ya know?"

"Well, can't say I recall too much of them particular stories, but if you like 'em I guess that's fine. But you get too damn cold or lonely over there, you just come on over. Maybe leave the Bible in your cabin, but you're welcome here. Don't reckon the men would mind, 'cept maybe steer clear of Curly. He's just mad as hell all the time at everybody, whether he got cause for it or no. And most of the time he don't."

"Reckon that's good advice. I'll probably stay in the cabin, but I thank you for offerin'. Right kind of you. Think I'll get back now, fire up the stove for the night."

"Sure 'nough. Glad we had a chance to talk a bit. Good night now."

"Good night. See you again soon I suppose."

***

Winter in the mountains evokes a terrifying beauty. The canyons hoard the sun's slim light; it brushes the eastern slopes, the southern snowfields, and teases glaciated western and northern facing slopes. On clear nights crystalline stars and the wandering moon orchestrate a dance of shimmering light that pirouettes endlessly over sparkling snow-bound peaks. Wind drives the cold ever deeper into clefts and crevices, freezing every drop of moisture. A landscape equally dazzling and deadly.

Yet here, as much in defiance as in determination, Jeremiah ventured often in the winter of 1867. More alone now than at any time since coming to Green River, he sought out these desolate canyons north and east of the river, especially the seemingly endless maze of side canyons carved by streams cascading from peaks surrounding Reiser Canyon. On many winter mornings he sought the solitude and the cold, always the cold, of the nearly sunless canyons, as if preparing himself for a mission that demanded purification and pain. As he rode deeper into the forbidding valleys, he sensed a gradual calming, an almost involuntary purging as if bits of an image in his mind's eye were slowly fading. After a particularly long ride he would often remain in his cabin for several days, sometimes even missing meals in the bunkhouse, brooding and confused, equally drawn back to the canyon lands yet resisting further ventures. Fewer were the nights when he saw his wife and child tied to stakes in a burning barn and terrified screams awakened him.

Endless snow-capped peaks of the White Mountains, glimmering in the early morning light, greeted Jeremiah on a bright Sunday morning in early February as he slowly rode northeast through fresh snow, following the contour of the Green River toward Reiser Canyon. Coming upon a trail junction just over a small ridge, he stopped, sensing familiarity with the area but not sure why. Hearing running water to his right, despite the cold, he turned his horse toward it and rode for another twenty minutes before encountering yet another trail that led due east toward a wall of jagged, protruding rocks. He followed this latter trail and fifteen minutes later recognized the rock outcropping as Casper's Bluff, below which a stream from high above him cascaded into Eagle Canyon.

Jeremiah slowly steered his horse toward the canyon entrance, ever mindful of the slippery surface of the rocks from the freezing spray billowing off the stream. He rode for several minutes, not sure exactly why, but again sensing that he must proceed further into the canyon, as if searching for something waiting there that had previously eluded him. About fifty yards down, Jeremiah stopped when his horse stumbled slightly. After settling the horse, he sat upright in the saddle and looked across the canyon to his right.

Enveloped in brilliant winter light the Indian woman and her son appeared to him on the ledge where he had seen them months before at the canyon. This time she did not run from him. Rather, she held out her arms in supplication, as if seeking protection and, Jeremiah believed, the salvation that only he could offer her. As he gazed upon them the words of the prophet that his father had read to him long ago came to him again, and he believed they were now his destiny, for he had borne witness to terrible evil: "Therefore will I scatter them as the stubble that passeth away by the wind of the wilderness." Besides the rippling waters of Eagle Canyon Jeremiah heard his calling from the Lord and saw in the woman and child those whom he believed he must now lead away from evil and into salvation. Baptized they would be, and blessed they would become, and with them he would erase forever from his mind the terrifying fires that had haunted him. With them he would obliterate knowing that he could not protect his wife and child or quell the rage of men who hated without reason and killed without mercy. "My God, my God," he cried, "surely thou has tested me because thou has called me and found me worthy!" Again he heard the voice of the Lord calling to him: "Before I formed thee in the belly I knew thee: and before thou camest forth out of the womb I sanctified thee, and I ordained thee a prophet unto the nations." For the Lord commanded him: "Take the wine cup of this fury at my hand, and cause all the nations, to whom I send thee, to drink it. And they shall drink, and be moved, and be mad, because of the sword that I will send among them."

The vision slowly faded. For several seconds Jeremiah sat trembling in his saddle. Then a great wave swept over him, and drained his fear. His breathing calmed, and warmth filled his body. He turned his horse and headed back up the trail through the snow and slippery rocks toward the junction. Twenty-five minutes later he came to the initial crossing, then pointed his horse south toward his cabin.

23
Confrontations

By mid February Brent Tompkin had rounded up nearly two hundred head of cattle from his scattered grazing areas on the vast snow-covered plains beneath the mountains to the east and up along the canyons to the north. He had shipped livestock in early December as far east as Chicago. Trains were running fairly frequently now, their cattle cars full with herds from several western ranchers. Indian raids on trains and their efforts to rip up tracks had been partly halted by contingents of Union soldiers deployed in the western territories after the war. Pockets of Indian resistance remained, especially in remote areas of the Dakota and Colorado Territories, such as the plains and mountains around Green River and further west. Tompkin was determined to get his cattle to market without interference of any kind. However, after the latest confrontation with Sheriff Talbot and his deputy at his cabin Tompkin was almost more worried about him than he was about another Indian raid. He also realized that all his men now knew about the murder of Staggart's family, and he wondered how any man could endure what Staggart had seen when he returned to his torched Tennessee homestead. Sympathy aside, he wondered if Staggart could be trusted, and how, or when, or against whom a man so deeply wounded might seek revenge.

Tompkin's men continued to lead his cattle over much of the frozen prairies during January and into February. They watered the herd wherever they could find flowing streams, and often stashed piles of hay near watering holes so the animals could remain in one location for several days. This made tending them easier for the men, and Tompkin told them that in the spring he planned to start fencing in much of the land where his cows now grazed. He was determined to include much of the land around Eagle Canyon, where he knew there was running water nearly year-round. "Drive 'em there," he told his men. "Don't give a shit 'bout no sacred nothin'!"

During an early thaw the first week of March Curly, Williams, and Mitchell were sitting around a camp fire near a stream about three miles from Eagle Canyon. Williams had driven a wagon full of hay they intended for the large herd there along the stream they knew would be flowing.

The first bullet grazed Mitchell's shoulder and sent him sprawling. Curly and Williams dove to the ground and began firing their pistols wildly, not sure from which direction the shot had come. A second shot caromed off the small fire pit and just missed William's left arm as he rolled over trying to avoid any more bullets.

"Crazy red bastards. Where the hell are they?" yelled Curly. "I can't hardly see 'em!"

"Up there, along that ridge, behind them rocks!" cried Williams. "Musta shot from there!"

"Red bastards! Savages!" Curly screamed as he scrambled to his horse, pulled down his rifle, ran behind the wagon and began firing at two large boulders at the top of a ridge line thirty yards away. Under cover of Curly's firing Williams and Mitchell dashed to the wagon and Mitchell lay behind a wheel while Williams grabbed a rifle from the driver's seat and began firing from behind the wagon.

"Mitchell, you hurt bad?" Williams cried out.

"Nah, just a scratch on my right shoulder. Ain't too deep, not much blood."

"How many of 'em ya think?" yelled Williams.

"Can't rightly tell," screamed Curly, ducking a bullet that ricocheted off the wagon driver's seat. "Fuckers can shoot all right!"

Seeing one of the Indians suddenly dart toward a third boulder, Williams fired immediately and hit him squarely in the chest. The Indian screamed and fell backward, and when the other warriors ceased firing for several seconds, Williams cautiously stepped out from behind the back of the wagon.

"Williams, get down!"

A single bullet splintered Williams's skull. In the shattering silence that followed all Curly heard was his own terrified breathing.

***

Curly sat trembling by the stove in the bunkhouse, pounding a table and almost too angry to speak. "Brent, I told you! I Don't fuckin' know! Two, maybe three, four! They ambushed us, two, three miles from Eagle Canyon. Never saw 'em 'till they started firing from behind boulders up on a ridge. Williams hit one of 'em, then like a damn fool stood out from behind the wagon for a quick look and they musta know'd that would happen, 'cause one of 'em drilled Williams square in the head. Killed him with one shot. Never had a chance. Shit! Shit! Told him to get down, but he never heard me. God damnit! The lousy cowards rode away so me and Mitchell loaded Williams' body onto the wagon and came right back."

Tompkin pounded his fists on the table. "That's it! That's it! I ain't waitin' no longer. I'm goin' to O'Sullivan again and we're gettin' ready. I'm sorry for Williams, but I wasn't real sure he would've been with us anyway. We need to have a meeting here in the bunkhouse when everyone gets back. Set this up, and make sure everyone now is with us."

"And just what do you plan on doin' with Staggart now? He in on this?" Mitchell asked.

"Don't rightly see how. I don't like his ridin' out to the canyons like he says he does. Can't figure that no way, seein' as how it must be so god damn cold up there. But I figure he can't do no damage all by himself. Far as I can see he ain't talkin' to no one, 'specially now that Williams is dead. Hardly no one else ever spoke to him. Who the hell would he talk to up in all that snow in them valleys? Man's hurt, I know, but he's more nutty than hurt if you ask me. We keep him here, tendin' the horses, make sure we know what he's up to, though. Just leave him be and watch him, that's all."

"Well, if'n you say so, Brent," Curly grumbled, "but if he gets in our way, I'll kill him sure as shit. Ain't no two ways 'bout that."

"I hear you, Curly. Just watch him is all. I got to get back to O'Sullivan. It's time. I'm not about to lose any more men, and I ain't fixin' to waste any more time either!"

24
Cleansing Spring Waters

When Jeremiah returned to his farm on leave in the spring of 1863 he had found blood dried on stones among scorched fields. Many nights since, in his dreams of fire and bones, all the land lay covered in blood. Now, in early spring 1867 Jeremiah traversed the warming wilderness alone, day after day, seeking the deepest canyons where melting snows fed numerous rushing streams. He knew that if the Lord were calling him, he and the land must first be cleansed. Guilt must be washed clean that one might be justified and others might be saved, even though some would be lost. As he rode, Jeremiah recalled the cry of the Psalmist: "Search me out, O God, and know my heart; try me and know my restless thoughts."

On a beautifully clear morning in early March, after a ride of several miles, Jeremiah stopped beside a swollen stream foaming over rocks. Suddenly he was convinced that at this spot the voice of the Lord was calling to him. He dismounted, stripped naked, and waded in. Stumbling forward he invoked the swirling waters: "Water, oh blessed water, run over me, run through me, cleanse my heart, that I may be purified and know at last that I am sanctified!" He hurled himself headlong into the cold, churning water, emerging seconds later shivering violently and cursing the fire that scorched his soul but could not comfort his flesh. He fell headlong onto rocks and lay exhausted, coughing rattling his bones. After several minutes he crawled toward his pile of clothes and began wiping his body with his shirt. He turned his face toward the sun, suddenly aware of its warmth. Then Jeremiah stood and cried unto his Lord, "Righteous art thou, O Lord, when I plead with thee: yet let me talk with thee of thy judgments: Wherefore doth the way of the wicked prosper?" And he fell to his knees, lay upon rocks and cried, and his body shook until he could neither cry nor shake any longer.

He awoke twenty minutes later, his legs drawn into his chest and his arms over his head. The sun burned high overhead, telling him that most of the day lay ahead of him. He felt surprisingly calm; as he began dressing his clothes felt dry and comforting. The stream to his right ran clean toward its rendezvous with the Green River at the bottom of the canyon that Jeremiah knew well. Surely, he thought, the Lord has brought me to this place for his purposes. Surely, my daddy long ago gave me a prophet's name because I was born to lead people to salvation. Surely now I know my course. The innocent must no longer suffer at the hands of the wicked.

He walked to his horse waiting several yards away. Strange, he thought, it had barely moved since he had dismounted, which now seemed very long ago. He took from his saddlebag a slab of bacon and a tin cup, walked to the edge of the stream, and sat down. Upriver several large boulders diverted a second channel that settled into a small, still pond before overflowing its rocky banks into the main channel. Below him to his right Jeremiah saw green fields emerging from under the rapidly melting snow as spring loosened winter's prolonged grip. Sitting calmly in the soothing sun, content in his solitude as he had not been for many months, Jeremiah ate the bacon slabs rapidly, satisfying a clawing hunger deep in his bones. He lowered his cup into the stream and drank his fill of the cold, pure water.

Three hours later Jeremiah approached the entrance to Eagle Canyon. The gentle stream he recalled from his visit in February had become a torrent of snow melt from high in the White Mountains. Sitting straight in his saddle, transfixed by the cascading water, he sensed the Lord's mastery of the rapidly changing landscape. Jeremiah recalled the Lord's rebuff to Job: "Where wast thou when...?"

The woman's scream shattered his reverie. To his right and twenty yards below him at the near bank of the stream an Indian woman was desperately trying to hold onto a young child who had slipped into the swollen river. Jeremiah dismounted and raced toward them. The woman was holding the child with her right arm while digging her left hand into the sand and rocks along the bank. Jeremiah jumped into the river and picked up the child in his arms, then swung him over his right shoulder and lifted the woman up with his left arm, pulling her away from the treacherous bank of the swollen stream. He set the child down and steadied the woman, and only then did he recognize them as the woman and child he had seen washing clothes last fall when they had run from him, and who had appeared to him on the ledge on his February visit to the canyon. Now, the woman just stared at him, and her son clung desperately to his mother's skirt, terrified more perhaps by the white man before him than by his near drowning.

Jeremiah was so startled at seeing this woman and child again that he did not hear the two Cheyenne warriors approaching from behind on horseback. They dismounted, and saw immediately the terror in the child's face and the woman's blank stare. Assuming that Jeremiah had attempted to harm them, the warriors pushed him aside and raised their rifles to his chest. Jeremiah stood still, staring down the rifles. From her frantic gestures and the look on her face, and the gradual change in the warriors' glare, Jeremiah believed that she was explaining what had happened.

"No!" the woman cried in response to an angry question from one of the warriors. "He save boy," she screamed, "Save boy." Still staring down the rifles, Jeremiah pointed to the river, mimicked pulling the boy out of the water, and, tapping his chest, nodded and said "Yes, I saved the boy." The warrior next to the woman looked at her, she nodded, and then she placed her left arm on the barrel of his rifle and lowered it. The other Indian lowered his also. Jeremiah stepped back, and exhaled deeply.

The woman stepped slowly toward Jeremiah, and extended her right hand. "I thank," she whispered, and Jeremiah, looking first warily at the two warriors still holding their rifles, took her hand in his. "You're welcome," he said quietly, not sure she understood what he said, although sure she did understand his hesitant smile. She quickly squeezed his hand, then she and her son walked swiftly back with the warriors to their waiting horses. Each mounted behind one of the warriors, and as they rode off she looked back at Jeremiah until they disappeared around a bend in the trail.

From his visions the woman and her son had now appeared to him in the flesh. Riding back to his cabin Jeremiah was exalted, convinced now that the Lord had indeed fashioned him as a savior and that soon in this vast wilderness he would fulfill the destiny that his father had prophesied for him.

25
Search Parties

In Tompkin's new bunkhouse Luke O'Sullivan sat around a table with him and Curly. "Ten, maybe a few more. Most I can say for now," O'Sullivan said. "I ain't seen no map of these canyons yet, but the men figured the Indians know this territory a damn sight better'n whites ever will. Men ain't figurin' on suicide. Fightin' maybe, but not suicide."

"Won't be no damn suicide. I got six to seven herders I can round up, maybe a few more men from town, some loggers and maybe some miners been tryin' to stake claims up some of these canyons and tired of gettin' shot at. They's fixin' to take revenge themselves 'cause like me they're fed up with this damn patsy sheriff. Maybe all told we can get twenty men or so. Don't rightly know how many Indian warriors are left up these canyons, but they's for sure Cheyenne, and I know some of their warriors are crazy fierce fighters. They got ten rifles plus a lot of ammunition they took from Bridges after they scalped the poor bastard, so I know they got at least that many guns. Don't know how many more. No tellin' who else they might have ambushed to get guns this winter. Not sayin' this will be easy, we just got to be well armed and prepared."

"So, what you're tellin' me is that this is a reglar ole crap shoot! That right?"

"Won't be no crap shoot if we can find out where their main camp is and surprise 'em. That's what I'm plannin'. Gonna be sendin' out men on search parties into the canyons soon, try to figure out the best place to attack. So far they've surprised us, especially at the corral, and now it's our turn to surprise them."

"Well, all right," said O'Sullivan as he stood up slowly and pushed his chair back from the table. "But you don't really know what they's capable of, and you don't know the lay of the land up there like they do, and you also don't know what that damn sheriff is liable to do if'n he hears what we're plannin'. So you just better be sure you know what the hell you're doin' with this surprise attack idea. Could be a god damn fuckin' disaster."

"I'll see that don't happen," snapped Tompkin. "You just get me as many committed men as you can, and those rifles you said you got stored in your bunkhouses, and we'll have nothin' to worry about, Talbot included.

Once it's done, it's done, and there won't be a damn thing he can do about it. We'll fix it so's no blame can fall on us. Ain't that hard to do when it's savages we're dealin' with."

"Well, you let me know. I'll keep talkin' to my men, and you send out them search parties of yours, and you let me know what they find out. By the way, when exactly you figurin' to do all this? We got to get back to work pretty soon, seein' as how the snow's meltin' and we can get back to grading and laying track again."

"Soon as I get my reports from the searchers. They're goin' out in a few days, maybe two or three."

"Right. Well, like I said, you let me know. I'll see you around I reckon."

At the door, O'Sullivan turned around. "Talbot, huh? What you figurin' to do about him?"

"Leave him to me. Let's just say I got plans for him."

"Right. Guess I'll hear about them plans later then."

"Yeah, you will."

Luke O'Sullivan shook Tompkin's hand, then turned and walked out of the bunkhouse. He rode swiftly down the path between the bunkhouse and Staggart's cabin toward town, and did not notice that Jeremiah had seen him ride past.

Curly turned to Tompkin. "Now that you got your reinforcements I got one question for you. Like I asked you before, you figurin' on includin' Staggart in this operation? You remember after he told us about how the Yanks killed his wife and kid and burned down his place, said only those who would kill the innocent like that were from hell? Well, this ain't quite the same thing. Maybe he don't think they're savages from hell. You notice what he's been doin' all winter? Rides out alone, gone all day and half the night, other days just sits in that cabin over there readin' the Bible I saw in there one day. Shit, whole bunch of pages turned down, like he's been studyin' the same places over and over. He don't hardly say much anymore either."

"Yeah, I noticed," Tompkin said. "But he still guards the place when he's here on days we're out with the herd, and I trust him that far anyway. He's hurt real bad, like you said, but I don't think he's plum loco just 'cause he don't say much and spends too much time alone or ridin' up in them mountains or wherever he goes."

"Well, maybe not, but if I was you I'd be real damn careful what you tell him. He don't need to know too much of what we're plannin'. Not by a long shot."

"Agreed," added Tompkin. "When all this is over, I'll get rid of him. He ain't all that necessary now. We got others close by can mind the corral. Days he's here he's still useful, keeps the guns and grub organized in the bunkhouse. For now I still think we got to keep him close. Now let's get out with the herd and tell the men what O'Sullivan said."

***

Eight days later Curly sank into a chair by the stove. "Most of 'em are settled up around Greens Canyon, just like you thought, northeast of Reiser Canyon. Whole bunch of 'em, warriors, women, kids runnin' around. All hold up there. Mitchell and I spied 'em from a ridge. Look real peaceful from above. Got a big stone circle in the center, built real nice. Big long house, looks like it's made of wood and bunch of tree branches all tied together, bunch of teepees. They got some elk and deer strung up dryin', stream runnin' by, seems kinda peaceful for savages."

"How many?" Tompkin asked.

"Don't rightly know."

"Well can you guess?"

"Maybe all told thirty, thirty-five, includin' womenfolk. No sense countin' kids. Them's easy killin'."

"Right. I'll get back to O'Sullivan now. The time to plan our own little raid is comin' on."

26
Jeremiah's Turn

The heavy spring rains muddying the dusty streets of Green River heralded renewed life in town. Miners were staking claims and loggers were cutting timber for construction of new houses and a rebuilt depot for the approaching railroad, and expansion of the one room school house. The railroad gangs were back to grading and laying track east of town along the planned route of the Union Pacific, and Richards Brothers' general store was bustling. Josh Stanton, the blacksmith whose shop was one street over from Milly's saloon, was extra busy shoeing horses for everybody in town, including many of the herders, and repairing buggies and "carriages," as Doc Johnson insisted on calling his. Tom Courtney, the local carpenter, seemed suddenly to be making furniture for everybody in town, including Milly, whose winter had been surprisingly profitable and who was busy replacing all the furniture damaged in last September's raid. As for the Green River Saloon itself, the varied services she and her employees offered were in steady demand from the local shop owners, bankers, and the more genteel of Green River's citizens. With the warmer weather and lingering daylight the railroad gangs, loggers, and miners often worked much longer hours, and the few such who preferred Milly's generally arrived later in the evenings and often needed considerable encouragement from Milly and Frank to leave the premises at closing time.

However, customers seeking poker games, whiskey and enchanting ladies could still be found inside the swinging doors, especially on weekend evenings. Johnny Redfeather occasionally appeared, from where no one knew, spent a day or two with Courtney Dillard, aka Miss Darla, the young lady he especially fancied, then ghost-like disappeared as he had been doing since he accompanied Sheriff Talbot to his meeting with Running Bear. His itinerary was unpredictable and, as he made clear to Milly after the raid in September, he preferred it to remain that way. Snuffy still prowled the saloon, chawing baccy and boldly defying decorum and the wishes of the several young women who pretended to be "raising her," a task they all admitted was impossible. The Reverend Bartholomew Aloysius Simpson, frustrated that he and Miss St. Clair and their righteous brigade had failed to save even one lost soul during the long winter, retired to his study on Sunday evenings and diligently rearranged his list of sins and commandments, seeking the most effective way to lead the denizens of Milly's Saloon to salvation on a future occasion.

Miss Milly meanwhile aspired, like politicians in Cheyenne and Laramie who had begun as saloon keepers, to become mayor of Green River. She believed she would have the backing of Sheriff Talbot and his deputy Butch Grogan, who had become quite popular among Milly's girls, and also of her regular customers at the saloon. She and Frank continued to donate money to the local school, to maintain Sheriff Talbot's favorite sculpture and its arch at the round-about up the street from her place, and they even contributed $50.00 to a repair fund for Reverend Simpson's church, which had been seriously damaged by two winter storms. Milly rightly calculated that these and similar charitable endeavors would elevate her in the public eye above any other possible candidates in town come the next elections.

"Ain't that good strategy, Sam?" Milly would carp on Friday nights when business picked up and several men and her ladies were dancing to the irregularly tuned endeavors of Old Willie and Charley.

"Yup, sure is Miss Milly. Like you always say, you can fry bacon on that one!"

Sheriff Talbot continued to work the night shift at Milly's, especially on weekends, while he sent his deputies Grogan, Devonshire, and Cunningham to roam the town, making sure they learned as much as possible about its not so fine establishments, including Hal's, as quickly as possible. On quiet nights at Milly's Sheriff Talbot could often be seen sitting and chatting softly with Marilee, who had recovered completely from her wounds. True, every night "Gentleman Jim," as Marilee began calling him, still could be seen leaving the Green River Saloon alone, but not before holding Marilee briefly in his arms and kissing her gently on her cheek. Milly, who pretended not to notice but always did, would insist that, as the days grew longer and the weather warmed, Sheriff Talbot's embraces were becoming a bit longer and his kisses a bit more, Milly would say, lingering. But Frank was quick to remind her, as he had forcefully on New Year's Eve, that she had no right to meddle in Sheriff Talbot's personal business.

"You let the man be, Milly!" Frank scolded her on a busy Friday night. "Just let him be! Run this here saloon and run for mayor if you like, but the sheriff's business is his own. It ain't none of yours. And Marilee's ain't either. She's doin' tables just fine. She don't need to do nothin' more now."

"Yeah, I reckon you're right, Frank. Just seems them two is workin' up to somethin' and I thought maybe I could help along whatever it might get up to be. But I know it ain't really none of my business. Guess that's flat all right. Now let's get them new whiskey bottles open. It's gettin' right lively in here tonight."

***

In the sullen gray of a rainy afternoon in mid March Jeremiah, Sheriff Talbot, and Deputy Grogan sat around a small table in the sheriff's office three doors down from the round-about. Talbot had just poured them all a cup of strong, steaming coffee. Jeremiah sipped his while Talbot took a big gulp. Grogan politely declined.

"You're sure what you saw, Jeremiah? Curly and Mitchell, you're sure you recognized them?"

"Jim, I am sure. I been riding in these canyons for months, lookin', you know, for some peace, 'cause of what I told you back at Tompkin's cabin 'bout my family. Somehow I feel better out there, cleansed maybe, I don't know, almost free. Anyway, I been ridin' out there a lot, and I know the canyons and the trails real good now. And I spotted these two guys on a bluff overlooking Greens Canyon, where I knowed the Cheyenne have their settlement. One of them, Curly, wanted to shoot you when you and your men visited Tompkin's bunkhouse once. He's mean as hell. After you left Tompkin said somethin' like 'Bide your time, Curly, it will come,' meanin' I take it, time to shoot and kill. I know there's been killin' on both sides, and I think you know Williams got shot out near Eagle Canyon by a Cheyenne hunting party near two weeks ago. So I think maybe Tompkin's fixin' to attack. Why else have his men spying on the Indians? This don't have to be. There's women and children there. I know."

Talbot squirmed in his chair. "Yes, I heard about Williams. One of Tompkin's herders was in town several days ago and told me, said they buried him and they aren't planning to bury any more men. I've telegraphed the Marshall in Fort Collins, sayin' I might need a contingent real quick and to get men and arms ready in case I do, and Cunningham and Devonshire are still in town. I also know that Running Bear's dog soldiers are fierce warriors. If they are attacked, they will never surrender."

"Another thing," Jeremiah added. "Not too long ago I seen riding away from Tompkin's bunkhouse this huge guy who I remember once talkin' to in Milly's, Irish guy I think who said he works for the railroad. Don't recall his name, but I'm sure it was the same guy. So damn big you can't miss him. Hadn't knowed Tompkin to be doin' business with railroad men."

"O'Sullivan!" Talbot shouted immediately. "Man has a voracious appetite for whiskey and violence and a fierce hatred of Indians. They been fightin' the advance of the railroad for years, especially since after the war. My predecessor had to designate a posse twice to stop skirmishes between the

Cheyenne and the railroad workers just east of town. Now listen to me, both of you. If Tompkin recruits a gang of railroad workers, we could easily have a serious battle on our hands in no time. I still suspect that some of the mob that shot up Milly's last fall were railroad men, though I can't prove that, just as I'll never know whose bullet killed Abigail. But I can't go back to that. We just got to worry about what Tompkin might be plannin' now."

"Sheriff," said Grogan, "I still feel for your loss. I sure wish that was somethin' I could help fix for you. Especially now."

"Me too, Sheriff," added Jeremiah. "What we lost can't hardly be explained any which way."

"I'm right grateful for that to both of you. And to you Jeremiah for this information. But listen here. We both know you been working for Tompkin since last summer. I know you shot that Indian that died at Doc's, and mostly I know about your loss, so you and I got something terrible in common, and that makes me want to trust what you say. But I don't trust Tompkin, not from here to the moon, especially now given what you just told me. But there's no way I can know exactly what your motivation is for coming here to tell me what you claim you saw at Greens Canyon, or why you believe Tompkin's men were up there. This could all be a lie, a plan to trap me and my deputies up in some god forsaken canyon somewhere, since you know these canyons so well. What I can believe is that Tompkin is capable of any terrible scheme to eliminate those Indians 'cause he's crazy enough to believe he can take over all this land around here. And the railroad men sure as hell don't want to deal with any more Indians rippin' up ties and rails. I can understand that. And I can also understand why the Cheyenne hate the 'fire wagons' coming through their land, but I still believe avoiding all-out war here is possible. But if what you're telling me is true, it looks like I need to deputize a posse quick, which I can certainly do."

Sheriff Talbot paused, then leaned forward in his chair. "But now, Jeremiah, you got to be careful. Real damn careful! It's not clear to me exactly whose side you're actually on here, mine or Tompkin's or the Indians', or maybe nobody's. But when you get back to your cabin you got to lay low. If everything you're telling me is true, and you're trying to stop a surprise attack on Running Bear, if Tompkin finds out you have betrayed him, or that crazy O'Sullivan, one of them will kill you. And it won't be a quick death. Especially if O'Sullivan gets his hands on you. So you better have a real good story to tell when you get back. Anyone know you're in town?"

"Far as I know they're all out on the range. I'm supposed to be guardin' the horses they left behind, but I rode out here soon as I could, and yeah, I got to get back. There's more light now and they're out later every day. I'll be all right."

"I hope so. Assuming all this is true, I expect I'll hear from you again. But a bit of advice: don't think you can play me, or Deputy Grogan here, for fools. You know what I've lost, and that makes a man real hard inside, reckless, not always believing there's reason to live. No tellin' what a man with a deep hurt will do if he thinks he's been duped. Just so you know."

"I sure understand that, Sheriff. And I hear ya!"

"I sure hope so."

It was suddenly quiet around the sheriff's table as the men stared down at the cups in their hands.

"That coffee's right strong," Jeremiah observed. "You make that, or get it from Milly's?"

"No, I made it. Can't you tell? My Abigail could make a darn fine cup of coffee, but I have yet to master that art." Grogan laughed softly.

"Yeah, I know what you mean. My wife Samantha was pretty good at that too."

The two men looked each other in the eye, then down at the floor.

"Right. You better get goin' back now. Remember everything I said."

"I will, Sheriff. I promise."

They stood, shook hands, and Jeremiah walked quickly out the door to his waiting horse. Sheriff Talbot sank into his chair as tears flooded his eyes. "Abigail, Abigail," he murmured softly. Grogan stood and gently placed his hands on the sheriff's shoulders.

27
Developing Storms

At four o'clock two days later Sheriff Talbot sat in Mark Johnson's office. "The problem, Doc, is that I'm just not sure I can trust Staggart. I don't know what to believe about where he sits with Tompkin, or why he's tellin' me all this. Tompkin is ruthless and dangerous as hell. We sure don't need another all-out shooting war out here, not with Running Bear's Cheyenne or the Arapaho or any other tribe. Had enough killing back in that damn war, as you and I both know all too well. It's basically my job to stop whatever Staggart thinks Tompkin may be planning, and I'm bettin' that he's trying to recruit some of the railroad men, seeing as how Staggart saw this O'Sullivan brute leaving Tompkin's cabin a few days back. No telling what that Irish lunatic might be up to. And after that damn drunk firing from Hal's and the mob shoot up last September at Milly's, I'm not sure I'd put anything past a bunch of those liquored-up railroad workers. I know they're fed up with the Indians too."

At Talbot's sudden, spontaneous mention of that lethal night in July that brought pain to both men, Doc Johnson reached across the table and briefly held the sheriff's right hand.

"Besides, Doc," Talbot continued, "Staggart's got what you'd rightly call a wound, a hurt, worse than mine. I lost my Abigail, but he lost his wife and his child in a god awful way. He told me at his cabin when I visited last fall that he returned to his place in Tennessee on leave and found everything burned down and the skeletons of his wife and boy inside the barn. Just bones, he said. Nothing more. I've learned to cope, I guess, but that doesn't mean there aren't nights when I'm wondering how I'll get through to morning, and whether there's even any point in waiting for it. Come morning Abigail will still be dead. No sunrise can change that. Imagine adding a child onto that! And that's what Staggart carries around with him every day."

At the mention of Abigail's death Johnson leaned back in his chair, head down, wondering again about the wisdom of telling Talbot everything that single bullet had cost him. What right as a physician did he have to keep that information from a man? How would Talbot react if he learned that he and Staggart, whose mental stability the sheriff was seriously doubting, shared the intolerable loss of a child? Would he be stronger? Weaker? Since

Abigail's death Mark Johnson had begun to believe that Sheriff Talbot had guts of steel, but he had practiced medicine long enough, and in the most deplorable circumstances, to know that every man has a breaking point. And he feared that telling Talbot now, in the middle of a developing storm, might push him beyond that point. Should he risk inflicting more pain on the sheriff when many lives might depend on his ability to lead? No, he decided; not yet.

"What about those deputies you took with us when we met Running Bear and then you took to Tompkin's cabin? Where'd you say they came from?"

"Rock Springs, not far away. Most they could spare. Got their hands full with whites rioting over the railroad hiring Chinese miners in the coal fields. I got Cunningham and Devonshire for at least another month or two, depending on the situations there I guess. But no tellin' where that's headed. Butch Grogan is permanent, and I am very grateful for him. Real steady man. Hell of a shot too. But I can't rely on that small company in Rock Springs for too many men. Best bet is Fort Laramie, where there's a cavalry contingent, but that's nearly 150 miles away. Take a while for men and guns to get here once I wired for them."

"And here's another thing," Johnson interjected. "If we really do get wind of Tompkin planning a raid, and we can't head it off with a posse or even a cavalry, don't we somehow have to warn the Indians? There are women and children in their encampment, not just Running Bear's warriors, his dog soldiers. If Tompkin is as murderous as you think he is, Jim, no telling what he might be willing to do. Could be a terrible bloodbath."

"The Cheyenne's raid at Tompkin's corral, where Staggart was damn near killed, would enrage any man, but he is just as blood-thirsty as those Indians he calls savages. Won't listen to reason about his damn cattle, and can't or won't see that he has caused a lot of this trouble himself. Maybe he thinks now his only solution is revenge. There's just no way to predict what he's willing to do."

"What about Johnny Redfeather? He went with us to meet Running Bear. Where's he these days? Maybe send him to the Chief to warn him if necessary?"

"I don't always know where he is or when he'll be in town. He's gone for days at a time then suddenly shows up at Milly's, playing around with the women and that Snuffy kid who he calls his 'lieutenant.' He might be able to warn Running Bear if this situation gets out of our control, but sometimes I think he's no more reliable than a rattlesnake."

"Well, I think you should at least telegraph the commander in Fort Laramie, and ask him to set aside guns and ammo just in case you need to get a good-size posse up here in a hurry. Still going to take five to six days. And how exactly you expect to track Tompkin's doings? Especially if you're not sure you can trust Staggart to tell you the truth? As you said, you can't know where he sits with Tompkin.

"Staggart said he would get back to me if he learns anything more about Tompkin's doings. At this point I guess I have to trust him. I don't quite know what else to do. I came here because I wanted you to know what I've been hearing, and because I know you've had some dealings with the Indian women, and you were with me when we met Running Bear. In case something happens to me, someone else has to know what Staggart told me, and contact Deputy Grogan and then the garrison at Fort Laramie. I'm sure you understand all this."

"I do, Jim, and I thank you for taking me into your confidence. But let's discard all that kind of talk about you, and focus on doing whatever we can to calm this situation. You send that telegram to Laramie, and I'll keep my ears and eyes open and let you know anything I learn."

"I sure appreciate that, Doc. See you around town, maybe at Milly's for a drink."

"My buggy, as Johnny Redfeather calls it, needs some work, so I'll be around. I'll stop by your office."

"Sure thing. See you then. Thanks again."

"You bet."

28
Further Wanderings

As he had done during the winter months, but now more often in early spring and with a renewed purpose, Jeremiah continued to ride alone into the mountains. He often met the rising sun a mile or so from his cabin as he headed north and east toward the complex of canyons he had come to know so well. Now past the spring equinox the sun blazed in the high mountains, sending water crashing into the valleys below. He thrilled at the vastness of the landscape and the wildlife he saw everywhere, rejoicing in the budding trees and flowers. The Lord, Jeremiah thought, is refreshing His land, blessing it and preparing it for the cleansing and benediction to come when righteousness would prevail and evil be vanquished. Jeremiah looked over the land into which he rode and believed that it could be made pure again. The mountains soared toward the sky, and at night outside his cabin he marveled at the trillions of torches igniting the heavens.

Near the sloping entrance to Eagle Canyon on an afternoon in late March Jeremiah dismounted and stood gazing into the craggy walls the sun was painting crimson and gold. In this most peaceful place, conflicting images haunted his mind. He recalled his previous visits to this canyon, his two encounters with the Indian woman and her son, and especially his recent rescue of the boy from the swollen river. He had gone to Sheriff Talbot because, he believed, Tompkin was about to attack the Indians, and although he had witnessed the assault on Tompkin's corral and had narrowly missed being killed himself, he believed now that he must prevent a surprise assault on the Indian settlement that would surely result in another massacre, another field of blood. He had seen one too many of these, and knew all too well the fate of women and children consumed in the furnace of war. Might not the Lord provide for him, as eventually he did for Job, if he could prevent such madness? While he did not know exactly what Tompkin was planning, or why Curly and Mitchell had been spying on the Indians at Greens Canyon, he suspected the worst. Perhaps he could not save the whole tribe of the Southern Cheyenne; perhaps the evil he sensed growing within Tompkin was beyond his and the sheriff's control. But had he not been cleansed in the rushing waters the Lord had sent, then warmed by this refreshing sun? And therefore could he not at least save some, somewhere in the bewildering maze of these mesmerizing canyons? He must find the place of rescue and convey whom he could to the safety and salvation he became convinced only he could provide.

One week after talking to Sheriff Talbot, during another ride to Greens Canyon, Jeremiah spotted two men crouched high on a ridge overlooking the valley below. Fifty yards away from them he dismounted, and tied his horse behind a clump of trees. He crept cautiously toward the ridge up a western facing slope below an outcropping that he kept between himself and the men. When he was within about fifteen yards of the ridge top he stopped. The two men were talking feverishly, and although he could not understand everything they said, he was close enough to recognize Curly's voice. He was able to hear enough words between them to be certain now that Tompkin was planning a raid on Running Bear's settlement.

Jeremiah turned around, and as he headed back down the slope his left foot dislodged a rock that rolled several feet before stopping. He stopped. Above him the voices ceased, and he pressed his body flat against the rock face, just out of sight from the ridge top. Curly yelled "Anybody there?" After several agonizing seconds, when he did not hear anyone moving toward him, Jeremiah lowered himself and, keeping as close to the rock outcropping as possible, crept gingerly down the slope toward his waiting horse. Only when he had mounted the horse and begun riding slowly away did it whinny. Jeremiah hoped by then he was far enough away that the men wouldn't have been able to hear the sound, and he was sure he was well out of sight from the top of the ridge. Once back on the trail he rode swiftly back toward his cabin. He knew that he had to arrive well ahead of Curly and his companion in order to deflect any suspicion that he had seen them anywhere near Greens Canyon. He also knew that he had to get back to Sheriff Talbot immediately.

29
Curly's Anger

"I told you, Brent, we didn't see no one. I heard some kinda noise below, maybe some rocks fallin' but just figured it was an animal. I don't think anyone knows we was up there. Why'd you ask, anyway?"

"I saw Staggart ride in last night. He got back just before you did. Just seems strange, that's all. I asked him where he was and where he goes and he always says he's just out ridin' in the canyons up north. Sometimes the herders see him, but not too often. He says it's peaceful there, and I guess he's still dealin' with his loss, which I think maybe I can understand, but I'm just not sure what to make of him after all these months. He's been here now since, when, last August? If you ask me he's still not right in the head. And maybe won't ever be. He was in the old bunkhouse when Talbot came by after seein' Running Bear, and after he left you barked out about killin' the sheriff and I said the time would come. I never should have said that with Staggart in the room. He's got his own idea of who's evil, and I don't reckon we and him see eye to eye on how to deal with these Indians. I just have this strange feeling that he's shadowin' us here, and maybe up in the canyons too."

"Beats me. I ain't never seen him out in the canyons by himself, just around here. Ever since that meeting with Talbot I've pretty much avoided him. Figured he was a bit loony, like you said. Just never knew what he meant when he said somethin' 'bout 'the time surely will come,' or some such horse shit. He was all right for a while, like after that raid where I know he killed a redskin, but since he let on about losin' his wife and kid at this farm and his talkin' about evil and hell, he ain't hardly been the same. Seems like he's got his own ideas about everythin' out here. Now all this ridin' out into them canyons alone, 'specially since the warm weather got here. I ain't never connected that to anything we're plannin' here. Maybe I should have."

"Yeah," Tompkin added, "and maybe you should have investigated that rock you heard rollin' around up on that ridge, or whatever or whoever that was. And kept a'hold of Benny on New Year's too! Maybe do a better job next time you're up there."

"Yeah, reckon you're right. If'n there is a next time. When you fixin' on getting this done? Seems we should be gettin' on with it if we're gonna do it. What's O'Sullivan say? Ain't they pretty much back to gradin' and layin' track now rather than just sittin' around gettin' drunk up at the saloons?"

"Yeah, they're back to work all right. O'Sullivan says give him three days notice and he'll have ten, maybe twelve men armed with rifles ready to go. Says he'll arrange it. Figure we leave just at dawn, maybe a bit before. The trail ain't too hard to follow from here. Get to the settlement in a few hours, surprise the hell out of 'em. Running Bear won't know whether to shit or go blind. It will be over in minutes if we plan this thing right. That's why I sent you and Mitchell up there, to scout the lay of the land and get some vantages for an attack so we know where to place our men. We have to be sure there's no place to escape. So, what did you see?"

"Gimme some paper and I'll show you what I think will work."

30
The Last Battle

Thirteen days later Sheriff Talbot was awakened just before sunrise by a frantic pounding on the door of his office in town. Imagining the worst, he rolled out of bed, grabbed his gun from under the bed, and crept cautiously toward the door.

"Who is it?" he asked wearily.

"It's me, Jeremiah. I gotta talk to you quick!"

Talbot placed his revolver on a nearby table and, barely half-awake, opened the door. Jeremiah burst inside.

"Sheriff, listen, I promised you I would let you know if anything developed over at Tompkin's place. Well, earlier this morning I saw a gang of men up by the bunkhouse, I figure near twenty or so. After some minutes they all rode off and I watched them go north toward the canyons. They had plenty of rifles. I'm guessin' they were headed for Greens Canyon, where I saw Curly and that other man like I told you. I figure they're up to no good, goin' after the Indians' camp up there. You got that posse together yet? Seems like you're gonna need it today, so I hope it's ready!"

"I got twelve men up from Fort Laramie, arrived just four days ago, plus Grogan, and also Devonshire and Cunningham I took when we met Running Bear. They're all holed up at the hotel, but I'm guessin' they've been hanging around Milly's, probably havin' a good old time what with the whiskey and women. Maybe not the smartest idea, but as long as they can stand upright and shoot straight this early in the morning that's about all I care about right now. I'll rouse them and we'll get up to Greens Canyon. I'll stop at Doc's office. He usually bunks there during the week. You recall about where you saw Tompkin's men?"

"You bet I can. I know exactly where I spotted 'em, and I know these canyons up there real well. Let me ride along and I'll show you where to take advantage. This is my battle too."

"Yeah, how's that exactly? What stake you got in this?"

"Just let me come along. I know more than you might think about gun fightin'. Trust me, you're gonna need me up there."

Sheriff Talbot dressed quickly and grabbed a pistol, his Spenser rifle, and a box of extra ammunition. "Well, if you say so. Just do what I say and try not to get yourself hurt. No tellin' how this is gonna end up now. You ride with us, and once we get up there, any help you can provide on the Indians' whereabouts in the canyon or trails will be appreciated. But if shooting starts, and I'm guessin' now it sure will, you keep close and do what I tell you. That's an order!"

"Yes, Sheriff. I get that."

Three hours later, after a furious ride, Sheriff Talbot, Jeremiah, Grogan, Cunningham and Devonshire, plus twelve soldiers from Fort Laramie led by Captain Xavier Wheeler, stopped at the top of Sandy Bluff overlooking the west entrance to Greens Canyon. A stream ran through the valley floor at the base of the canyon between the north and south walls.

"There's a ridge higher up on the north side of the canyon," Jeremiah said. "You can get there by following a lower valley west of here then going up a lower ridge without being seen from here. From up there you can see clear across the whole valley below. There's a break in the trees, and a rough trail leads to the valley floor. I've ridden it many times. You can ride down it without being seen until you're almost at the bottom. If Tompkin is planning an attack, I'm bettin' he's got his men yonder up on that north ridge. He got a good head start on us. They'll come down that opening, be on the Indians in no time, Sheriff. We got to get down there, rescue them folks 'fore it's too late. Now!"

"Jeremiah, let me handle this!" Talbot barked. "We have to do this right!"

From his vantage point on the bluff Sheriff Talbot surveyed the Indian settlement half a mile below. In front of a cluster of teepees and a large log structure covered with bound sheaves, several women were cooking over open fires in the middle of a stone circle. Men tended to horses in a corral, while others shook out blankets and clothes and laid them on rocks near the stream to dry. Older children gathered wood or carried pots of water to the women, while younger children, screaming in delight, threw rocks into the water trying to splash each other on opposite sides of the stream.

"Wheeler," Talbot yelled at the posse captain, "take six of your men, plus Cunningham, and head directly down from here. Jeremiah, what's the most direct route down on this side?"

"Just east of here a bit. There's a gradual slope down to the valley below. Ain't hard ridin'."

"Wheeler," Talbot ordered," head down that route now. Go!" Wheeler and his men hurried up the slight rise, then rode as quickly as they could toward the Indian encampment below.

"Grogan, Devonshire and the rest of you, come with me. We'll go down to our left and try to encircle Tompkin's men from the west before they attack. That's our only hope, that and some small element of surprise. I'm guessin' they don't know we're here. Jeremiah, you stay put! Remember what I told you back at my place."

"Yeah, I remember. Just make sure you save the innocent, the wives and children. Don't forget what I said!"

"I'm forgetting nothing and remembering too much. Just stay put!"

The first shots came from several of Tompkin's men who fired on the Indians from behind trees and boulders on the ridge above the northern perimeter of the settlement. After the initial volley they charged down a bluff toward the stone circle where moments before women had been preparing the morning meal. Many Indians fell immediately and bullets sprayed the creek where children had been playing. Five lay dead, while others, including three bleeding from arm wounds, screamed and raced toward their terrified mothers who tried frantically to lead them into the log house. Attackers fired randomly into teepees and the log house and at wailing women and children racing across the field. Unnoticed initially by the Indians in the sudden chaos two men spread kerosene around some teepees and lighted it, setting them and the surrounding vegetation ablaze

Several of Running Bear's warriors, armed with rifles, came running to the largest teepees and the log dwelling. Shrieks of wounded women and children shattered the sunlight. Bullets crisscrossed the field as desperate warriors sprawled on the ground and fired at the attackers. Knowing that trying to rescue wounded braves would be suicidal, warriors just tried to save their chief and the remaining women and children. Six of O'Sullivan's workers, heedless of danger and drunk on killing, charged headlong down from the bluff in a second wave of attack near the structure. They were met suddenly by a thunderous volley from Wheeler's men positioned to the left of the log house and equipped with Spenser breach-loading rapid-fire rifles. They opened fire on O'Sullivan's attackers, their shots mixing with those of the remaining Cheyenne warriors.

"Fuckin' Jesus!" screamed Tompkin from behind a tree at the base of the slope north of the stone circle. "Where'd they come from?"

"It's Staggart, you dumb ass hole! I warned you 'bout him!" Curly yelled. "He musta know'd somehow we was plannin' this. I warned you, didn't I? I told ya he weren't right in the head! He betrayed us! That's what he did!"

"Shut up, Curly! Just keep firin'!"

"Fuck this! I'm outta here!" Curly yelled as he dashed back up the slope then ran east through a grove of huge fir trees well behind the log dwelling and Wheeler's posse toward the creek.

Sheriff Talbot and his men reached the western edge of the encampment and spread out behind large boulders and trees. Once positioned they opened fire on Tompkin's attackers from behind near the stone ring, killing several and scattering others trapped between the Indians and Wheeler's men firing from the east and Talbot's from the west. As they desperately tried to evade Talbot's sudden onslaught, many tried to gain the slope back up to the north ridge, but Wheeler's men and several Indians, sprawled on the ground and wounded but refusing to surrender, fired at them as they careened into a hail of bullets. As Mitchell raced among the fleeing attackers toward the slope away from the stone circle he stumbled over a young warrior, badly wounded and lying in a pool of blood. He stood up, screamed "Savage!" and emptied his pistol into the man's face.

"You beast!" Talbot yelled as he came out from behind a boulder and with a single rifle shot killed Mitchell. As he crumbled, from the far side of the log structure another volley suddenly erupted. Cunningham and four of Wheeler's soldiers emerged from among huge trees near the log house to kill O'Sullivan and five of his railroad workers who had retreated, they thought safely, to a rock formation after their initial raid. With most of Tompkin's and O'Sullivan's men dead or wounded, except for a few scattered back up the north ridge, Sheriff Talbot stood up from behind a boulder to survey the carnage. Before him lay dozens of dead and wounded bodies—men, women, and children—and a rapidly spreading blaze.

As Talbot stepped forward Tompkin, bleeding from his left shoulder and crippled by a wound in his thigh, sprang from behind a large tree fifteen yards in front of him. "Talbot, I'm givin' you just enough time to know who's killin' you!" As he raised his rifle a ten-inch hunting knife swept across his throat from behind and he fell back, gulping blood and gripping his neck.

"Nah, I don't think so," shouted Johnny Redfeather, decked out in his Confederate Greys. "Not this time anyway."

"Red, where the hell did you come from?"

"I'll be all go to hell man, I was out front at Milly's, saw you and the boys ridin' out. I figured here. Fuckin' hell, Sheriff! Seen Running Bear?"

"No! Come on! That fire's spreadin'!"

31
The Final Fire

The instant Jeremiah saw the flames erupt he had ridden rapidly up the small ridge to his right, then down the slope that Wheeler's men had taken to the valley below. Once there he dismounted and stood, horrified and helpless, well behind Wheeler's men as the battle raged. Blazing before him were the stark terror of Chickamauga and satanic fire of Tennessee, and he knew that this time he could not run. As flames scorched the side of a teepee a woman carrying a child in her arms burst forth and ran screaming toward the back of the log structure. Seeing her racing toward him, Jeremiah suddenly understood as never before the words of the Lord: "Before I formed thee in the belly I knew thee; and before thou camest forth out of the womb I sanctified thee." He had not been able to prevent the slaughter of men, women, and children whose butchered bodies lay everywhere in the valley. The Lord had proclaimed, "Out of the north an evil shall break forth upon all the inhabitants of the land." Yet had he not brought forth the righteous to trample it? Had not the Lord's judgment racked his bones and found him worthy of redemption, and from amid these flames was he not justified now to rescue his wife and child?

As the woman ran toward him he cried "Samantha, Seth," and caught them in his arms. "I am Jeremiah! I am here! I have come for you this time! I have come to save you! We must run now, up the valley and away. Come with me! We will be saved!"

Jeremiah grabbed the boy away from his mother. She looked at him in utter terror, and screaming "No, no!" tried vainly to wrest her son from him. "We must leave!" he cried. The woman looked again at Jeremiah, then back at the bodies scattered across the burning land. Suddenly recognizing him as the man who had saved her child at Eagle Canyon, she turned to him, and, crying profusely, said quietly "Yes, ride now, away," and mounted his horse. Holding the child in his left arm, Jeremiah deftly swung up onto the horse, and, still cradling the boy to his chest, urged his horse forward as all three began riding east away from the flaming fury behind them.

32
Fathers and Sons

As soon as the shooting stopped, Talbot's and Wheeler's men had advanced toward the center of the settlement and worked furiously to control the flames before they spread to the log house. A few soldiers began the grisly task of combing the remains of the burned teepees. Inside several they found charred bodies of women and children, and in those they had saved from the flames many wounded women and children but also some braves. The bodies of dead Cheyenne warriors lay strewn around the bloody ground in front of the log house where they had fallen trying to defend their chief. The bodies of Tompkin's invaders, including O'Sullivan's frenzied killers, littered the north and west edges of the settlement.

"Better get into the house," Talbot said, turning to Redfeather as they walked forward. "We still haven't seen Running Bear. And those brutes were firing into it before we could stop them."

As they strode toward the stone circle, Running Bear emerged from the log house carrying a young boy in his arms. He moved past the rim of the circle and stopped at its center. He knelt, kissed the boy's forehead, then laid the body down. From his shoulder he removed a blanket and placed it over the boy's bloodied body. Sheriff Talbot and Johnny Redfeather gazed at the chief, then bowed their heads and began walking slowly toward him, stepping over dead bodies of Indians and whites. When they reached the chief inside the circle they stopped, knelt, and Talbot touched the blanket. "I'm sorry," he said. "We tried to stop this." Redfeather bent over and cried.

"White man kill son. Cheyenne die now."

Redfeather looked up and, taking Running Bear's hands in his, told him in the Cheyenne language that the sheriff had genuinely hoped to prevent this attack. Running Bear looked at Talbot and whispered, "Late." Talbot bowed his head and, choking back tears, gently placed his right hand on Running Bear's forearm. The few remaining warriors gathered around their chief and knelt. Running Bear slowly raised his head, then emitted a long, wrenching howl.

A moment later Talbot heard horses behind him and turned to see Doctor Johnson riding toward them in his carriage with Maggie, Jim and Maria. He was not surprised that Doc had brought them, remembering their care after the shoot-up at Milly's saloon. Still, he had to admire Johnson's tenacity and their courage. Johnson pulled up when he saw the small gathering in the stone circle, and Sheriff Talbot rose and walked out of the circle to greet him.

"Doc, thanks for coming. Not sure there's much you can do now, except help us bury a whole lot of dead people. Been a terrible slaughter of innocents, women and children included. I'm sick we got here too late. I, ... I just didn't think.... Should have. Stinking brutes! Jeremiah warned me, and I got the posse all right, but just too damn late. Speaking of Jeremiah, did you see him up at that bluff where I left him?"

"I didn't see anyone up there, but because we had the carriage and supplies we swung wide and came up the canyon further west. So I didn't get a close look. Christ almighty, Jim! We're all too late. This looks and sounds like what we both thought we would never experience again. Never!"

"Not your fault. You were smart to bring help, and Maggie, Jim and Maria are downright brave to have come with you. Ladies, Jim, you are welcome. Hopefully there won't be any more shooting here, so guess you can do what you can for the wounded. They're women and children been badly wounded, as you can see and hear."

"We best get to work, Jim. Maybe we can save some of the wounded before it's too late."

"Doc, Running Bear is there inside the stone circle. His son is dead, and Johnny Redfeather is with him."

"Redfeather! What's he doing here?"

"He saw us leavin' town, figured we'd be here. Tompkin was about to shoot me, Red came up behind and slit his throat. No figurin' Red! Downright spooky!"

"My god, Jim, you're lucky."

"Yeah, probably more lucky than I deserve I'd say. You better go to Running Bear. No medicine can help him now, but some words might, even a white man's. Especially yours. I'll leave Grogan and my men here with you. Wheeler will also stay here.

"Right, we'll do what we can."

"I'll see about Jeremiah. I'll ride back up to the bluff, and if I don't see him I'll scout around, maybe up the valley. Just be careful."

"And you likewise. Not sure riding out alone anywhere in this valley is a good idea right now."

"Oh, I'll be all right. I could use a few minutes alone anyway. Tell Redfeather to stay with Running Bear. I'll be back soon. Keep Grogan close. He's a hell of a shot. Nobody gets by him."

"Sure thing. Thanks."

***

A mile from the Indian settlement, around a bend in the trail, Jeremiah had stopped his horse by a small, still pond in the stream. Still cradling the Indian boy, he dismounted, put the boy down, then helped the Indian woman off his horse. "Drink," he said to her. The woman knelt and drank deeply, then cupped water in her hands as she helped her son drink. Jeremiah knelt and drank beside them, and gazing east he saw a light shining brightly upon a small farm, and he knew finally that the Lord had judged him worthy. Through suffering he had been redeemed and justified and had found all that had been lost. He believed righteousness would now be upon him for all of his days. He cupped water in his hands and poured small amounts over the head of the woman and then her son. He gently placed a hand on each of their heads, and said quietly, "I baptize thee in the name of the Lord."

"Staggart, you fucking traitor, turn around!" Jeremiah whirled to face Curly who stumbled toward him, bleeding from a bullet wound in his right leg and pointing a rifle directly at his chest. The Indian woman screamed, grabbed her son, and instinctively stood behind Jeremiah, who held his arms out wide as if to protect them. Curly stopped a few yards in front of them.

"Christ but you're disgusting, you know that? You ratted on us, didn't you? Uh? Didn't you? I told Tompkin not to trust you, but of course he was too god damn smart to listen to me. Now they's all dead, and that's what you and these filthy redskins are gonna be right quick here."

"Curly, let us go. We're just ridin' to our little farm back up this stream east to Tennessee. Ain't just too far from here now, maybe two, three miles or so. Not gonna hurt nobody now. Just us three."

"Tennessee? You dumb shit! What the hell you goin' on about? You're not just a god damn traitor, you're plum loco to boot! I know'd there was somethin' strange about you after that time Talbot came to Tompkin's cabin, and you mumbled somethin' about time will come, and got up and walked out. Well, guess what? Your time has come!"

Curly heard the horse before he saw it. He swiveled on his right leg, howled in pain, and, seeing Talbot charging toward him around the bend, turned and fired two shots just as Jeremiah reached for his gun. Jeremiah tumbled backward into the woman and child, who collapsed and cowered on the ground. Before Curly could pull the trigger again, Sheriff Talbot fired a rifle shot from his horse that killed him instantly. The Indian woman and child, blood-spattered and terrified, sprawled on the ground and wept helplessly as Talbot approached. He dismounted, walked to the woman, knelt by her, and gently stroked her shoulder. "I will not hurt you," he said softly.

Talbot determined immediately that Jeremiah was dead and, pointing to the stream, said gently to the Indian woman, "Wash." He removed Jeremiah's shirt and, kneeling at the bank, rinsed out the blood from two chest wounds. "Right through the heart," he mused. He wanted to cleanse Jeremiah's wounds as best he could before placing the body on his horse. He gestured to the Indian boy to remove his shirt and when he did, Talbot washed it in the stream before returning it to him. Talbot looked at the woman, gestured to the stream and repeated, "Wash," then walked away and stood with his back to the stream. Several minutes later the woman stood to his right, her clothing dripping wet and cleansed of dust and Jeremiah's blood.

Sheriff Talbot helped the Indian woman onto his horse, then holding the boy mounted himself. They began riding slowly back toward the settlement. The Indian woman rode behind Talbot with her arms wrapped tightly around his waist. The boy rode in front, cradled in the sheriff's left arm with his hands on the reins. The body of Jeremiah Staggart lay strapped across his horse's saddle.

33
The Aftermath

By the time Sheriff Talbot and his passengers reached the remains of the Indian village nearly half an hour later, a soft rain was falling. The blood of Indians and whites pooled in the dusty earth. The very air seemed to weep blood. Bodies of dead and wounded lay scattered like so many stones across the desolate landscape. Cries of wounded men, women, and a few children greeted Doc Johnson, Maria, Jim and Maggie as they desperately attended those whom they believed could benefit from whatever primitive treatment they could provide. Others, whom Doc realized were beyond his or any mortal's care, were simply left to die. Amid the drizzle Talbot's and Wheeler's soldiers moved like silent sentinels in the graveyard, carrying bodies of dead Indians into the log house for burial when and according to what rituals Chief Running Bear dictated. The following day they would return to bury the Cheyenne and whatever was left of Tompkin's killers.

As disgusted as he was by what he had seen on the battlefield, Doctor Johnson was nonetheless stunned when he saw Jim ride up to the bullet ridden log structure and dismount. "God help us, Jim. What happened?"

Sheriff Talbot dismounted, carefully lowering the boy to the ground, then helped the woman down. Seeing the desolation, they broke free and immediately ran into the log house. From inside Jim and Doc heard a horrid scream, followed by wailing and sobbing.

"That bastard Curly shot Jeremiah 'bout a mile from here by a bend in the stream, then I shot him just as he was about to kill the woman and child. They were with Jeremiah, but I can't fathom how or why. Maybe he managed to rescue them from the shooting, or maybe the fires, I don't know. Where he thought he was taking them I can't figure either. Maybe just away from here, away from the battle for a while, but east up that stream there's nothing I know of for miles. Maybe he really was just plain crazy after all. Maybe there's no figurin' what he thought he was up to."

"Maybe it had something to do with those two passengers you had on your horse. Woman, child. Maybe he thought.... Oh hell, who knows what he thought? Like you said, no figuring."

"Yeah, maybe he thought the three of them could just keep riding east and never have to stop or even look back. Like he thought there really was someplace for them that the rest of us could not see."

"Or understand. Well, right now we got to get on with what we can do here. Not much anymore, but got to try. Sure could use your help. Let's get Jeremiah off your horse. He deserves a decent burial."

Just then Johnny Redfeather and Chief Running Bear, holding the boy he had carried earlier to the stone circle, emerged from the log house accompanied by the woman Talbot had saved from Curly, her son, and a few warriors who carried blankets, clothing, a small head-dress, and some jewelry. They walked back to the stone circle and stopped. Redfeather motioned Sheriff Talbot to join them.

"Sheriff, Chief Running Bear wants to bury his son now. His spirit must go on a journey to Seana, up in Milky Way, to find rest. We'll go off alone. No soldiers, okay?"

"Sure thing. I understand. I'll tell Wheeler and Grogan to stay away. Where to?"

"Back up the stream a bit. He'll leave the body for a few days so the spirit can roam, then come back for burial. We'll be a while."

"We'll be busy here quite a spell, I reckon. No sense rushing anything now."

Sheriff Talbot and Doctor Johnson watched as Johnny Redfeather, Chief Running Bear, and the surviving warriors, plus several women, walked slowly past them heading west along the winding stream away from the canyon entrance. In the rain and enveloping gloom they resembled ghosts walking into nowhere.

34
Eagle Canyon

At noon two weeks later Sheriff Talbot and Johnny Redfeather rode together to the rim of Eagle Canyon. From Redfeather's chosen vantage point they could see the mammoth canyon walls plunge steeply into the long valley below. From above Casper Bluff the stream, flush with spring snow melt, swept down the canyon. Spray exploded into a hundred hues as it danced in sunlight above boulders amid the madly rushing water. Redfeather likened the view from this plateau to the long, slow flight of an eagle descending to the bottom of the valley. Ever since arriving in these mountains he had loved to sit here on his horse, watching the canyon pull the last light of day into its depths. From the ridge the canyon seemed so long and so deep that he wondered how the morning light ever escaped its clutches.

Redfeather had mentioned this canyon to Talbot a few times, and he had hinted that it was somehow connected to the death of Colonel Swanson, though he was never quite sure what the connection was. What Redfeather did know was that this canyon was sacred to Chief Running Bear and the Cheyenne, and that white men were not wanted anywhere within its walls.

The men sat silently on their horses, gazing into what they both recognized as an enchanting and beautiful place. "So, Johnny Redfeather, what now? You brought me out here. What's on your mind? You been to see Running Bear, I hear."

"Yeah, been once, spent a few days there. Helped him bury the braves, women, children. Doc and his women been there too. Many rituals got to be done for the spirits' journeys. Important to Indians. White men usually don't get that sort of thing. Think it's silly, but it ain't silly to Indians. Course there's a whole lot white men don't get about Indians, you know?"

"Yes Red, I know. Or at least I think I do. What about Running Bear?"

"Ain't the same man no more. Why the hell would he be? He and whoever's left of his tribe will have to move. Can't stay where so many have died. Somewhere further up in the canyons, maybe go east. Don't know. What about Tompkin's men and their god damn cattle?"

"The men are scattered, as far as I know. Not many of his original herders left, or at least I haven't seen any that I recognize in town. O'Sullivan and his gang are dead, and Wheeler and his soldiers will be here for quite a spell now. Grogan is for sure assigned here now, and for a while also Cunningham and Devonshire. Just in case. Someone else is running Tompkin's herds, don't rightly know who, but at least for now they're staying out of Indian lands. Suppose that's the best we can hope for. Try to enforce the latest treaty rights, agreements. Don't know much beyond that."

Redfeather shifted in his saddle. "Listen, Sheriff, I know you tried to prevent that massacre, and Running Bear knows that, but that ain't the real problem here. The real problem is much deeper, and you and I both know we can't really do much about that. Indians know white man's treatise ain't worth a bucket of piss, and one good man wearin' a tin badge and tryin' to reason with men like Tompkin won't prevent more killin'. You ever bury a woman, a child?"

"Yes, Johnny, I've buried a woman. My wife. Guess you did not know that. Shot in town last summer by some lunatic drunk. Doc couldn't save her. Running Bear's loss is far, far greater, I know. Lost his son, just like Jeremiah in the war, come to think of it, plus most of his tribe. But yeah, I've buried someone I loved."

Redfeather looked down into the canyon, its crimson walls resplendent in sunlight. "Sheriff, Jim, I never did know that. I'm right sorry."

"I'm sure you are. I don't pretend to have lost nearly as much as Running Bear has. But I carry a pain everyday that nothing can shake. Nothing! But anyway, none of this is why you brought me up here today."

"Guess I wanted you to see this canyon with me, in spring, when I'm stone sober, see the high sun on these walls and the stream runnin' wild. 'Cause maybe this is all that's left for the Indians. A place white men can't destroy. Might fuckin' try, but they can't! Just thought I'd show you this, seein' as how it's up to me now. If Running Bear ever returns here, it'll just be to die. He'll die at the bottom of the canyon, along with the sunlight, and wait for the eagles to carry his spirit to the next world, where no one can harm him or his people anymore."

"Johnny, I tried..."

"I know you tried, Jim, and I ain't judgin' you on that. Running Bear ain't either, or least I don't think he is. But we both know you was too damn late with your posse, though I reckon they could shoot straight enough when they had to. Seems as if you trusted Tompkin one damn day too many, and now that village up in Greens Canyon is a huge Indian burial ground. Ain't none of them little braves ever comin' back to this canyon again."

Sheriff Talbot removed his Stetson and ran his fingers down the middle cleft, then smoothed out the brim. He reset it on his head, stared into the canyon, then turned to Redfeather.

"Johnny, I owe you my..."

"You owe me nothin', white man! I mighta saved your pale ass a few times 'cause Tompkin or some hired thug wanted your scalp, but like I said to you at Milly's that night, once a brother fightin' evil, always a brother. That's that. But now you gotta leave me alone."

Redfeather nudged his horse next to Talbot's and extended his right arm. The sheriff leaned to his left, reached across, and with his right hand grasped Red's forearm. Redfeather seized Talbot's forearm, and for a few moments both men squeezed hard.

Talbot released his grip and settled into his saddle. "Guess then I'll head back to town, see what Milly's up to. Might see about Marilee. Maybe stop at Doc's. See how he's doin'. Rattlesnakes slithering all over the place now. What you fixin' to do?"

"Dunno for sure. Me and Snuffy maybe take off somewhere, maybe take Old Willie too. Likely visit Running Bear again, seein' as how he ain't hardly right in the head. Man needs help real bad. Might could do some good back there for a while."

"You're a damn fine man, Johnny Redfeather. I wish you well, and hope we meet again."

"Ain't just too likely, but ya never know. Maybe Milly's sometime. Might wander back. Try to stay out of trouble for a while. I can't always show up at the last minute, ya know."

"Right. Guess nobody can. Goodbye for now, Johnny Redfeather."

"So long, Jim Talbot. Been right good knowin' ya."

Talbot tipped his hat, turned his horse, and headed back toward Green River.

Johnny Redfeather dismounted, tethered his horse to a large boulder, and walked slowly toward the rim of Eagle Canyon. After several paces he stopped, and stood a long time staring into the canyon's depth.

From a bluff above the stream on the opposite side of the canyon, a lone Indian woman, her son by her side, gazed at Johnny Redfeather and the silence of Eagle Canyon. A soft rain began falling.

Readers Guide

1. The Preface to *Green River Saga* identifies it as an "historical novel." What does this term indicate about the contents of such a novel? For *GRS*, how do the authors use historical information from the late 1860s as essential background and structure for the principal events of the novel?

2. Although Black Kettle, the historical Cheyenne Chief, does not actually appear in the novel, the attack on his encampment at Sand Creek is the motivation for the novel's fictional Cheyenne Chief, Running Bear, to flee to the mountains and valleys near Green River. Why is the history of Colonel John Chivington's attack on Black Kettle important for understanding Running Bear's motives in the novel, especially at Sandy Bluff where he meets Sheriff Talbot and Johnny Redfeather?

3. Investigate the history of the Union Pacific Railroad as it expanded west in the 1860s. How did the UPRR exploit foreign laborers, especially Chinese, and how does the history of this exploitation affect the attitudes of the railroad workers in the novel, especially the crew leader Luke O'Sullivan?

4. How is the topography of the setting essential to the novel and its main characters? How many crucial scenes, and at what points in the novel, occur in the mountains and valleys northeast of Green River?

5. Where in the story are there echoes of the Twenty-third Psalm. Given their placement, how do these become ironic?

6. Early on the authors employ a flashback structure for the three main characters, all of whose first names begin with the letter "J": Jeremiah Staggart, Jim Talbot, and Johnny Redfeather. How do these three characters eventually become fatefully, even tragically, entwined with Brett Tompkin and Chief Running Bear?

7. How closely does the novel's Jeremiah follow his Biblical namesake?

8. Besides the Book of Jeremiah, how is the book of Job important for understanding Jeremiah's character?

9. Why does Jeremiah flee after the battle of Chickamagua and during the battle of Chattanooga in November, 1863? How has the war and the way he lost his family affected him?

10. Why does Jeremiah seek forgiveness and "justification"? Does he ever believe he achieves such judgment from the Lord, and if so, where in the book? Why does Jeremiah venture so often into the mountains and valleys? What is he searching for?

11. At several crucial points in the novel Jeremiah encounters a Cheyenne woman and her son. Who does he eventually come to believe they are; how does this conviction grow; and what events contribute to this final conviction? Plot this development in Jeremiah's mind very carefully; it is crucial to understanding his character.

12. Where and why does Jeremiah finally break from loyalty to Tompkin? How is this break related to whom he believes the Indian woman and her son are?

13. Why does he insist on riding to the battle with Sheriff Talbot? How does his conviction about the Indian woman and her son lead to his actions in the final battle scene?

14. Why does Jeremiah head east on his horse with the Indian woman and her son as they flee the battle scene? Where does he believe they are going?

15. Is Jeremiah mad, sane, or somewhere in between at the end? Is he a genuinely tragic character?

16. Fire can be a complex symbol, indicating death but also purgation, and it has deep Biblical roots. How is fire central to understanding Jeremiah's actions up to and including the final scene?

17. Why has Jim Talbot come west? What does he hope to find in Green River?

18. How does his wife Abigail die, and how does her death affect him for the rest of the story?

19. Why does Talbot reject the advances of Marilee at Millie's New Year's Eve party?

20. Talbot often reflects on the statue at the round-about that Millie and her husband erected in Green River. What does this statue symbolize for him?

21. What is Talbot's major mistake regarding Tompkin's intentions, and how culpable is he in the book's tragic ending?

22. Whom does Tompkin hire to kill Sheriff Talbot, and why? What does the killer mean when he says, just before he dies, "Got you both"?

23. What does Talbot mean when he says to Jeremiah, just before the final battle, "I'm forgetting nothing and remembering too much"?

24. Johnny Redfeather is a "half-breed," born in Florida of Cheyenne heritage. What was his history in the Civil War, and how has it affected him and his relationship with Sheriff Talbot? Why does he say to Talbot after the raid on Millie's Saloon that he and Talbot are "sworn brothers"?

25. How many times does Johnny save Talbot's life? Why does he say he does this?

26. Why does Johnny tell Sheriff Talbot at Sandy Bluff, as they face Chief Running Bear's armed braves, that he is not the Chief's "favorite Indian"? Is Johnny Redfeather a tragic character? Why is hope so important to him? Why is he so fond of Snuffy, the "house orphan," at Milly's Saloon?

27. In the final scene at Eagle Valley, Johnny says he might "take off" and take Old Willie and Snuffy with him. Why is this possibility symbolically important in the novel? Who was Snuffy's mother? Father? How many men in *GRS* lose their family, and how? Finally, when Johnny Redfeather says to Talbot "It's up to me now," what does he mean?

28. How is Tompkin's outright racial hatred reflected in contemporary American society? Who in the novel should see and address this evil, but does not?

29. Who is the literary ancestor of Curly, one of Tompkin's truly murderous herders?

30. How is the meeting between Talbot, with his posse, including Johnny Redfeather and Doctor Mark Johnson, and Running Bear and his armed braves at Sandy Bluff a turning point in the novel? Why doesn't Redfeather's presence convince Running Bear to negotiate with Talbot? What is Talbot's mistake here?

31. Discuss the roles of women in the novel: Abigail, Milly, Marilee, Maria Santa Anna, and Maggie, the Indian woman, and the women who become "Johnny Redfeather's Army" at Milly's Saloon.

www.ingramcontent.com/pod-product-compliance
Lightning Source LLC
Chambersburg PA
CBHW030614310726
48979CB00003B/718
9781632934123